PRAISE FOR *ON THE W*

"These sweet, sassy, sparkling Christmas reads will brighten your day!"
—NANCY THAYER, *NEW YORK TIMES*
BESTSELLING AUTHOR OF *SUMMER LOVE*

"*On the Way to Christmas* is a triple treat of Christmas charm with three heartfelt, hopeful holiday romances about the power of love and never giving up on your dreams."
—KAREN SCHALER, WRITER OF *CHRISTMAS CAMP*
THE NOVEL AND HALLMARK MOVIE

"*On the Way to Christmas* features three heartwarming holiday tales by beloved authors. Travel home for the holidays in a charming friends-to-more romance. Get whisked away for adventure and romance on the Christmas Express. And escape to North Carolina to find love in the form of a former classmate. These festive reads are sure to make you merry and bright!"
—DENISE HUNTER, BESTSELLING AUTHOR OF
THE RIVERBEND ROMANCE SERIES

"In the hands of today's most accomplished sweet romance authors, the trials and tribulations of three different women come to life in vivid detail—and a sleigh-full of fun! Filled with love and bursting with cheer, *On the Way to Christmas* is *the* book to get readers in the spirit this holiday season. A tinsel-covered treat for everyone on your shopping list—including yourself—guaranteed to make it feel like the most wonderful time of the year."
—KRISTY WOODSON HARVEY, *NEW YORK TIMES*
BESTSELLING AUTHOR OF *THE WEDDING VEIL*

"Sheila Roberts, Melissa Ferguson, and Amy Clipston have served up a stocking-worthy trio of sweet holiday romances you don't want to miss. Filled with Christmas spirit, and a little chaos, too, all three stories left my heart filled with joy. Short enough to juggle during your busy Christmas schedule for life balance too. The realistic holiday challenges are well done, and each romance is as sweet as Christmas candy that left me eager to binge on the next. Five stars overall!"

—NANCY NAIGLE, *USA TODAY* BESTSELLING AUTHOR

On the Way to Christmas

Other Books by the Authors

Sheila Roberts

Stand-Alone Novels
Bikini Season
Love in Bloom
Angel Lane
Small Change

Life in Icicle Falls Series
Welcome to Icicle Falls
Sweet Dreams on Center Street (formerly *Better Than Chocolate*)
Romance on Mountain View Road (formerly *What She Wants*)
Merry Ex-mas
The Cottage on Juniper Ridge
The Tea Shop on Lavender Lane
The Lodge on Holly Road
Starting Over on Blackberry Lane
A Wedding on Primrose Street
Christmas on Candy Cane Lane
Home on Apple Blossom Road
Christmas in Icicle Falls

Moonlight Harbor Series
Sand Dollar Lane
Welcome to Moonlight Harbor
Winter at the Beach
The Summer Retreat

NONFICTION
The Gift of Love

On the Way to Christmas

SHEILA ROBERTS
MELISSA FERGUSON
AMY CLIPSTON

THOMAS NELSON
Since 1798

Published in Nashville, Tennessee, by Thomas Nelson. Thomas Nelson is a registered trademark of HarperCollins Christian Publishing, Inc.

Thomas Nelson titles may be purchased in bulk for educational, business, fundraising, or sales promotional use. For information, please email SpecialMarkets@ ThomasNelson.com.

Publisher's Note: This novel is a work of fiction. Names, characters, places, and incidents are either products of the authors' imaginations or used fictitiously. All characters are fictional, and any similarity to people living or dead is purely coincidental.

Library of Congress Cataloging-in-Publication Data

Names: Roberts, Sheila, 1951- Christmas do-over. | Ferguson, Melissa (Assistant professor) Dashing through the snow. | Clipston, Amy. Perfectly splendid Christmas.

Title: On the way to Christmas / Sheila Roberts, Melissa Ferguson, Amy Clipston.

Description: Nashville, Tennessee : Thomas Nelson, [2022] | Summary: "From three beloved romance authors come sweet and heartwarming stories about Christmas and the joy of finding home"-- Provided by publisher.

Identifiers: LCCN 2022010753 (print) | LCCN 2022010754 (ebook) | ISBN 9780840701572 (paperback) | ISBN 9780840702234 (epub) | ISBN 9780840702463

Subjects: LCSH: Christmas stories, American. | Christian fiction, American. | LCGFT: Christmas fiction. | Christian fiction. | Short stories.

Classification: LCC PS648.C45 O48 2022 (print) | LCC PS648.C45 (ebook) | DDC 813/.0108334--dc23/eng/20220422

LC record available at https://lccn.loc.gov/2022010753

LC ebook record available at https://lccn.loc.gov/2022010754

Printed in the United States of America

22 23 24 25 26 LSC 5 4 3 2 1

CONTENTS

A Christmas Do-Over

SHEILA ROBERTS

For Rose, who's as far from mean as a girl can get

Chapter 1

Going home for the holidays wasn't all happy smiles and Christmas carols when everywhere you looked you were bound to see smoldering bridges. And when you were Darby Brown, there were a lot of them.

Of course, Mom and Dad wanted to see Darby. But they were parents, and parents were prejudiced. They, and probably her little brother, were about the only ones. Fa-la-yuck!

Darby had no one but herself to blame for this, and she wanted to fix it, really. But she wasn't sure how.

"You'll figure it out," said Josh White, the man who was supposed to have fallen at her feet in adoration but had stubbornly remained upright.

She'd met him in a Starbucks in the fall, when the weather in New York was cooling down and pumpkin lattes were on the menu. She'd flirted with him while they waited in line for their drinks, and she'd charmed him because, well, that was what she did. And he'd charmed her. So they'd gone out. A few times.

He'd listened to her work woes and nodded thoughtfully when she told him about her awful boss who hated her because she was young and pretty, and the coworker who was sabotaging her. Yes, sabotaging her. (She knew what sabotage looked like—gossip and backbiting. She'd done her share of both.) He'd nodded thoughtfully again when she told him about her idiot neighbor who was always snarling at her about something. Then, when they met for drinks after she got fired—fired!—and she went on another rant about how awful her boss was and the revenge she was going to take, he'd stopped calling. Was everyone in New York a jerk?

It turned out that, no, not everyone was. But someone was. Darby.

"Really?" Josh responded when she ran into him at a different Starbucks and informed him that he'd shown incredibly poor taste by ghosting her. "Maybe it was more a case of seeing that we're not a match," he suggested.

"What's that supposed to mean?" she demanded.

"Different priorities, different value systems."

"I have values. I don't cheat on my income taxes."

"Good for you."

What a tool.

Still, she'd stayed right there in Starbucks and kept talking to him. More like listening to him, really. Or maybe it wasn't really him speaking to her. Maybe he was a tool of a different kind. He didn't ask her out, but he offered to take her to church. Next thing she knew, she was doing some serious thinking about her life, her attitudes, and what was important.

Josh kept them at the friendship level, explaining that Darby needed to do some work on herself before he or anybody could really be with her. That hurt. But then, painful truths often do.

Now, here she was, coming home for the holidays, even though she didn't want to.

"It's been three years," Mom had reminded her when they'd talked on the phone. "You can't make a habit of staying away."

Sure she could. Her sister would as soon never see her again. And then there were . . . others. Anyway, Mom and Dad already had two kids to play with at Christmas. They didn't really need her.

"You have no excuse now," Mom had added.

Yeah, she did. "How about no money? You don't have it when you don't have a job, Mom." Okay, that had come out snotty. Old habits were hard to break.

"That's why we're sending you a ticket. We miss you, Darby Doll. Come home."

So much for the can't-afford-it excuse.

Now, here she was at Sea-Tac International Airport, waiting for her brother, Cole, to pick her up. She had a swarm of butterflies (did butterflies swarm?) in her stomach, and she half-wished she could turn right around and fly back to New York where she had . . . no one and nothing waiting for her.

No one and nothing was preferable to what was probably waiting in Eagledale, the small town way, way north of Seattle. She was standing in front of the Alaska Airlines passenger pickup area when Cole pulled up in his pride and joy—a red Chevy truck, which, of course, every guy finishing up a master's degree in construction management needed.

He screeched to a stop and hopped out. "Hey, sis! About time you came home."

"Just for a visit," she clarified.

"Why go back? You lost your job."

"Thanks for reminding me," she muttered as he picked up her suitcase and carry-on and stowed them.

"So, what happened?" he asked as they pulled away from the curb.

Great. Was everyone going to ask her this? "It didn't work out." Only a month ago she'd had a different take on things—one that blamed her threatened boss and jealous, sabotaging coworker. Now she had a more balanced version, and it wasn't a story she was all that ready to tell.

"Got anything else lined up?"

"Not yet," she said.

She'd updated her LinkedIn profile, sent out résumés, made calls, and haunted job boards, so far with no success. Every blog she read said her best bet was to be a referenced candidate, but she hadn't figured out how to find any company insider to help her with that.

She'd so easily fallen into her job in New York—got it through a friend of a friend—both men, naturally. Women hated her. (As if she could help it that she had perfect hair, symmetrical features, and good taste in clothes!) Other than Josh and a couple of his buddies, the pool of people with helping hands stretched out was proving to be very shallow.

Like you are, whispered the new-and-improving Darby. She sighed.

"It'll work out," Cole said easily. "There's tons of ad agencies in Seattle, and probably lots of companies that need writers. And words are your thing."

"Yeah, you're right," she said. It was a gift.

One she'd misused often in high school and then again when she went away to college. She had a lot of rebuilding to do.

"How's school going?" she asked. "You going to graduate cum laude?"

"I'm gonna graduate," he replied with a cheeky grin.

Cole was a loveable goof—a people person and the king of charm. He'd be fine. He'd probably be a construction manager before he turned twenty-five.

"If you stay here awhile, you won't have to come all the way back for the ceremony. You are coming to my graduation, right?"

"Of course." She'd come to Erika's graduation too. Not that Erika cared about Darby being anywhere near her anymore. Who could blame her?

"Rika's already at the house. Mom made that peppermint divinity you like, and she's planning on you guys all baking cookies together tomorrow."

Yes, Mom had a whole week of fun activities planned. Cookie baking, tree decorating, a neighborhood open house. That was scheduled for Sunday, the day after next.

"Who all's coming to the open house?" she asked. *Please don't say* Gregory.

Sweet, loyal Gregory. Her heart gave a sick flop over how she'd treated her former childhood boy bestie. She had a lot of mean to make up for, but she hated the idea of atoning for her past by being publicly snubbed and humiliated, even if she had it coming.

Cole started rattling off names. A couple of neighbor girls she'd ignored, Mrs. Williams from two doors down. "And the Colliers," he finished.

"As in Gregory?"

"Yep. Him too."

Ugh. She wished she'd stayed in New York.

"He bought the Henrys' old place."

"I didn't know that," Darby said.

There was a lot she didn't know anymore about Gregory Collier, former nerd turned teacher. Like why he chose to remain in Small Town, USA.

"That's what happens when you stay away," said Cole. "You miss out on what's going on. Not that there's that much going on in Eagledale."

"Not even for you? Why don't you have a serious girl-friend yet?"

"It's hard to pick when so many want me," he said, flashing that grin again.

He'd meant it as a joke, but Darby could believe it. Her brother was as good-looking as he was good-natured.

Her sister was also good-looking and good-natured. Well, except when it came to Darby. Erika's animosity was well deserved.

What had happened to Darby? Why had she chosen to be a mean girl?

Oh, yeah. She'd taken to heart the old saying that the best defense was a good offense and found that donning the mean girl persona was a great defense against all kinds of insecurity. Plus she'd thought it was cool, almost like a superpower that left lesser mortals running scared. Lower others and raise yourself. The attitude and the snarky remarks became so habitual she never noticed them. They became who she was.

Who you were, she reminded herself. *Not who you are anymore.*

She suspected she was going to have a hard time proving it.

Chapter 2

Eagledale was a small town, surrounded by pasture and farms with mountains in the distance and the Canadian border not far away. In keeping with the holiday spirit, snow had fallen, carpeting streets and frosting roofs. Daylight was fading and Christmas lights were winking on. Smoke curled up from chimneys. Welcome to Norman Rockwell Land.

Darby's family's house, a two-story Craftsman-style home on a corner lot, sat on a nice street with nice homes and nice people living in them. It came complete with a long front porch, a fireplace (perfect for hanging stockings at Christmas), and a large front yard where Darby and her friends had played freeze tag when they were kids. It had three bedrooms, one of which Darby and Erika had always shared. With only a two-year difference between the sisters, it had meant no privacy and plenty of fights over who controlled the TV their parents had let them have in their room. Darby almost always won.

They'd be sharing that room again. This year, Erika could watch whatever she wanted whenever she wanted. Hopefully the sound would fill the vacuum between them.

Mom knew all was not well between the sisters. When Darby had protested having to return to childhood and share a room, she'd merely said, "This will be good for you two."

Right. In a parallel universe.

"I told your sister the same thing."

So, Darby hadn't been the only one who wasn't thrilled with the sleeping arrangements. But, of course, being the perfect one, Erika must have acquiesced. Anyway, when it came to mapping things out for everyone for the holidays, Mom was a force to be reckoned with.

Darby walked into the house and was greeted by the aroma of pot roast. Her favorite. That meant there would be carrots and potatoes and Mom's homemade biscuits. Their old dog, Jackal, a golden lab, hobbled up to her, tail wagging, and she knelt to give him a hug and a face rub.

"Hey, you old boy," she said, and he moved in to give her a doggy kiss. Good old Jackal, he'd always loved her.

"Our girl is here!"

She looked up to see her mother rushing toward her, arms outstretched. Mom wasn't as slender as she'd been when Darby was little. She'd packed on some pounds and hadn't bothered to unpack them.

Darby had found it rather embarrassing when she was a teen fashionista. She'd outgrown that, though, and now there was something comforting about seeing this fifty-three-year-old woman with a thick waist and thick brown hair with threads of gray sneaking in. Crinkles now formed at the corners of her mother's eyes, looking at Darby with such love. Mom could have been in a greeting card commercial. Her very appearance said Home and Love.

By the time Darcy stood, Mom was on her, hugging her like the prodigal she was. "It's so good to have you home."

Darcy hugged her back. "It's good to be home." *Sort of.* At least, it was good to see her mom.

Other facets of her holiday return were a different matter. She felt like an ill-prepared cage fighter getting ready to step into the cage with the champ. Only a few months ago, she'd been so snatched, so cool, so confident. That was sure gone. Would there be any merry in this Christmas?

"Put your things away, then come on out to the kitchen," Mom said. "Erika's in there. She's got her hands in pie dough at the moment."

Of course she did. Erika was the artsy one. She was probably shaping dough into little trees to top the pie crust.

"It's the last of the blackberries from the freezer, by the way," Mom added. "I've been saving them for when you came home."

A traffic jam of emotion clogged Darby's throat, making it hard to get out a thank-you.

"Hey, it's not just for you," pointed out her brother. He would obviously help keep her humble while she was home.

Cole lugged her suitcase upstairs, leaving her to bring the carry-on. She freshened up, then put away her things in the same old dresser and closet she and Rika had used when they shared the room. Rika had taken the two bottom drawers, just as she had when they were growing up, and the rest of her clothes—properly stylish for an up-and-coming movie production assistant—were hanging in her side of the closet. Darby hung up hers, then took a deep breath and went back downstairs.

Only Mom and Erika were in the kitchen. Mom had a cup of tea already on the table for Darby, along with a small plate holding two pieces of pink divinity. Darby's favorite.

Mom was back at the stove, stirring a pot with the pie filling, as Erika put the bottom layer of crust in a fluted pie pan.

She barely looked up as she worked. "Hi, Darb."

"Hi, Rika." The exchange was stiff and chilly. Darby attempted to warm it. "You look great."

She did. Her reddish hair was cut in a midlength shag with bangs. She looked like an influencer ready for a shoot in her designer jeans and shirt. Erika had always been cute, but since getting the job as a production assistant in LA, she'd gone from cute to polished. Maybe part of her new look was simply confidence. She was doing what she'd always wanted to.

But she was minus the boyfriend she'd had last time she and Darby had been home together. Ugh.

"Thanks," Erika said.

Okay, this wasn't simply standoffish chilly. It was a deep freeze. Who could blame her?

For all appearances, though, it was a happy family dinner

that evening once Dad came home from work, with some jok-
ing back and forth between him and Cole and compliments
for Erika and Mom on the pie.

Then came the questions Darby was uncomfortable trying to answer. Like, what had happened to the hotshot copy-
writer position?

"I thought it was supposed to be such a great job," Erika
jabbed.

It should have been—working for a big-name clothing
manufacturer headquartered in NYC. Talk about a dream job.

"It was," Darby said. "My boss . . . " *Hated me. Was a jerk.*
She reined in her anger, knowing the bulk of it needed to be
turned on herself. "It just didn't work out."

"What are you going to do now?" her father wanted to
know.

"I'm not sure."

"You should come home for good," Mom said. "You're
too far away out there on the East Coast. Family should be
together."

Darby stole a look at her sister. Erika was concentrating
on finishing her pie, in no hurry to second that motion.

"I don't know what I'm going to do," Darby said.

At least not that far in the future. She knew what she
needed to do while she was home, though, and she had a tough
job ahead of her.

After dinner Mom shooed the three siblings out the door.
"Go have a good time. But don't stay out too late. We have
things to do tomorrow."

Yes, cookie baking and tree decorating. And Sunday would be the big neighborhood open house. Oh, goody.

"Let's go over to Bruno's," Cole suggested.

A favorite hangout of the town's millennials and Gen Zers, Bruno's offered mile-high burgers and the world's best onion rings, along with drinks and pool tables. It was Eagledale's answer to Match.com and the last place Darby wanted to go. She was bound to run into someone she didn't want to see.

Cole offered to drive. Any excuse to spend time with his beloved, the truck.

"I'm going to stay home," Erika said once they reached the front hall.

"Come on, don't be a lemon," Cole coaxed, slinging an arm around her. Clueless.

She frowned and wiggled out from under him. "You guys have fun."

"We will. Your loss," he said. "Come on, Darb."

When it came to choosing time with her brother and risking a chance encounter with someone she didn't want to see, or an evening at home with her sister, who was probably already contemplating smothering her with a pillow, Darby opted for going out with her bro.

"Look at this snow," he said. "They're expecting four inches at Snoqualmie. Good snowboarding. We should go."

At least her brother wanted to spend time with her. "Good idea," she said.

Bruno's was the same as it had always been—rustic, noisy, and packed with people. The heady aroma of old-fashioned greasy pub food was almost enough to make Darby forget she'd already eaten.

"Looks like there's a free table," Cole said, pointing to one of three pool tables lined up on the far side of the room. "Grab it and I'll get the drinks."

She nodded and started for the pool tables. On her way, though, she spotted her two best friends from high school. Ainsley and Laurel, both sporting similar pastel colors in hair that had cost them a fortune, were casual in jeans and sweaters and trendy boots, their coats thrown over the backs of their seats. Two out of the old foursome, back home and taking center stage. It had always been that way with Darby and her posse. Every boy had wanted them, and every girl had wished she could be one of them.

Darcy had lost track of one of the girls, but she'd kept in touch with Ainsley and Laurel, who were both living in Seattle. Well, until things had started going south at that impressive job she'd bragged about.

Ainsley was an influencer now, with a growing following, and Laurel owned her own business staging houses for Realtors. Then there was Darby, who was unemployed. She hadn't told either one she was coming home for the holidays. She certainly hadn't told either one that she'd been fired, especially after making such a big deal about her fancy job in New York (entry-level unimpressive, but nobody needed to know that) and her amazing life in the city.

Darby tried to slip past them but Ainsley said, "Darby! Am I hallucinating?"

She should have bolted for the door the minute she saw them. Now she was trapped. She stopped and flashed her famous Darby smile.

"What are you doing in town?" Ainsley asked. "And you brat. Why didn't you tell me you were coming?"

"I thought you'd eighty-sixed Eagledale," said Laurel.

Darby shrugged. "You have to come back for the holidays. Family."

Ainsley rolled her eyes. "Everyone's curse." She shoved out a wooden chair with the toe of her boot. "Sit."

Since when did Ainsley tell people to sit? The old Darby returned like the Ghost of Christmas Past and cocked a perfectly penciled eyebrow.

Ainsley changed tack and donned a more humble tone of voice. "Come on."

That was more like it. "Can't. I'm with the brother."

"Ooh," Laurel cooed. "Baby Bro can join us. I'm in between."

Baby Bro, their nickname for Cole when they were in high school. They had enjoyed teasing him and making him blush. Now Cole was a big boy who didn't blush, but Darby still didn't want her brother getting eaten alive by Laurel.

"I think not. I don't need you two gnawing down his ego," Darby said, and Laurel snickered.

"Coffee Monday?" Ainsley suggested. "We so need to catch up."

Even if her sister didn't want to hang with her, at least someone did. She could fall right back in with her old posse and nurse the wounds to her pride that had been inflicted by her New York fail. It would make the holidays a lot merrier, for sure.

"Okay," she said. "I assume Brewed Awakening is still in business."

"Oh, yeah," Ainsley assured her. "And wait 'til you see who's running the place now."

"Who?"

Ainsley shook her head. "Nuh-uh. You'll have to wait and see."

"All right. Ten on Monday," Darby said, then moved away. She saw a guy gaping at her and gave her long, blond hair a shake just to give him a thrill—yes, she still could rock a joint—then joined her brother.

Cole was already at the pool table with a Coke for her and a beer for himself. "Looks like the princesses are in town for the holidays," he observed as he chalked the tip of his cue stick. "You gonna hang out with them?"

She shrugged. "I might."

"They haven't changed," he said as he leaned over the table. It wasn't a compliment. "I'll break."

Darby mostly ignored her two old friends, concentrated on her shots, smack-talked her brother, drank pop, and after a while, made room for some onion rings. She couldn't help noticing how the cutest guys in the room drifted toward Laurel and Ainsley's table, bought them drinks, and generally drooled over them. They'd have been drooling over Darby, too, if she'd been at that table, and she'd have been flirting and letting them buy her goodies as well. And, in the end, blowing them off . . . just like Ainsley and Laurel would end up doing. Because, after all, they were only locals and, therefore, not worthy.

Except now her conscience nibbled away at the idea of behaving like that. The feeling made her uncomfortable. Did she want to go through the rest of her life using people?

The ride home with her brother was companionable and filled her with the kind of warmth all those ads for jewelry and home goods told people they were supposed to feel during the holidays. It even injected hope into her heart that she could repair the damage she'd done to her relationship with her sister. Christmas was, after all, about miracles. They were both laughing by the time they pulled into the driveway, finishing the last chorus of "Grandma Got Run Over by a Reindeer."

The happiness switch got flipped off when she slipped into the bedroom she and Erika were sharing. Her sister was still awake in bed, propped up against pillows and texting on her phone. She didn't even look in Darby's direction.

"I wish you'd have come with us," Darby ventured.

"I had things to do. That's how it works when you have a job."

The jab hurt. Darby forced herself to ignore it. "Aren't you in between movies?"

"It doesn't mean I don't have work. Or a life."

It was more than Darby could say for herself.

"Anyway, I'm going to be stuck with you enough just sharing a room," Erika added, each word chipped from ice.

The same room they'd always shared. Every time they returned to it, it felt smaller.

Her sister's words drove away the last of the happy-happys from earlier. Darby dug her toothbrush out of her toiletry bag and slumped down the hall to the bathroom. Coming home had been a mistake.

Chapter 3

Baking cookies together had always been a family tradition, and when Darby was a kid, she'd loved it. Mom always saved out a few to decorate tastefully, but for the most part gave both her and Erika free creative rein. Erika had the artistic eye, and while Mom was an equal opportunity praise-giver, Darby had known whose cookies she liked best.

As the sisters grew up it began to feel like Mom preferred everything Erika did—from the high school play she'd done the set designs for to those stupid cookies. Darby had written an essay her last year in middle school that won first place in a school-wide competition ("Anyone Can Be Beautiful"), and Mom had framed it, which had been great validation.

And then tucked it away somewhere, never to be seen again.

"For safekeeping," she'd said. Who knew where it had wound up?

And so, somewhere along the way, Erika went from the little sister Darby told fairy tales to and tried to carry around to the pest who was always eavesdropping on Darby's conversations with her friends. And to the one Mom liked best.

Of course, Mom liked Erika best as they got older because Erika never gave her grief. That had been Darby's job. As the oldest, she was the trailblazer, fighting for later curfews and earlier dating privileges. Two years younger, Erika could do no wrong. Darby had been the prettier one, but Erika had been the good girl. Darby had been clever, but Erika had been adored. The sliver of resentment burrowed deep and festered. Not that Darby ever acknowledged it. Young girls weren't that skilled in self-analysis. Neither were grown girls, it seemed, as there'd been little enough of that on her last visit home.

Here it was—time to bake cookies again—and Erika would, of course, outdo Darby. Well, good luck with that. Darby watched the Food Network. She knew a thing or two now.

"I thought, in addition to our rolled cookies and snowball cookies, we could make bar cookies," Mom said when Darby and Erika reported for duty. "I found a great recipe that has a shortbread base and uses raspberry jam and white chocolate. I think you'd really like that one, Darby Doll," she said, using Darby's old nickname.

"It does sound good," Darby said.

"How about you make those and the snowballs while Erika and I work on the sugar cookies?"

So Erika and Mom would work together with Darby

relegated to the bar cookie corner. "I can help decorate," she said.

"Of course you can, if you want," Mom said.

"Because you'll do it so much better," Erika added in her snotty sister voice.

"I didn't say that," Darby shot back.

"Now, girls. No squabbling. It's Christmas," Mom said, smiling at both of them.

"Sorry," Erika muttered.

"Sorry," said Darby, although she had nothing to be sorry about. Well, not at the moment, anyway.

"How your grandma would have loved this," Mom said later from her post at the kitchen counter where she mixed frosting as Darby put a pan in the oven.

Another reason Darby hadn't been all that thrilled to come home. It wasn't the same without Grandma. She'd been Darby's biggest fan. It had been Grandma who told her she was the prettiest girl in Eagledale, Grandma who told her she could be anything she wanted to be when she grew up—maybe even the next Danielle Steele. Mom had just told her to clean her room and be nice to her little sister.

Like you were so abused, she scolded herself. She hadn't exactly suffered growing up.

Mom raved over how lovely the bar cookies turned out and gave Darby's snowball cookies a thumbs-up, but Erika's frosted trees and bells and snowflakes were works of art. She could have her own Insta following. Cookie queen, successful career woman—Erika had it all going for her. And here was

Darby, going . . . nowhere. She'd always thought she was so special. Was she going to be one of those people whose best years were behind her before she even hit thirty? It was a humbling thought.

One of Erika's friends called, and she left to meet her for lunch, after assuring Mom she'd be back in plenty of time to help decorate the tree later. Then it was just Darby and Mom, sitting down for a cup of coffee before starting lunch.

"It's a treat to have you girls home again," Mom said as they settled at the kitchen table. "I hate that you're both so far away. You especially."

"Me?" Funny how when you came back home you picked up the same old habits. Like eye-rolling.

"Yes, you. You feel so out of reach all the way out on the East Coast. And texting isn't the same as being together in person," Mom added before Darby could point out that she texted regularly. Dutifully. "You're so talented. I'm sure you could get a job here in Washington."

"Frosting that particular cookie a little thick, aren't you, Mom?"

Her mother looked puzzled. "Why would you say that?"

Darby gazed at the dark liquid in her mug, looking for the right words. She couldn't find them, so she settled for, "Erika's the one you think is talented."

Mom looked both surprised and disgusted. "You're both talented, and I'm proud of each of you."

Darby nodded, took a sip of her coffee. There wasn't much she could say to that.

Mom did some gazing of her own, giving her mug a thoughtful turn. "Some people have favorites when it comes to their children. I've never understood that."

"You could have fooled me," Darby blurted, making her mother's brows come together in an angry *V*. Okay, finding the right words was overrated. "Erika never got in trouble like I did," she added.

Mom actually laughed. "You are twenty-eight years old, and we're just now having this conversation? Erika never drove me nuts like you did. I swear, I think every time she saw you getting in trouble, she said to herself, 'Okay, I'm not going to do that.'" Mom shook her head, took another sip from her mug. "You definitely gave me the most gray hairs, especially in high school. You were such a stinker. But I loved you like crazy. I always have and I always will."

"Yeah?" Darby challenged. "If we were all drowning, who would you save?"

"All three of you. Your father would have to fend for himself." Mom smiled at her and reached across the table to lay a hand on her arm. "Never doubt my love for you, because that would be a waste of time."

Other than consoling each other after Grandma's death, it was the most intimate conversation they'd had in a long time, and Darby felt tears coming to her eyes. She saw the same teary sparkle in her mother's.

This time she did find the right words. "Thanks, Mom."

Lunch consisted of BLTs, which both Dad and Cole gobbled up before going outside to tackle hanging Christmas lights. Mom had cleaning to do before the big open house the next day, and Darby offered to help her.

"Great. How about dusting?" Mom suggested.

One of the most boring jobs ever. "Okay," Darby said, and sighed inwardly.

Her mother loved her knickknacks, and when it came to holiday decorations, she went crazy. She had a nativity set composed of a cast of thousands—Mary and Joseph and baby Jesus, of course, and the wise men, but also shepherds, sheep, cows, oxen. And camels. You couldn't forget the camels. Then there were the little ceramic angels and Santas and elves and gnomes perched on every available surface—from the mantel to the buffet. Add to all that the furniture, including all the dining table chairs, and dusting would keep her busy for the afternoon.

It did. Then, after dinner, and after Erika returned home, it was time to haul out the many boxes of ornaments and decorate the tree—a giant monster Dad and Cole had brought home from the local tree lot.

Getting the thing into the living room required a team effort. It took a swing at Erika with one of its branches coming through the door—*You'll never take me alive*—and tried to KO the mechanical Santa standing in the hallway, tipping it over and starting it ho-ho-ho-ing. Darby was able to duck just before Killer Tree could whack her in the face.

"Careful!" Mom scolded the men.

It was her favorite word when it came to tree trimming.

She seasoned every other sentence with it as they worked, Jackal supervising. "Careful with those gold glass beads. They're antiques." As if they didn't know this. She told them every year. "Be careful with those pine cone lights. Grandma got those in Germany when she was living there . . . And be careful with that ornament. It's from the fifties."

"I know, Mom," Darby said after about the fifth careful.

"I know you know. Just . . . be careful."

And Darby was. Then she picked up the one ornament she should have never even gone near. The fragile blown glass ballerina was an early present to Erika from their grandmother, back when Erika had been taking ballet lessons. It was beautiful and exquisite, full of sentimental value.

Darby watched in horror as it slipped from her fingers and landed on the hardwood floor. The ballerina's head went one way, and her legs went dancing off the other. A delicately extended arm waved good-bye to the rest of her.

Erika turned at the sound, saw the dead ballerina, and gasped. "You broke her!"

Darby had just added the cherry to the hate cupcake. "I'm sorry," she said. *Sorry* could be such a flimsy word.

"Whoa, she's toast," said Cole. "Jack, get away from that." He shooed Jackal away as the dog came up to inspect the damage.

"I'll get the broom," Dad said, probably as an excuse to escape the female drama.

"You did that on purpose," Erika accused Darby.

"I didn't. I really didn't."

"Darling, I'm sure she didn't mean to," said Mom, stepping in as peacemaker.

"Why were *you* hanging her anyway?" Erika demanded.

"I . . . don't know." What a dumb thing to do. "I just didn't think."

"Yeah, well, there's a surprise," Erika snapped, her eyes practically burning into her sister. "You never think about anyone but yourself."

What could Darby say to that? Sadly, it was true. Jackal began to whimper. She wanted to join in with him.

"I'm done with this." Erika tossed the cloth teddy bear ornament she'd been holding into the ornament box and stormed off.

Mom hurried after her, leaving Cole with Darby, the ballerina destroyer. "I didn't do it on purpose," she said to him.

"I know," he said. "Rika's always been a drama queen."

But sometimes that drama was understandable. This was about way more than breaking an ornament. Darby had broken something much more valuable on her last visit. She just kept racking up the evil sister points.

She fell into the nearest chair. She could almost see the angel at the top of the tree shaking her head in disappointment. Jackal came and laid his head in her lap. Dogs were so forgiving. Why couldn't everyone be more like dogs?

From upstairs the sound of a raised voice (Erika's) drifted down to them. The words were muffled, but the anger came through loud and clear.

"I think she's done helping," Cole said.

I think she's done with me, Darby thought.

Sure enough, Erika came stomping down the stairs a moment later. She grabbed her coat from the coat closet, yanked open the front door, and slammed it behind her.

Dad came back with the broom and began sweeping up. Mom returned and picked up a fresh ornament from the box, saying, "She'll get over it."

Darby had her doubts.

"So much for family time," Dad muttered as he walked away with the dustpan.

"We are still having family time," Mom insisted. "I didn't buy all that pizza for nothing."

Later, as they sat around the living room eating pizza and streaming old Christmas movies, Darby texted her pal Josh back in New York. Thomas Wolfe was right. U can't go home again.

It wasn't until the start of the next movie that Josh's reply came through. He'd probably been out with his nice friends, having a nice time, like he deserved.

Sure U can. It worked for the prodigal son.

Not workin for the prodigal daughter.

What U going to do about that?

Don't know.

I do. Try again. ☺

Easy for him to say. To try again you had to have some idea of where to start. She texted Thanks a lot and set her phone aside.

On the TV, Nicolas Cage was having a serious discussion with a very strange angel. "You're workin' on a new deal now, baby," the angel informed him.

He wasn't the only one. Darby picked her phone back up and began looking around online for some kind of olive branch—what kind, she wasn't quite sure.

Suddenly she saw it. Yes. That was what she was looking for.

It was a silver ornament in the shape of a wreath. In the middle of the wreath hung a smaller circle trimmed with cubic zirconia and stating "I ♥ my sister." She did, but she had a long way to go to prove it.

What was that saying about the longest journey starting with a single step? Well, here was her first step, and one step at a time would have to do.

Two Christmas movies was all she could take, and she was in no mood to laugh at the antics in *Elf*. She went up to their shared room to wait for Erika to come home. She'd apologize again, promise to make it up to her. She tried to read the latest book she'd downloaded, but in the end, the time difference between coasts caught up with her and she fell asleep. By the time she awoke the next morning, Erika was already gone and she was alone.

She came down to breakfast to find everyone already at the kitchen table, downing bacon and eggs. "We didn't want to wake you," Mom said.

Erika said nothing. No surprise there. Darby counted herself lucky that her sister hadn't put a pillow over her head in the night.

"What time does the circus start?" Dad asked as he helped himself to another cup of coffee.

"Two," Mom said. "I told you, Frank."

"I forgot."

"Never marry a man who doesn't listen to you," Mom joked.

"It's hard to keep up when there's that much talking," Dad shot back. "Too much for my ears to hold."

"I'm getting your hearing tested," Mom informed him. It was an ongoing threat.

Her parents cracked Darby up. They loved to trade insults, but they were so there for each other. They'd gone through their share of trials, but instead of dividing them, the challenges had made them stronger. They'd lost a baby in between Erika and Cole. Mom had survived breast cancer. Both of them had lost their parents. No matter what life threw at them, they stayed together. How did you find love like that? Darcy wished she knew.

Breakfast was long and leisurely, but once the dishes were cleared Mom turned into a drill sergeant. The men were put to work bringing up folding chairs from the basement and wiping them down, and the women got busy making appetizers and putting together cookie platters to set on the dining table, along with red paper plates and holiday napkins. The glass punch bowl was brought out and eggnog punch made. Scented candles were lit, background music was started, and soon the Browns' residence looked and smelled a lot like Christmas.

At ten minutes to two, their first guest dropped in. Mrs. Williams was an eightysomething who had been widowed for as long as Darby could remember. She loved to wear red sweaters and bright red lipstick to match, drawn on well beyond her lip line. The effort made her look like the world's oldest clown. Darby and her friends had made fun of her for years.

Why had they done that? Looking at the woman, so frail and glad to join them, she couldn't remember.

"It's so good to see both of your darling daughters," Mrs. Williams said to Mom, beaming at Erika and Darby.

Oh yes, what darlings.

Erika had been giving Darby the silent treatment all day, but now it was lights, camera, action, and she was all warm smiles and happiness. "You look great, Mrs. Williams," she said to the older woman.

Okay, that was stretching it. "How are you, Mrs. Williams?" Darby asked as she took the woman's coat.

The elderly woman waved a hand. "Don't ask. I'm turning into a dry old stick. Never get old, dears."

What to say to that? "I'll try not to," Darby said. Then added, "And nobody thinks you're a dry old stick." Somebody—her—used to, but Mrs. Williams didn't need to know that.

The doorbell rang, signaling another arrival. "Find a seat, Mrs. Williams," Mom said. "One of the girls will get you some punch."

Mom opened the door and there stood Mrs. Collier. And Gregory.

Darby's heart jumped to attention. It had been a few years since Darby had seen him. Still, she hadn't expected such a transformation. This was Gregory? Where were his glasses? And why wasn't he skinny and nerdy-looking anymore?

And why was her mouth suddenly dry?

"I'll get your punch," she said to the old woman. Mrs. Williams wasn't the only one who could use a drink.

Chapter 4

Darby fetched punch for Mrs. Williams and filled her a plate with mini quiches, crackers, and slices from the cheeseball Mom had made. She visited with another neighbor who had come in, then took Mrs. Williams her plate and punch. She tried to feign interest in Mr. Larson's latest skirmish with his cable provider. Then she brought Mrs. Williams a fresh plate with cookies. She did everything she could think to do to avoid making contact with Gregory Collier.

Finally, his mother cornered her and asked her how she was enjoying New York. Good ol' Mrs. Collier, who never knew what a snotball Darby had been to her son. He'd never ratted her out, and Mrs. Collier had probably assumed they'd grown apart as they got older.

There was an understatement. They'd gone from best buddies in grade school to princess and commoner in middle school. After that, it was never the twain shall meet.

Except his mother, envisioning a happy reunion, had summoned him to her side. Now here he was, standing in front of Darby and looking down on her. Physically, that was. Probably in other ways as well.

"I hear you lost your job," he said.

His mother looked at him in surprise, then at Darby, equally surprised. "Oh, I didn't know. Your mother didn't say."

"It was pretty recent," Darby said. Then, to Gregory, "How did you hear?" As soon as the words were out of her mouth, she knew the answer.

"Erika told me."

Of course she did. Happy to announce her sister's failure to the world. Who else had Rika told? All her friends, for sure. *Darby finally got what she deserved.*

"It didn't work out," Darby said.

"Sorry about that," he said, and it sounded sincere. Hardly surprising. Gregory had always been sincere.

"If it didn't work out, then it wasn't meant to be," Mrs. Collier said. She gave Darby a little pat on the arm. "Something better will come along. Who knows? Maybe you'll move back here and find a job. Or write a book? A lot of people are doing that these days."

"Maybe," Darby said. Back in high school, she'd thought she might like to become a novelist. After getting fired she'd toyed with the idea of writing a book about her evil boss. Except Lauren Weisberger had beaten her to the punch with *The Devil Wears Prada.*

"Oh, there's Annalise," Mrs. Collier said, excusing herself. She flitted away, leaving Darby to face Gregory all by herself.

If she didn't have so much to feel guilty about, she'd have loved facing him. Why had she never noticed what a strong jawline he had? And that curly hair she used to make fun of— now it added an element of boyish charm. Though there was nothing boyish about those pecs.

"I hear you're still here," she said. Okay, that probably sounded snobby. "Teaching," she added.

"I am. I like it."

"And I bet the kids like you."

He shrugged. "They seem to."

They could stand there forever in Awkward Land or she could get them over the border fast. It was time to start repairing those burned bridges.

"Gregory," she began.

It was as far as she got. One of their other neighbors, Arielle, who'd been a couple years behind them in school, interrupted the moment. Arielle was short and cute, with a round little face and a round little butt. Darby had ignored her once upon a time. It was hard to ignore her now as she stepped in between Darby and Gregory and flipped her long, fantasy-dyed hair.

"Hi, Gregory," she said, her voice filled with warmth. The warmth died when she added, "Hi, Darby." She might as well have added, "Don't you have some appetizers to serve up somewhere?"

"Hi, Arielle." It would have been polite to ask Arielle how

she was doing, but the girl wasn't exactly putting Darby in the mood to be polite.

"I'm home for the holidays," Arielle added, smiling up at Gregory.

Well, duh. And, obviously, she had hopes of spending a lot of that time with him. Darby couldn't say she blamed her. Gregory had come into his own in the last few years. He'd always been quiet, never a star on the football field or the basketball court, which had disqualified him from breathing the same rarefied air as Darby's crowd. But now that quietness came across as confidence, and he'd obviously been doing something to stay fit. With those new-and-improved pecs, probably working out at the gym. Snowboarding as well. Like her, he'd spent a lot of time on the slopes as a kid.

"We should do something," Arielle said. As her back was half-turned on Darby and she looked straight at Gregory, it wasn't hard to tell who she wanted to do something with.

"Sure," he said. "We'll have to see what we can work out."

Arielle wasn't going to let him get away with such a vague response. "How about hitting the slopes tomorrow? Fresh powder."

He looked a little like a fish that had closed its mouth on something tempting, only to realize it was a hook. "Uh, sure."

"How about Tuesday instead?" Darby suggested.

"You can't make tomorrow? Too bad," Arielle said. Then, to Gregory, "Do you want to drive, or should I?"

"I can drive," he said.

"Okay. Pick me up at eight."

And that was that. Darby had met her match.

She frowned as another neighbor mom summoned Arielle over for a chat. "The little snot," Darby muttered.

Remind you of anyone you know? came the thought.

She pushed it away. "You didn't have to say yes, you know," she said to Gregory.

"Arielle's a force to be reckoned with," he replied. "Anyway, why not? She wants to be with me."

His tone of voice was a challenge, and the implication was plain. It had been a long time since Darby had wanted to be with him. Stupid her.

"Gregory," she began, "I need to—"

Once more she was cut off by the arrival of yet another pest. This time it was Pete Davies, another neighbor she'd palled around with . . . before she became too cool. She'd heard he'd gone into commercial real estate and was doing well. He'd invested in all the right stocks. He'd bought a Harley and become the quintessential cool dude—well-off and good-looking enough to be on the cover of a romance novel.

And to think she used to tease him about the collection of zits he once sported. Petey Pus. Lovely nickname. Yep, she'd been something. Standing there between two sweet guys who had turned into spectacular men, she made up a nickname for herself: Dopey Darby.

Pete looked at her with mild dislike. "Look who came back to town."

"Lucky you," she said in a vain attempt to mock her former superior self.

"Yeah, right," he sneered, then turned to Gregory. "Hey, I hear you guys are hitting the slopes tomorrow. Got room for me?"

"Sure," said Gregory.

Cole joined them, his plate piled high with chips. "I hear you and Arielle are going snowboarding tomorrow. Want a wingman?"

"Sure," Gregory said.

Great. Now everyone was going snowboarding without her. She was never that good, either on a snowboard or skis, but she still liked spending time on the slopes. So this was what it felt like to be on the outside looking in. Darby couldn't help feeling a little sorry for herself.

She left them talking and made for the refreshment table. *Bring on the cookies.*

She had plans anyway. She was having coffee with Ainsley and Laurel. Her posse. Her girls. Her gang.

Fa-la-yuck.

"It's snowing again," one of the moms announced, and two little boys yelled, "Snowball fight!"

"Oh, yeah," said Cole. "Come on, Darb. Let's see how tough you are. Rika! Come on!" he called to their sister, who was on the other side of the room drinking punch, talking to Mom's friend, Mrs. Jones, and doing an excellent job of hiding her boredom. "Get your coat."

Darby had always been able to wield her tongue like a sword, but never won when it came to snowball wars. "Oh, no," she said.

"Guess you're just too cool for that," Gregory taunted.

She sighed and fetched her coat.

Once outside, running around with both the people she'd grown up with and the young ones coming up, she remembered how much fun it had been to be a kid, chasing one another around with abandon, slipping and sliding, falling down, getting snow shoved down the back of her coat. Hitting Erika on the butt with a snowball. Oh, yeah. The years fell away.

"Hey, Darb," called her brother.

She looked back over her shoulder and received a hard-pack snowball in the face. It caught her on the nose and made her see stars. She let out a shriek.

Cole came running up, followed by Erika and Gregory. "Darb, are you okay?"

"No, I'm not okay," she snarled. She was in agony! "I think my nose is broken. And even worse, I'm getting blood on my coat," she howled.

"Crap," he muttered. "Come on, I'll take you to the emergency room."

"Good luck in your mission," said Gregory.

Erika just stood there, saying nothing.

Whoever wrote that song about it being nice to be home for the holidays was deluded. So far this was turning out to be anything but nice. Darby's sister had built the Berlin Wall between them, and her brother had tried to take her out with a snowball. Oh, yeah, what a fun visit this was turning out to be.

Sure enough, her nose was broken. The emergency room

doctor examined it and assured her it wasn't severe—only a minor fracture—but warned that she'd have swelling.

"Put an ice or cold pack on it for ten to twenty minutes at a time but don't apply too much pressure," he told her. "Acetaminophen for pain."

"Sorry, sis," Cole said for what had to be the hundredth time as they walked back to the truck.

She scowled at him. "You are such a brick brain."

Once inside the truck she turned on the dome light and checked out her face in the visor mirror. "I look grotesque," she said with a groan.

"You do look a little, uh, dinged up," he said. "I really am sorry."

He sounded downright miserable. Good. Let him. She said nothing and they rode back to the house in silence.

But by the time they pulled into the driveway, she was feeling as ugly on the inside as she looked on the outside. She laid a hand on his arm. "I'm sorry I was a jerk. I know it was an accident."

"And we can always forgive accidents," Cole finished with her.

It was one of their mother's favorite sayings. If only a certain accident with a glass ballerina could be forgiven.

She shoved aside the thought and returned her attention to her brother. "Anyway, I'll live. But you owe me big-time," she added, not wanting to totally let him off the hook. "So you'll be on dish patrol when it's my turn to load the dishwasher?"

He grinned. "You got it. Come on, we'd better get some ice on your face."

The party was long over, and their parents and Erika were in the living room watching *It's a Wonderful Life*. "Your poor face," Mom cried at the sight of Darby's swollen nose.

Darby almost said, "It's ruined." But she was aware of her brother right behind her. "It's okay."

"And you have blood on your coat. Give it to me. I bet I can get that out with baking soda. Cole, get the cool pack. You go lie down," Mom commanded Darby. "Erika, help your sister upstairs."

First a broken nose, and now some cozy one-on-one time with her sister—who probably wished *she* could've been the one to break Darby's nose. Happy holidays.

Chapter 5

"D" oes it hurt?" Erika asked as she walked upstairs with Darby.

"Yes," Darby said. Of course it hurt. What a dumb question.

"You're going to look really bad tomorrow," Erika predicted.

"Going to?" She already looked like she should be designing her own personal Phantom of the Opera mask.

"Poetic justice," Erika murmured.

Mom appeared with painkillers and water, and Cole arrived with ice for her schnoz. He apologized yet again, and Darby eased his conscience with a "Don't worry about it." Mom laid her out with the ice pack, kissed her cheek, and promised to come back and check on her. Then all three abandoned her to suffer alone. Solitary confinement.

She pulled her journal out of the pocket of her carry-on and began to write.

I am living proof that you reap what you sow. I could almost feel sorry for myself if not for the fact that I know I deserve the lumps of coal falling on me. Between that little twit Arielle invading my world and stealing Gregory out from under my nose—which, thanks to my brother, now has me looking like a female Cyrano de Bergerac—this is not going well. If only I was as noble as Cyrano! I'm trying to steer my life in a new and better direction, but I feel like the steering wheel is broken.

Her phone dinged with a text. How's it going? Josh texted.

Rotten. Broke my nose.

Free nose job?

Wasn't he the comic? She scowled. Snowball fight.

To this she got the old laughing-'til-I-cry emoticon.

Happy to amuse, she texted back. What am I doing here?

Growing spiritually. Hang in there. ☺

She didn't want to hang in there, and she didn't particularly want to grow. Growth is overrated.

It's not, trust me. You will look back on all this and be glad it happened.

She doubted that, but she thanked him for checking up on her. Things may not have worked out for them romantically, but he was proving to be a really good friend.

That night she dreamed her nose swelled to the size of a watermelon and she found herself in downtown Eagledale wandering the streets dressed as a clown. "And she thought she was so cool," she heard someone say. She whirled around to find a crowd standing behind her. It was comprised of all the people she'd mocked or put down in the past, regarding her with superior smirks.

"You reap what you sow," said Pete, echoing what she'd written in her journal. "What goes around comes around."

"Yes, it does," said a voice from the back of the crowd. "What goes around comes around. What goes around comes around."

Soon the entire crowd was chanting it, pointing fingers at her.

"I'm sorry," she cried. "I'm sorry!" She woke up with the words still on her lips.

She was really sorry when she checked out her reflection in the bathroom mirror. Her bruised and swollen nose made her look like a freak. How was she supposed to go out looking like this? By hoping nobody she knew would recognize her.

Erika and Cole were already gone, and Dad had left for work, so it was just her and Mom sitting at the kitchen table. Mom worked on her second cup of coffee, Darby on her first, icing her nose and staring morosely at the pastry on her plate.

"What are your plans for today?" Mom asked.

"I'm supposed to meet Ainsley and Laurel for coffee," she said. "But I'm going to cancel."

"Nonsense," Mom said. "You don't look that bad."

"Compared to what, roadkill?"

Her mother shook her head at her. "Your friends won't care."

"I should have them come here." That would work. She could hide out in the house all week.

"Sorry, darling, but I've got a full house today. The mah-jongg girls are coming over to play and have lunch."

Oh, yes, Mom's crazy friends. They'd be wearing Rudolph noses and reindeer antlers and ugly sweaters, and they'd all want to know every detail of Darby's life to date. She was better off risking the coffee shop.

So at ten thirty she walked into Brewed Awakenings, determined to brazen it out. After all, she was Darby Brown. And a little thing like a dinged-up nose didn't make her any less . . . fabulous. Mom had gotten the bloodstains out of her coat, and she'd worn her most stylish clothes under it.

The Phantom does fashion. She hoped she wouldn't run into anyone she knew.

She did. To her surprise, when she walked up to the counter to order her favorite eggnog latte, there was Janice Jenkins, one of her favorite targets way-back-when. She had seen neither hide nor hair of Janice on her visits home and had assumed she moved away . . . never to return again. But here she was, behind the counter, ready to take Darby's order.

She'd slimmed down some, but the old Darby still would have judged her for her less-than-perfect figure. Her nose was still her worst feature (but who was Darby to talk about noses!), but her complexion had cleared—and somewhere along the way she'd finally gotten her teeth straightened and had gained the confidence to smile.

Although the one she gave Darby was barely welcoming. Who could blame her?

"What can I get you?" she asked. *Arsenic? Cyanide?*

Darby placed her order, then fished around for something to say. "So, you still live in Eagledale?" Okay, did that imply failure? Good grief. She was the queen of words. Why were the right ones deserting her now?

"I do." Janice's chin lifted just a little. "I own this place."

"Wow. Really?" As if Janice wasn't capable of owning and running a coffee shop. Okay, that hadn't come out right.

"Yeah, really," Janice said. "For here or to-go?"

"Here." *Where I'm so popular.*

Janice rang up the sale, then turned her back on Darby and got busy with her order.

"I love how you fixed the place up. It looks great," Darby said to Janice's back.

The coffee shop's original décor had looked like Grandma's kitchen, with old-fashioned curtains at the window and cute little percolators and vintage alarm clocks in the windowsills—kitschy but not necessarily appealing to people Darby's age. Now it was slick with sepia-colored wall art depicting mugs and coffee beans, along with simply framed black-and-white photos of elegant people at sidewalk cafés sipping cappuccinos. The cat wall clock with eyes that moved from side to side had been replaced by a brown one shaped like a steaming cup of coffee.

"Thanks," Janice said. Formal and cold. She returned with the order, a work of art in a thick, cream-colored ceramic mug.

"Gorgeous," Darby said appreciatively.

"High praise coming from Darby Brown. I'll have to share that on Facebook."

A well-deserved slam. Darby was about to say something when the coffee shop door jingled, and she turned and saw her mean girl besties coming in, dressed like they were ready for a photo shoot for *Vogue*. With their superior expressions they were Ugliness Past, and she wished she hadn't committed to meeting them. She could feel her smile fading.

Janice saw it and probably figured Darby was deflating for a different reason—embarrassment over being caught visiting with her. The moment of almost bonding fled, and Janice's expression iced over once more.

Ainsley and Laurel walked to the counter like models on the catwalk. Not that any of the other customers were paying attention. The three teenagers seated at a table beneath the coffee cup clock were too busy with their own conversation and their muffins, and the old geezer drinking coffee and reading his paper had more important things on his mind.

"What. On. Earth?" Ainsley greeted Darby. "Did you forget Halloween is over?"

"Very funny. I broke my nose."

"Getting clumsy in her old age," cracked Laurel.

"Not so clumsy I can't take you out," Darby threatened, the old Darby rearing her ugly head.

"Small coffee, black," Ainsley said shortly, tossing a five-dollar bill on the counter. She left Laurel to give her order, turning her back on Janice and directing her attention once more to Darby.

"Your poor nose," Laurel said as they all took their drinks to a table by the window. "You look like . . ."

"Janice," Ainsley supplied, and the two of them burst into giggles.

Darby frowned at them, disgusted. "That was a nasty thing to say."

"What?" Ainsley demanded.

"About Janice."

Ainsley shrugged. "Just kidding. So, what happened?"

"My brother took me out with a snowball. And not on purpose," Darby added, just to be clear.

"Is it going to be crooked?" Laurel asked.

There was a lovely thought. Darby pushed away her drink.

"You should see a good plastic surgeon the minute you get back to New York," Ainsley advised.

Darby decided not to share with them the fact that she no longer had her glitzy job in New York. Which hadn't been all that glitzy in the first place, since she'd been on the bottom rung of the ladder. Actually, she wasn't sure what, if anything, she wanted to share with these two women. They suddenly felt like a foreign species.

It didn't matter. They had plenty to share on their own, happily spilling tea about Janice.

"She got the place for next to nothing," Laurel said. "You know, her aunt and uncle owned it. Remember what a dump it was?"

"So they retired?" Darby asked.

"Not hardly. Uncle ran off with the teller at First National and the aunt had a nervous breakdown. I think Janice's parents bought the place for her. God knows she wouldn't be able to get a job doing much of anything else."

Janice was hardly stupid. "Why is that?" Darby asked.

Ainsley rolled her eyes. "Oh, come on. Look at her. She's hardly executive material, and she'll sure never be an influencer."

"I guess she's got some influence. We're here drinking her coffee," Darby pointed out.

"Until we get a Starbucks," Ainsley said. She narrowed her eyes. "What is your problem? Did that snowball damage your brain?"

"What do you mean by that?" Darby demanded.

"You're suddenly Miss Congeniality," Ainsley said in disgust.

God help her, she had been just like Ainsley—and not that long ago. Talking to her was like thinking you had a clean house until someone turned on the lights.

Darby shook her head. "You really should stop and listen to yourself sometime."

"Oh, Saint Darby," Ainsley taunted.

"I'm going home," Darby said. "I need to ice my nose, and I've got a headache."

"Fine with me 'cause you're giving me one," said Ainsley.

Darby rolled her eyes. "Pathetic," she said, standing.

"You sure are," Ainsley said, determined to have the last word. "Call us once the aliens vacate your body."

"What's with her?" she heard Laurel ask as she headed for the door.

She didn't hear what Ainsley said in reply. And she didn't want to.

She sighed as she got into her mom's car, which Mom was letting her use. Who was she to sit in judgment on her friends? She'd been just like them for so long—and still had a long way to go.

Chapter 6

Darby's parents were hospitable to a fault, and when the snowboard party returned, all were invited to stay and share the giant pot of chili Mom had made. Darby found herself irritated watching Arielle in action, flattering Gregory until it was a wonder his head didn't blow up and float off like a Macy's Thanksgiving Day Parade balloon. He was amazing on the slopes. She couldn't keep up. And everyone knew he was the smartest man in Eagledale. Gack.

Darby reached a point where it was all she could do not to shriek, "Will you just shut up?"

Okay, she was cranky. She wasn't in physical pain thanks to the painkillers, but her nose was a mess and she felt ugly.

And she was jealous, which brought a pain all its own. Gregory had, once upon a time, been crazy about her. She wanted him to be once again, even though she didn't deserve his admiration. Instead, she had to watch some other woman moving in on him like a stealth bomber. Except there was nothing stealthy about the way Arielle was behaving. Darby watched and ground her teeth . . . which did nothing to make her unhappy heart feel any better.

How many girls had watched her in action over the years and experienced the same pangs? How many boyfriends had she stolen? She thought of what she'd done to her own sister and cringed. Sometimes it was hard not to think of herself as beyond redemption. Thank God for Josh, who had assured her that she wasn't.

She half-wished he was with her to nod approvingly as she held back the many verbal barbs that came to mind.

"It's too bad you had to miss today," Arielle said to her. It was a taunt, and they both knew it. The up-and-coming mean girl challenging the former queen of Mean Hill. "Just as well, though, 'cause you would have fallen on your nose."

With the way you snowboard, it's a wonder you didn't fall on yours. Darby clamped her lips down on the retort, keeping it firmly corralled.

She shrugged. "Oh, well. Sounds like you all had a good time." She added a smile to make sure everyone knew she didn't feel left out.

Although, of course, she did, and she couldn't help wondering if anyone (well, other than Cole, who was clueless) would have wanted her along even if she hadn't broken her nose. And, really, since when did a broken nose stop a girl from snowboarding?

"Hey, we should play spoons," Cole said.

"Oh, yeah," agreed Pete.

Soon all of them were at the dining table, playing the card equivalent of musical chairs, trying to match cards and grab from a pile of spoons that was one short. Darby always excelled at the game.

Not this time. She got in a battle over a spoon with Arielle, each tugging fiercely. Arielle had a great sense of timing. She let go just when Darby was pulling with the most force, and Darby wound up whacking herself. In the nose. Oh, look, the stars were out. She said one of those words her mother would have washed her mouth out for saying when she was a kid and probably still would.

"Gross. Your nose is bleeding," Arielle cried.

Lovely.

As Darby dashed for the kitchen and a paper towel, she could hear the little snot say, "Sorry." She knew that tone of voice. It *really* said, "No, I'm not."

"You okay, Dar?" Cole called from the other room.

Yeah, I like standing with my head back, catching blood in a paper towel. "I'm fine," she called back. "No harm." One foul.

The game went on without her, and by the time her nose felt better and she replaced her sweater with a clean one, everyone had moved into the den to stream a movie.

"We need popcorn to go with it," Cole said. "You guys want something to drink?"

Of course everyone did, and both Erika and Darby wound up helping Cole get the snacks ready. Meanwhile, Arielle plopped herself on the couch next to Gregory and did nothing to help. Sheesh. Even at her meanest, Darby had the manners to help out at a party.

By the time the movie was over, she was tired. She was especially tired of Arielle.

"She'll have Collier tied down by Valentine's Day," Cole predicted.

Poor Gregory. "He deserves way better than her," Darby said.

"Yeah? Like who?"

"Dar, of course," Erika said with a sneer. "I'm going to bed."

Her brother, who paid little enough attention to undercurrents, could see that the sisterly love wasn't happening. "Better sleep with one eye open," he advised Darby.

Darby sighed and followed her sister up to bed.

"Arielle should have been your sister," said Erika, folding down the covers. "You two are exactly alike." Then Erika shut off the bedside lamp and plunged them into darkness.

Ugh.

Mom didn't have much planned for the next day, which left the siblings free to do whatever they wanted. Cole vanished with some of his friends, and Erika and one of hers went shopping. Darby . . . read and watched old episodes of *Friends* on her phone with Jackal by her side. Pathetic.

Her present for Erika arrived that afternoon, and she showed it to Mom. "Think she'll like it?"

"It's lovely. Of course she will. And, more important, she'll appreciate the sentiment behind it," Mom said. It was encouraging, although maybe not accurate.

Darby set the ornament on Erika's pillow, hoping her sister wouldn't throw it in the garbage. She filled more of her day by writing in her journal—*I'm pathetic. I have no idea how to erase the past!*—scrolling through her Facebook feed, snacking on cookies (who needed a waist, anyway?), and generally feeling sorry for herself. When it got late enough in the afternoon, she texted Josh, figuring he'd be off work.

What are U doing?

Going out with Vince and Lissa.

Of course. Josh was a nice guy. Josh had friends.

U OK?

My life sucks.

☺ Better get busy unsucking it.

Thanx. A lot. Will get right on that.

Good luck.

How, exactly, did you go about unsucking your life? So far she hadn't found a way.

She couldn't mope around the house forever though. She needed to get out and . . . do what? With whom?

She didn't *need* to do anything with anyone. She could handle being alone. With the new-and-improving her. She decided to take a walk.

The street had been cleared and the sidewalk was slushy, but the houses still looked pretty with thick blankets of snow on their roofs. Her yard and the ones nearest it were torn up from Sunday's snowball fight, but farther down the street a few lawns were relatively pristine.

She walked by one house where two little girls were in the front yard, building a snowman. She didn't recognize them and wondered if the family was new to their neighborhood.

"Your snowman's lookin' good," she said to them.

"We're rebuilding him," said the littlest girl. "Billy Watkins knocked his head off."

"That wasn't very nice," said Darby.

"Billy Watkins is a poopy head," the girl informed her.

The older girl cocked her head and studied Darby. "What happened to your nose?"

"I got hit with a snowball."

"Does it hurt?" asked the younger one.

"Not so much now," Darby said.

The older girl made a face. "You look ugly."

A future mean girl. "Yeah, well, one thing I'm learning—it's better to look ugly than to be ugly," Darby said, then moved on down the street. A turn around the corner, down a couple more blocks, and lo and behold, she found herself in front of the house Gregory Collier had bought.

Unlike most of the houses around him, he hadn't put up Christmas lights, but an inflatable green snail with a Santa hat and a house on its back that looked like a peppermint candy was camped out on the lawn. Gregory sure marched to his own quirky drumbeat.

She saw lights on inside. Was he home? She could march up the walk, ring the doorbell, and make her apology. Get it over with and get on with her life. Without Gregory, probably.

He would, hopefully, forgive her, but she doubted he'd want to have anything to do with her going forward. Not with her track record.

She couldn't erase the past. That was a stupid wish. Your past was your past, and you carried it with you just like that snail carried its house. There were no do-overs. But there was such a thing as do-better. If she told him she was working on that, would he believe her?

Was he alone in there? What if Arielle was over?

She stood on the front walk for a very long time, gnawing on her lip. What to do? The light was fading, and porch lights and Christmas lights were blinking on. It was getting cold. She should go home before she turned into a pillar of ice.

The front door opened and there he stood, looking at her. "Are you stalking me?"

"That's right," she said.

"Well, you're caught now. You may as well come in."

Her feet moved slowly, but her heart began to race. She suddenly wished she'd stayed in the house with Jennifer Aniston and her friends.

"What are you doing here? Slumming?" he asked once she'd reached the porch.

Sounded like Gregory had picked up the snotty remarks she'd dropped from her lexicon. "No, actually, I made some humble pie and wanted to bring you a great big slice."

More like the whole pie. Not only did she look awful, but also she sounded ridiculous with her nasal voice.

Both of his eyebrows shot up. "Yeah? This sounds interesting." He stepped aside and gestured for her to enter. "Want something to drink?" he offered as he led her into the living room.

"No, thanks."

She wasn't going to stay that long. She'd say what she needed to say and then run for it.

His living room sure looked inviting though. It was simply furnished with a couch upholstered in a sturdy brown fabric and a couple of fake-leather easy chairs. A thick area carpet patterned in cream and brown covered much of the hardwood floor. She suspected the flooring was new. The fireplace had been refaced, and a framed color photo of the Grand Canyon hung over it. A Charlie Brown tree sat in a corner by the window, decorated with a few lights and a collection of Star Wars–themed ornaments.

"The house looks great," she said.

"Thanks. I did the floors and the fireplace myself."

"Hidden talents."

"I have a lot of talents you don't know about," he said. That sounded almost flirty, but more likely it was a subtle scold. Which she deserved.

She walked over to the fireplace, where a fire was burning, and checked out the picture. "You took this?" she guessed.

He came and stood next to her. "I did."

"It's great."

"Yeah, well, having done nerdy stuff like photography club in high school, I learned a few things."

Yep, this was *not* flirting. She could feel her face heating, and it had nothing to do with the fire in front of her.

She sat down on the nearest chair. A good decision, since the knocking together of her knees was distracting. She'd come to apologize. She needed to say something.

He dropped onto the couch, across from her. "How's the nose?"

"A mess." Rather like her life.

"You're not having a very good time of it here so far, are you?"

"Maybe it's time I got a cosmic punch in the nose," she said. *Okay, it's now or never.* "I'm sorry for what a snot I was to you."

He gave a snort. "Which time?"

"All of them."

"That's a lot of sorrys," he said softly.

"You're right. I was horrid." She wanted to say, "I've changed," but she knew that wasn't quite accurate. "I'm working on changing."

"Are you now?"

"While you guys were on the slopes yesterday, I met up with some old friends."

"Yeah?"

"It was like . . . looking in a magic mirror, showing me the kind of person I've been. I didn't like what I saw. I don't suppose you can forgive me," she ventured.

He shrugged.

She sighed. "I know. I don't deserve it."

"You were cool when we were kids. What happened to you?"

"I wanted to be cooler, I guess."

"Was that what you called it?"

"I thought it was. You had to hate me."

"I kind of did. And yet . . ." He shook his head. "Moth to the flame."

"I'm truly sorry." Would she ever be able to say it enough to make up for the person she'd been?

He shrugged again.

"You never should have helped me cheat on those math tests."

That brought a bitter chuckle. "You'd have flunked otherwise."

"Maybe I should have. It would have served me right."

"It would have," he agreed.

She winced. Eating humble pie was hard work.

"You know what the worst moment of my whole young life was?" he said.

She could guess. She braced herself.

"That first dance at Eagledale High School. You'd found your new friends that summer, but I still thought you'd dance with me. You weren't dancing with anyone else, so I took a chance."

Darby had seen him coming, then turned her back on him right before he reached her. She'd snubbed him in the halls when she was with her cool friends but hadn't been above using him when she needed help with math. Once she'd gotten through algebra, she'd pretended he was completely invisible.

"If I had it to do over again, I'd have danced with you."

"Too bad you can't go back," he said, unbending.

"But you can go forward," she said in a small voice. Knees still knocking, she rose from her chair, crossed the room, and stood in front of him. "Would you dance with me now?"

He looked at her suspiciously. "Okay, Darby, where's the punch line?"

"What?"

"This is some kind of sick joke."

"No, it's not," she said earnestly. "I am sorry, Gregory. I'm sorry I was so awful. I'm sorry I trampled on our friendship. On your kindness. On your heart. I deserve to go through life with a deformed nose to match my deformed heart." Oh, great. Now she was all teary and dopey. The ultimate humiliation.

He looked at her, apparently shocked. "Your nose is going to be deformed?"

"No, it's not that bad," she said. "I'm just trying to make a point. I'm trying to get you to like me again, just a little. Just enough that we can be friends and I can be a better person."

That did it. There came the tears. She should have made this speech in some public place so she could have been truly as humiliated as she'd made him back when they were kids.

His expression softened, and he stood and did something amazing. He put his arms around her. "Hey, don't cry. We were dumb kids."

"You were never dumb," she said, sniffing. She wiped at her nose and winced.

"Stay here," he said, and left the room.

He was back a moment later with a box of tissues.

"Thank you," she said, and took it.

While she oh-so-gently blew her nose, hoping it wouldn't start bleeding again, he picked up his phone and started streaming Tim McGraw's "It's Your Love." He held out his hand to her. "You do owe me a dance."

She started to cry all over again.

"Hey, stop it. You'll start bleeding, and I happen to like this shirt."

Which he filled out very nicely.

As they swayed back and forth, the last trickle of tears slid down Darby's face. She smiled, hoping it was the end of an era and the beginning of a new, better relationship. Later on, Gregory microwaved popcorn and made hot chocolate, and the two of them talked. About his past girlfriends, her past boyfriends, the job she lost, and the boss who'd hated her.

"I think I earned that," she said at last with a sigh.

"Maybe you did," he agreed. "But maybe things have a way of working out for the best too. Maybe the worst thing in your life leads you to something better."

"It's possible," she said, but she wasn't sure.

At last he shook his head.

"What?" she demanded.

"It's being with this new you. Or the old you come back. Either way, I can't wrap my head around it."

"Thanks," she said with a frown.

"But I always knew the old Darby was in there some-where."

"Maybe I didn't want to let her out. Maybe I didn't think she was, I don't know, good enough. Well, except when it came to the mouth. Being a verbal slasher had its own sick reward. I could make people feel like nothing, and I guess that made me feel like something."

It was a horrible thing to have to confess. She could feel the heat of embarrassment racing up her neck and flooding her cheeks. She suddenly couldn't look Gregory in the face. So ironic that the woman who had once thought she was way too fabulous for the likes of him now desperately wanted to make herself worthy of his friendship.

"We all do dumb stuff," he said.

"There's dumb and there's wicked."

"Okay, Wicked Witch of the West, I guess you're going to have to spend some time with me, making up for your bad behavior."

She heard it in his voice and looked up to confirm. Yep, he had a smile on his face.

"Anything you say," she said.

"Anything?" He waggled his eyebrows.

"Within reason."

"How about dinner tomorrow night?"

"Good idea. I'll pay."

"I might just let you," he said.

It was late when he finally walked her back to her house.

They stopped at her front walk and turned to face each other. "Thank you for giving me a second chance," she said.

"Thanks for finally asking for one," he replied. He gave her a final smile, then turned and headed back toward his home.

"Wow," she said, and sent up a quick prayer of thanks that everyone in Eagledale wasn't as mean as she'd once been.

She was still smiling when she checked in with her parents and told them good night, and even as she climbed the stairs to her shared bedroom. But once she reached the bedroom door, her smile turned wary. What would Erika think of her peace offering?

Chapter 7

Darby found out soon enough what her sister thought of her holiday olive branch. She found Erika in bed, watching a Hallmark Christmas movie on their old TV. She didn't even look Darby's way when she entered the room, and there was no sign of the ornament.

Until Darby plopped onto the edge of her bed and saw it in the wastebasket. Okay, that had gone well.

"Guess you didn't like the present," she ventured.

"Guess not," Erika replied.

"I couldn't find one like the one I broke."

"You thought you'd be able to?" her sister demanded.

"I'd hoped I'd be able to. I tried. Then I saw that one and thought maybe—"

"It would make up for ruining things with me and Ethan?" Her sister turned her attention away from the TV screen long enough to provide Darby with a visual of her scorn.

The hot chocolate and popcorn she'd had at Gregory's house suddenly weren't settling well in her stomach. What she'd done was unforgivable.

"Nothing can make up for that," Darby said.

"You just had to flirt with him, didn't you? Had to show how superior you are."

"Yes, I did," Darby admitted. "He was hot and I couldn't resist."

"Yeah, you could. You just didn't want to."

Darby bit her lip, unsure of where to go next. Her sister was right. She could have kept her distance, but she'd seen the way he looked at her and thought, *What the heck? How serious can it be if he's looking at me and drooling?*

"We'd started talking about getting married."

"You didn't have a ring," Darby said in her own defense.

"I brought him home for Christmas! Don't pretend you're too dense not to know what that means." Erika returned to staring at the TV, and Darby could see the glisten of tears in her eyes. "It's not about losing him. If a couple of days of exposure to you at Christmas was enough for him to behave that way, then he wasn't worth keeping around."

"Exactly," Darby said, feeling exonerated.

She wasn't. "But you're my sister. And you never said you were sorry." She looked toward Darby again, the hurt plain on her face. "All I really wanted was for you to acknowledge what a jerk you'd been. All I wanted was an apology. One heartfelt apology. But, of course, the great Darby Brown couldn't be bothered. Big surprise. I'd seen what you turned into. And here's another big surprise; you're still the same. So, hashtag: *done-with-my-sister*."

Arrow to the heart. And Darby deserved it. What she'd done was inexcusable.

She dropped to her knees in front of Erika. "I am so, so sorry. I was awful."

Erika looked down at her. "And those phony words on that ornament. What a joke."

"But they're true. I do love you."

Erika turned away, hunching her shoulders. "Yeah, right."

"For real. And I don't want to be the same person I used to be. I was a horror in high school and not much better in college."

"And beyond," Erika muttered.

"Yes, beyond," Darby admitted. "I just had to be . . ." How to put into words what she was coming to see about herself? "More than everyone. Better. You were always Mom's favorite."

Those last words had just spilled out. Now there they sat, like a big pointing finger, showing the true motive for so much of her unkind behavior to her sister when they were teenagers. And beyond. It was the worst kind of pain looking at such ugliness.

"I was not."

"Yeah, you were. I guess I took that sibling rivalry thing to the max."

"Sibling rivalry," Erika said in disgust. "That makes what you did sound so mild."

"I know it wasn't. I was horrible. I've been arrogant and

cruel, but I don't want to be that woman anymore, and I want my sister back. Desperately. Do you think we could start over?" She should add music and make those words her theme song. *Could we start over again? I really need a friend.* She needed more than a friend. She needed her sister back.

Erika squirmed a little. "I don't know. Are you worth it?"

"No."

That made her sister smile just a little, even made her mouth tremble.

Darby smiled, too, and shifted up to sit by Erika on the bed.

Erika looked away again, toward all the Hallmark happiness taking place on the screen. "You know what I loved when we were little? When you used to tell me fairy tales. Everything was perfect when we were little."

"I got stupid."

"Yeah, you did." There was still some bitterness lingering in Erika's voice.

Darby sighed. It was a good thing to have your eyes opened, but it was also a little like getting a shot. You needed it, but it hurt. All those bad choices she'd made had racked up the regrets.

They sat for a moment in silence. Then Darby slung an arm around Erika's shoulder. "Once upon a time there was a girl who had everything, but she didn't realize how much she had . . ."

It was a short tale, not very original, except for maybe the ending, where Darby pushed the mean girl into a campfire. "Her head was so fat and heavy she couldn't get out, even though everyone tried to rescue her with their hot dog forks. In the end there was nothing left of her but a bad smell."

That made Erika smile.

"They erected a monument at the site of the campfire."

"Of course they did," Erika said, shaking her head.

"They wrote on it: 'Here lies the meanest girl in town. Follow in her footsteps and you'll fall into a fire too.'"

"Good symbolism," Erika approved. "Words were always your thing."

And Darby vowed to use them more wisely in the future. She dug the ornament out of the wastebasket. "Will you take it now?"

Erika nodded solemnly and reached for it. "By the way, I'm with someone great now."

"Yeah?"

"And I'm not bringing him home to meet the family until I've got a ring on my finger," Erika added.

"Don't worry. I've learned my lesson," Darby assured her.

The movie had ended, so they started a new one together, squeezed side by side on Erika's bed. Later that night, long after her sister had fallen asleep, Darby was still awake.

She texted Josh: I have hope. The best Christmas present ever.

The next day she had happiness too. She and her siblings spent the day playing the board games they'd loved during childhood. Cole trounced them at Monopoly, but Erika was the star detective when they played Clue. Of course, Darby won when they played Scrabble.

"Everyone's a winner," she joked. She sure felt like one, on so many levels.

The winning continued when she and Gregory went to the Bird's Nest for dinner. It was hardly haute cuisine, but they made a clam chowder to die for. He ordered steak, and she asked for the chowder as well as the grilled salmon.

"Bet you don't get seafood like this in New York," Gregory said as they dug into their food.

"You can get everything in New York," Darby said.

"So, you like it." His tone of voice said he couldn't understand why.

"It's an exciting city. Always something going on."

"Hey, there's always something going on here. High school basketball and football, bingo at Our Lady of the Sacred Heart on Friday night, line dancing at the Eagle's Club. Something for everyone."

"I can see that," she said.

"And don't forget how close we are to Snoqualmie. Where can you go snowboarding in the city?"

"There are mountains back east, you know."

"Yeah? How close?"

"A couple hours away."

"Oh, sign me up."

She pointed her fork at him. "No sneering allowed."

He shook his head. "I guess I'm a provincial. I love it here."

"Actually, I'm beginning to love it here myself," Darby said.

Funny how you saw things in such a different light when your attitude changed. She'd looked down on her hometown, thinking she needed more out of life. More, of course, was somewhere else. Now she was coming to realize that she had gold in her own backyard.

Gregory Collier had a lot to do with that. In some ways, being with him felt so familiar. In others, it was like she was discovering a new man. She was also discovering new feelings for him, feelings that dug deeper into her heart than friendship.

They were halfway through their meal when she saw Laurel walk in with a date. She looked Darby's direction, and her eyebrows shot up. Gregory was hardly ugly. But he was still too many rungs down the social ladder for Laurel's approval.

Darby waved at her, determined to stay on the path of becoming a better person, but when the hostess led Laurel and her date to a table, Laurel didn't stop to say hello. Instead, as she passed, she tossed out a "Really?"

Gregory frowned. "At this rate, you're going to get kicked out of the club."

"Too late for that. I already left it. Was I really that bad?" She knew the answer before he said it. "Pretty much."

"Thanks for giving me a second chance. I am forgiven, right?"

"You are. I knew the real you was trapped in there somewhere. I'm glad you finally decided to set her free."

"Me too," said Darby.

"It might be hard for you, becoming one of us little people," he said.

"Hard because women like me make it hard." She grimaced. "Why did I think I was so special?"

"Because you were. You are. You're a living iridescent. You light up a room when you walk into it. You did that even when we were kids. Remember that show you and Erika put on when we were in fifth grade?"

"The Halloween one? Where I was Princess Pumpkin?"

She remembered that play. She'd helped Erika write the dialogue. Erika had draped her in orange fabric and stuck a cardboard toilet paper roll painted brown on top of her head to signify a stem. She'd wandered back and forth in the front yard in front of all their friends, crying, "Where are my pumpkins? How will we make jack-o'-lanterns and pumpkin pie without them?" Gregory had been drafted as Prince Pumpkin and had arrived just in time to save the day.

He smiled at the memory. "Yep. Even then you were a princess."

"And you were a prince. I can't believe I lost sight of that."

He got suddenly busy mashing the inside of his baked potato with his fork. "Have you gotten your sight back?"

"I have," she said.

"I hope so," was all he said in return.

Prince Pumpkin insisted on paying for the meal, reminding her that she was unemployed.

"Okay, how about I pay for lattes and blueberry scones tomorrow then?" she offered.

"It's a deal," he said.

As they drove home, she couldn't help wondering if he'd

try to kiss her. She wanted him to. After all, they were starting over. Shouldn't they seal the bargain with a kiss? Yet he
made no move to.

"You could kiss me good night, you know," she said.

"I could," he agreed.

"Then what are you waiting for?"

He leaned across her and opened her door. "Waiting to
make sure this is real."

"It is," she assured him.

But she didn't press. When it came to sowing humiliation
all around her, she'd done plenty—and she had no desire to
reap any more that night. Maybe, at some point, he'd see
that she really had changed. There was no hurry. It wasn't as
though she had a job to rush back to after the holidays.

Her father and Cole were in the den watching *Alien vs.
Predator*, a cheery little holiday movie, and Mom and Erika
were at the kitchen table playing gin rummy.

"How did it go?" Erika asked.

"Great. We're having coffee tomorrow."

"Lucky you," said Erika.

"Yes, lucky me," Darby agreed.

"It's nice to see you two connecting again," Mom said.

Way more than nice.

She went up to her room, pulled out her journal, and wrote:

I feel like a deflated balloon that just got a fresh shot of
helium. Forgiveness is the most amazing gift anyone can
give you. Nothing in Santa's bag of goodies can top it!

When Darby and Gregory arrived at Brewed Awakenings the next day, Janice had a smile for Gregory, but she looked less than thrilled to see Darby returning to her coffee shop. She cheerfully filled his order and silently handed Darby hers.

Here was a bridge that had not only burned but also completely washed away. There was no time like the present to haul in some more lumber and get to work.

"I see you're not busy now," Darby began.

That hadn't been the best way to begin. Oh, yes, she was so good with words.

Janice stiffened. "We just had our rush."

"That's what I figured. So, I'm hoping, since you're in between customers, you could spare a couple of minutes to talk." Right there, in front of Gregory. Pretty humiliating, but he wasn't going to hear anything new. He'd seen her past behavior.

Janice looked like she'd rather be doused with scalding coffee than chat with Darby. "So talk."

Darby got right to the point. "I owe you an apology. Well, more like a few hundred, really." She could feel Gregory staring at her, feel that heat of a blush running up her neck again.

"For what?" Janice knew, of course, but she wasn't about to let Darby off the hook.

"For the way I treated you in high school. And beyond," she added.

She'd been the queen of cocky when she returned from her first year of college. Lesser beings got snubbed. Some of them got tortured. Janice, manning the refreshment counter at the movie theater, had been one of the unlucky ones. Reamed out for not getting Darby's popcorn order right one night. *I paid for a large. Are you embezzling popcorn now? I can see you really need it.*

Ugh. Who was that girl? And why hadn't everyone in town cornered her in a dark alley and beaten her up yet?

"That's right, you do," Janice said, enough venom in her voice for ten snakes.

It was hard to continue looking her in the eye. Darby took a twenty-dollar bill from her purse and laid it on the counter. "Would you join us for a few minutes? The latte's on me. And anything else you want. Just keep the change."

For a moment she thought Janice was going to either throw the money in her face or turn her back on her. But she didn't. She took it with an unenthusiastic, "All right."

"Thanks," Darby said, then headed for a table in the middle of the room with four chairs around it.

"Did you bring me along for protection or as a witness?" Gregory said as they settled in.

"Maybe a little of both. I'm not sure how I'm going to make up for being so rotten to her, but I figure this is a good start."

"Yes, it is," he agreed.

It seemed to take forever for Janice to make her drink and join them at the table, and Darby began to shred her muffin as she waited. She hoped Janice wouldn't take advantage of their close proximity and pour the scalding drink in her lap.

Gregory finally laid a hand over hers. "You got this."

She was more sure that she was going to get it.

Janice arrived at the table, slipped into the seat next to Gregory, and turned to Darby, her face like stone.

"I wish I could travel back in time and take back every bad thing I ever said to you," Darby told her. "All I can do is say how sorry I am."

Janice's only reply to that was a shrug.

"I do want to make it up to you."

The bell on the shop door jingled, and Janice's stone face unfroze and morphed into a scowl. Darby turned to see who had come in. Ainsley and Laurel, of course.

Janice started to get up, but Darby put a hand on her arm and stopped her. "They can wait."

"They're customers. I can't make them wait," Janice said, shaking off her hand.

"She's gotta keep the customers happy," Gregory said to a frowning Darby as Janice returned to her position behind the counter.

"Nothing keeps those two happy like making someone else miserable," Darby said. "I know how they think."

Neither friend came over to the table to say hi after getting their order. Of course not, because Darby had broken the mean girl rules. She had fraternized with inferior people.

"Yep. Looks like you're off the team," Gregory said.

"I don't want to be a player anymore, anyway," she told him.

To her surprise, Janice returned to the table. "You were saying?"

Was this some sort of test? Probably. Darby knew her former posse was watching.

"I was saying that I can't undo the past, but I can be different in the future."

"How are you going to do that?" Janice scoffed.

"I can start by being your best customer. And by seeing if you're in the mood for pizza. Maybe the three of us can go to Gino's tonight."

Janice blinked in astonishment. "Who are you?"

"Meet me at Gino's and find out," Darby suggested. She turned to Gregory. "Are you interested?"

"Oh, yeah. I wouldn't miss this for the world."

Darby was aware of a presence looming at her back. She turned to see Ainsley looking down at her with scorn and disbelief.

Chapter 8

"What are you doing? Have you fallen on your head?" Ainsley demanded.

"Do you mind?" Darby said, matching her snotty tone. "I'm trying to have a meaningful conversation here. Which is more than I've ever had with you. Every time you open your mouth, nothing but air comes out."

Okay, not exactly gracious.

Ainsley's eyes grew to the size of saucers, and her cheeks took on a reddish tint.

Darby could feel heat on her own cheeks. "Okay, that was rude. Sorry."

"You sure are. In fact, you're pathetic," Ainsley said. Then, with an offended huff, she marched back to the window table. There she signaled to Laurel, and the two left the shop.

"Sorry, I think you just lost some business," Darby said. *Sorry*, now the most used word in her vocabulary.

"Their business I can do without," replied Janice. "You

know, I didn't believe what you said about wanting to be different. But I do now."

"I meant it. So, how about taking me up on the offer of pizza?"

"I'll pass on the pizza, but they make a great chopped chicken salad," Janice said.

"Salad works," Darby said, and smiled.

"Not for me. I want pizza," put in Gregory.

"That too," Darby said, still smiling. How much better the world was when you seasoned your days with kindness.

Both Cole and Erika joined the pizza expedition, and afterward everyone returned to the house to play games. Darby even drafted her parents into playing Pictionary with them. The evening was filled with laughter and camaraderie. Darby couldn't remember the last time she'd smiled so much—not the fake ones or the superior smirks she'd gotten so skilled at, but genuine, happy ones.

The next day she and Gregory hit the slopes. He received several texts from Arielle but ignored them all. Darby tried hard not to feel superior.

"This has been great," she said as they made their way to his SUV for the ride home.

"You're not bored yet?" he asked.

"Why would I be?"

"Not exactly the glamorous life you've been leading with all those big-city movers and shakers."

"No, I'm genuinely having fun."

"You really have changed, haven't you?" he said.

"Working on it. And don't sound so surprised. God can change anyone who's willing, right?"

"Right. So what else has changed about you, besides your behavior?"

"What do you mean?" she asked.

"I'm thinking of your taste in men. Still dating the top-of-the-line superstars with *GQ* wardrobes?"

Gregory was a casual dresser, tending toward jeans, T-shirts, and plaid flannel shirts that made him look a little like a lumberjack. But the shirts brought out the green in those hazel eyes of his. There was nothing wrong with the man himself either. Gregory was as kind and honest as he'd always been.

Once they reached the vehicle, she leaned against it and looked up at him. "I'm still greedy. I still want top-of-the-line. In character."

"Yeah? Got anyone in mind?"

Did she ever. "What do you think?"

He showed her. He cupped her face with his hands and leaned in. He smelled like fresh air, and the tiniest hint of the hot chocolate they'd enjoyed at the lodge lingered on his lips. His kiss was better than any she'd ever received from the jocks she'd dated in high school or players she'd gone with in college—so much better, even, than the last loser she'd kissed in New York. Gregory's kiss said commitment and happiness.

It had sure taken her long enough to figure out what was important. The kiss continued, and she slipped her hands up his chest and onto his shoulders. They felt amazingly solid. It was cold standing there in the ski resort parking lot, but with the fire he'd lit inside her, who cared?

"How was that?" he murmured as he gently pulled away.

"That was amazing," she said, her eyes still closed. "You are a fabulous kisser."

She opened her eyes to see that he, too, could master a superior smirk. "About time you gave me a chance to show you how good I am."

"I bet you've always been good," she said. "I've just been blind."

But no more.

That night they went back to the Bird's Nest. Ainsley was there with a date—Griff Moore—whom Darby had dated when she was a junior in high school. He'd dumped her right before her junior prom and had eventually gotten together with Ainsley, who'd been trying her best to steal him from Darby all along. That hadn't lasted long, either, and after she and Ainsley made up, Darby had been quick to point out that she knew it wouldn't.

Darby hadn't seen him in years, and it felt a little like déjà vu seeing him with Ainsley. Maybe she was finally going to get him. He was still fine looking, but not as hot as when he'd been captain of the football team.

"I thought he'd be married by now," she mused as she and Gregory waited for their server to take their order.

Gregory shrugged. "He married Marissa Fortunata." Fellow cheerleader and Darby's chief rival for queen of the hill way-back-when. "They got divorced a couple years ago."

"Where's Marissa now?"

"I hear she moved to Park City and married a ski instructor." Tired of the subject, Gregory returned to perusing the menu. "Think I'll have the prime rib," he said.

Think I'll have a good laugh, Darby thought, then corrected herself. She was no longer interested in revenge or taking delight in anyone else's failure. Hopefully Griff would do better next time around . . . unless he wound up with Ainsley.

The restaurant's lighting was low, but it wasn't so low her former friend and boyfriend couldn't see Darby. They both ignored her. Even when all four of them wound up leaving the restaurant at the same time.

As they walked out onto the sidewalk, a car zipped by and sent up a rooster tail of slush. "Look out," Gregory said, trying to move Darby out of the way.

Too late. It caught her on the legs and splashed muddy water on her boots, leggings, and coat as well, bringing about a relapse of bad words. She looked down and gave her coat a helpless shake. Ugh. First blood and now mud. The thing was doomed.

She heard a giggle and looked to see Ainsley delighting in the moment.

Griff, too, was smiling. "Merry Christmas," he called.

"Same to you," she called back, then scowled down at her poor coat. Was it her imagination, or was she turning into a target for crap?

Well, she'd thrown enough mud other people's way. It was about time she got some. She shook her head and chuckled.

"You're laughing?" Gregory asked in surprise.

"Only at the irony of it all. With all the humbling I dished out over the years, it's time I got a helping of it myself. Looks like I'm going to get several. Let's go back to my place. I need to get into some dry clothes."

Back at the Browns' home, Mom's eyes grew wide at the sight of Darby. "You are a magnet for mess this holiday season," she said when Darby showed her the coat. "I think we can get it clean though."

"I don't know," Darby said doubtfully. "Maybe I should just take it to the dry cleaners."

"Let me try first," Mom insisted, taking the coat from her. "It won't take long. Gregory, we're about to watch a classic movie. Why don't you stay and watch it with us?"

"Not *Alien*," Darby begged.

"Your mother vetoed it," her father said with a frown. "We have to stay on Christmas overload."

"Christmas only comes once a year," Mom reminded him.

"It's a good thing. Our bank account couldn't handle more than once a year," Dad retorted.

His wife ignored him. Darby followed her into the laundry room and watched as she went to work spot-cleaning the coat.

"I may as well resign myself to the fact that it's never going to be the same," she predicted. "That was a Vince." She'd gotten it at Bergdorf Goodman, and it had cost a pretty penny. Now that she was unemployed, she wished she had some of those pennies back.

"What's a Vince?" Mom asked, working away at the stains with her damp cloth.

"A brand of clothes I can't afford anymore. Oh, well."

"My, you are being calm and philosophical about this," Mom said.

Yes—there, too, was a change.

"All part of my steep learning curve," Darby quipped.

One thing she *was* learning at a rapid pace was to appreciate Gregory Collier. He'd been her best friend in grade school; she was finding her best friend all over again now that they were adults. Even better, after that kiss they'd shared, she dared to hope they could be a lot more than friends.

They'd just settled on the couch with popcorn and eggnog to watch *Christmas with the Kranks* when Gregory's phone pinged. Darby knew even without asking who the text was from. Arielle. Of course he'd ignore her, like he had all day.

He didn't. Darby, who had always been so confident, so self-assured, was suddenly hit by an avalanche of insecurity. She could feel that warm holiday feeling slipping away from her.

No, no, no. Between her broken nose, tonight's mud bath, and falling out with old friends, she was learning enough lessons. Losing Gregory just when she'd found him again would be taking this whole learning thing too far. She held her breath and surreptitiously looked over as he thumbed his response.

Chapter 9

Busy all week, he texted.

All right! "Yeah? With who?" Darby teased.

"Guess," he replied. "And what are you doing reading my texts?" he asked with a grin and a cocked eyebrow.

"I just happened to see," she said, returning the grin.

Of course, Arielle couldn't take such a subtle no for an answer. With???

Darby

U R nuts.

No, happy, he texted, then turned off his phone.

"Really?" she whispered, snuggling closer.

"Really," he whispered back. "I got my old friend again. Welcome back."

"It's good to be back."

"Hey, you two are going to miss something," said Dad, who was not a fan of multitasking when it came to watching movies.

They exchanged smiles and returned their attention to the movie, and he took her hand in his.

After her parents went to bed, they returned to paying attention to each other. The kiss he gave her before he left promised more than friendship. And to think she hadn't wanted to come home for the holidays!

On Christmas Eve, the family attended the candlelight service for one of the Brown family's twice-yearly church appearances: Christmas and Easter. The folks figured those two celebrations covered it all.

Darby was coming to believe that there were a lot of days she could fill in between those two, but she was happy to start with this special night.

And it was special. Gregory sat a couple rows over with his parents and older brother. He smiled at her, and her heart warmed. The cherry on top of the red velvet cupcake was sitting next to her sister, knowing that the barrier between them had started to come down.

"As we light our candles, can we say to each other, 'The Lord bless you'?" suggested Pastor Grant.

Darby sure could, with all her heart. "I mean it," she added after she'd lit her sister's candle.

"I know you do," Erika said, and that meant the world to Darby.

After the service, the Colliers hosted a caroling party, and even though Darby couldn't carry a tune for an inch, she happily stood next to Gregory and attempted to sing "Joy to the World." She sounded like a crow next to his beautiful tenor voice, but he didn't seem to care.

As they stood in the Colliers' living room with the rest of the carolers, drinking eggnog punch, she said to him, "When did you grow such a gorgeous voice?"

"After puberty," he replied.

"You should be on *The Voice*."

He shook his head. "I don't want to be a performer. I'm happy where I am, doing what I'm doing."

Making a difference in young lives. It was more than she could say for her own work. What was she doing with her life? What *could* she be doing? She had no idea.

"Lucky you," she said.

"Lucky because?"

"You're doing something important."

"Everyone can do something important for someone. You don't have to do good deeds for a living, you know. Just when the opportunity comes around."

She gave a snort. "Good deeds aren't exactly my forte."

"Could be. You know, there are a lot of kids at school who struggle with reading. Many of 'em will graduate by the skin of their teeth. College won't even be an option. How can it be when you can't read?"

"I can't imagine what it would be like to not be able to read," Darby said.

Carolyn Keene had showed her how to be a girl sleuth when she was a child, and Victoria Holt and Debbie Macomber had kept her dreaming about love once she got older. It was hard to wrap her mind around someone not being able to experience that enjoyment. And, yes, how could you make it through college if you could barely read?

"I know, right?" said Gregory. "But it's true. The school is putting together a volunteer program, matching up people with skills in English who can help. You'd be perfect."

"Except I don't live here anymore."

"You could though."

Coming back home. Once upon a delusion, she'd thought she was way too good to get stuck in Eagledale. Now she half-wondered if she was good enough yet to come back.

"Think about it," he urged, and she promised she would.

Was there a way she could bury the old Darby, her old reputation, and build a new life here? Even just tonight, two of the Colliers' guests had avoided her and moved to the other side of the room when they saw her coming.

"I don't know if I'd fit," she mused, looking their direction.

"The old you might not have. But I haven't seen her since you got back. Have you?"

"Glimpses. But she's on her way out."

"So who cares about her?"

"Not me," Darby said. "That's for sure."

"You had enough eggnog?" he asked. "Want to get out of here?"

"Sure. Where to?"

"Thought the new you might like to check out the Christmas lights."

"I would."

One neighborhood in particular had always been worth a visit when Darby was growing up, having dubbed itself Candy Cane Lane. For many consecutive Christmases, her parents drove her and her siblings to check it out when they were kids. It had been years since she'd gone to look at Christmas lights because, of course, by the age of fourteen she was simply too cool to be bothered. She wasn't that cool anymore.

Candy Cane Lane had gotten bigger and grander since she visited it years ago. As they approached, she could hear canned Christmas music playing. A giant twinkling Merry Christmas arch had been erected at the entrance to the housing development, held up by lit plastic candy canes.

"Wow, they've gotten serious about this," Darcy said, taking it in.

"Oh, yeah. Everybody who has kids comes here before Christmas," said Gregory.

Obviously. Several cars were crawling along in front of them.

Up ahead and down the street, every roofline, bush, and tree sparkled. It looked like a carnival. A man dressed as Santa was handing out candy canes, and Darby rolled down her window and accepted two from him.

"Ho, ho, hope you have a wonderful Christmas," he said after she thanked him.

"Ho, ho, hope you do too," she replied. Had she just said that?

"What, no smart-mouth answer?" Gregory teased.

"The new-and-improved me."

"The old you, found again," he said. "I'm glad."

"Me too," she said.

They checked out houses decked in multicolored jewel lights, and houses with reindeer prancing on their lawns alongside snow globes or elves. Every tree on the street was wrapped with lights—blue, gold, red. Nativities abounded, a good reminder of the reason for the season. And every house sported candy canes somewhere.

"You ready to move to Candy Cane Lane?" Gregory asked when they finally drove off to check out some other neighborhoods.

"No, thanks. That neighborhood has turned into Christmas Coney Island."

"So, no Christmas lights for you?"

"I didn't say that. I'd love to have those white icicles dangling from my roof. They're so pretty when it snows. Of course, first I have to have a house."

"I have a house," he said.

What was behind that comment? She wanted there to be something. Even though they'd just reconnected after so many years, she found herself envisioning a life in Eagledale, near her parents and living happily ever after with Gregory.

"You can string icicle lights on it anytime you want," he continued.

Okay, not quite the same vision she'd had. "You string 'em and I'll watch," she said, and he chuckled.

Back at her house, he stopped the car and turned to face her. "Okay, I gotta ask. Are you open to coming back to Eagledale, or am I just getting my hopes up for nothing?"

That confirmed it. She wasn't the only one with hopes. Merry Christmas!

"I mean, I know it's not New York," he said.

"No, it's not," she agreed. "Funny how not that many years ago I thought the last place I wanted to be was Eagledale."

"And now?" he prompted.

"I think the last place I want to be is anywhere that's not here," she said.

His face was shadowy under the streetlights, but she could still see his smile. "Come here," he said.

She did, and was rewarded with a kiss. Gregory, the little boy she'd played freeze tag with, the nerd she'd scorned when she was a teenage fool, had become a mature and confident man. Who knew how to turn a woman to marshmallow creme with those lips of his.

"Where did you learn to kiss like that?" she asked. If a cat could talk after having too much catnip, it would probably sound like her.

"Here and there. In between pining for you."

"I think you can stop pining now," she said, and went back for seconds.

Chapter 10

Christmas morning began with the traditional Brown family breakfast of waffles and Mom's famous egg casserole. Then it was off to gather around the tree with their mugs of hot chocolate to open presents. Darby smiled at the sight of the ornament she'd given Erika, hanging front and center on the tree.

She'd brought back all kinds of big-city treats for everyone. Sweatshirts for Dad and Cole and mugs for Mom and Erika that featured iconic New York sights—all painted in pretty pastels—as well as knockoff designer purses she'd gotten on Canal Street. And for Jackal, a squeaky dog toy shaped like a yellow taxi.

Cole gave her a Starbucks gift card—such originality.

"Hey, I figure you can use it when you go back," he said in his own defense.

"But maybe she'll be wanting one to Brewed Awakenings," Mom said, giving Darby a knowing smile.

Yes, maybe she would.

Her parents gave her a practical present—a Visa gift card. In addition to that, she and Erika both received personalized music boxes from Mom. The script on the top brought tears to Darby's eyes.

Daughter, wherever you go, know that my love goes with you. You are special, and you are my treasure.

Those tears spilled over as Darby hugged her mother and thanked her.

"I have one more present for you," Mom told her. "Although you don't have to haul it back to New York. I'm happy to keep it here for you if you want."

Darby opened the box, parted the red tissue paper, and saw that framed essay she'd written long ago. Mom had since dated it.

"I've had it in the hope chest all these years," she told Darby. "But I need to start downsizing. Anyway, I thought you might like a reminder of how talented you are. By the way, there is something under that."

Darby lifted the essay and saw something else framed—an enlarged picture of her in her Princess Pumpkin costume. In one corner of the picture Mom had written with a felt tipped pen: *Always our shining star.*

Darby was, to her amazement and everyone else's, speechless.

Until Erika finally said, "Maybe you need to start writing again."

Yes, but not on how to look good. How to be good.

That thought inspired more, and as Cole set up his new video game system with Dad and Erika texted with her man in California, Darby pulled out her phone and began to make some notes. And then to write.

A few minutes later, Mom joined her on the couch, carrying her new mug filled with coffee. "What are you working on?"

She turned the phone so her mother could read. "Maybe this needs to go on a music box," Mom said.

"What?" Erika stopped texting and came to sit on the other side of Darby to read it.

"You really have changed," she said when she was done.

Darby looked at it and reread what she'd written. Not bad for a first effort.

Tis the Season . . .
To see that, like Frosty the Snowman, our dreams can melt if we wait too long to make them come true
To understand that, like a certain red-nosed reindeer, everyone has potential and no one should be excluded
To be humble, like the Little Drummer Boy
To know that it's not the presents under the tree but the people gathered around it that matter
To realize that the best thing to ask for is forgiveness and the greatest gift we can give anyone is love.

Later that night she wound up at Gregory's house, comparing how their Christmas Day had gone.

"Mine was chaos, as usual," he said. "My nephews were

amped up on sugar, and they terrified my mom's cat. Then they broke the arm on Mom's mechanical waving Santa. His waving days are now over, I guess. Oh, and remember Aunt Bernice?"

"The ugly sweater queen?"

"She dropped the red velvet cake on the way to the table."

"Sounds pretty entertaining," Darby said.

"And my cousin brought a friend who she knew would be perfect for me."

Darby frowned at that. "Is she?"

"Uh, that would be a no. The Griswolds have nothing on us."

"Now, there's a Christmas movie I haven't watched in a while," Darby said.

"Don't ask me to watch it with you. My personal Griswold Christmas is still fresh in my mind."

She chuckled. "Okay, no *National Lampoon's Christmas Vacation* then."

"Now onward and upward, to New Year's Eve," he said. "Have you got plans?"

"Not yet . . ."

"You do now," he informed her, and kissed her. Then he sobered. "And how about after New Year's Day? Do you have to go back to the city?"

"Only to collect my things."

"Yeah?" He looked at her hopefully.

"I think I need to make a new start somewhere else."

"With someone else?"

"Do you have someone in mind?" she teased.

"I sure do," he said. "I met this girl recently."

Darby smiled at that. She'd met a new girl too. The one she looked at in the mirror only that morning was very different from the one she'd seen for so many years. She liked this new Darby and knew that—whatever the future held—this girl would walk into it with kindness.

Later that night she texted Josh. I got something great for Christmas.

Yeah? What?

A new start. It was the perfect Christmas gift.

Dashing Through the Snow

MELISSA FERGUSON

To Ben, the one who puts on the green tights and Elf hat to please me in all my Christmas-loving schemes. I pick you for every train adventure.

Chapter 1
PLEASE COME HOME FOR CHRISTMAS

There is something about frantically shielding yourself from a linebacker of a man throwing his body and belongings straight toward the quickest route of exit—which, in this case, is through you—that really puts a kick in your step at 5:00 a.m.

While newly arrived trains screech to a halt and yawn, tossing open their doors and throwing out their sleepy travelers, I cling to the handles of the two colossal, waist-high suitcases on either side of me and lug them another step forward. Meanwhile Linebacker Man with the desperate eyes and swinging suitcases is still coming at me, and with the bells of my elf slippers jingling in mockery at my situation, I jump backward as swiftly as I can.

The nearly empty coffee cup, which had hitherto been dangling between two spare fingers not devoted to suitcase handling, dances precariously, and I regrip it just in time.

He passes me with an inch to spare, then begins taking the stairs three at a time.

What could possibly be that important?

While my mind draws up a few imaginary scenarios, I turn back toward the Moynihan Train Hall station platform. My attention shifts, however, to an unmistakable tapping on my slippers. A *drip-drip* of what's left of the weak, tawny coffee leaving spots on my new shoes.

"*Shoot.*" I let out an exasperated sigh.

"Willow? What's happened now?" Elodie says, and I nearly jump remembering the Bluetooth in my ear.

"I spilled coffee on my slippers."

"Oh, honey, *no.*"

Elodie is the best roommate anyone could ask for. Immigrated with her professor parents to Erwin, Tennessee, from Southern France at eleven, she is the perfect combination of quiet intellect and lemme-catch-that-chicken-for-dinner hillbilly. Throw in the fact that she moved to New York at eighteen for university, and she's one great big concoction of refinement, empathy, and hard-hitting street smarts.

She bakes to self-soothe.

She clog dances at parties upon request.

She will crack her umbrella on the hood of a cab in stilettos in the rain while screaming, "Get off my back!" and in the next sentence slip her arm through your elbow when you're feeling low and coo, "Oh, sweetie. How about I make you some of that shepherd's pie you like so much?"

She glides through both life and work at the French

patisserie with unwitting Audrey Hepburn-level ease, spunk, and charm. Throws terms of endearment at total strangers like confetti. And best of all, loves me at my best, and my worst.

And the past three days, I've been at my worst.

"Did you pack your tissues?" Elodie says in such a motherly tone I can't help pursing my lips. "I told you to put those on the list."

"I'm looking now." I drop my purse onto the top of one suitcase and begin digging. It's ridiculous to care so much about shoes, but just . . . well, since the Jonas conversation, anything can flip me like a coin these days.

Which is why Elodie's concern for my shoes is comforting. She knows the Arrival Day shoes. She knows how much time and energy I'd spent finding the Arrival Day shoes. She knows just how much I've saved up from my less-than-affluent home health job to get the shoes. And she knows that no matter how ridiculous the emerald-green leather slippers and their near-constant jingling coming from the tips of the curlicue toes are, how also terrifyingly little it takes to make me lapse into tears right now.

It's pathetic, really.

I already wept on the way here spotting a rat beside an old Chinese takeout box, recalling the way I'd clung to Jonas the first time I'd seen one in the city.

Me. Just standing there on the curb at four thirty in the morning. My blinking Christmas tree sweater glowing in the dark as I stared longingly at a rat. Weeping.

I find an old receipt in my purse and commence wiping.

The liquid-resistant thermal paper proves worthless from the start, and while Elodie continues to mother me, I switch to using my palm. "Okay," she says, "it says here that if it starts to stain, you need to mix one part white vinegar with two parts water. Do you have any vinegar with you?"

I drop my head. "Sure, Elodie. There's a vinegar kiosk right by the bathrooms."

"Honey, I've got forty more baguettes to make before opening, and I'm juggling the miracle of internet research while up to my neck in dough. Productive words only, please. Did you at least find some tissues?"

I look down at my dripping palm. "More or less."

And while Elodie carries on, traipsing down a long path of vinegar substitutes I may be able to wrangle from the dining car once aboard, I become aware of the travelers bustling by, all hugging their black purses and briefcases against their black winter coats, no doubt heading for a cup of coffee before driving themselves straight into the madness of New York City during Christmas. I am aware of how their gait slows as they pass me and my ensemble, and how their gazes drag. At least two follow with a sweep of the concrete floor around me, looking no doubt for some sort of hat or box detailing where to leave tips for the entertainer should she jump into performance.

Well. This is what I get for being early.

I must've sighed again, because the next moment Elodie is talking in my ear.

"You really should try to get some sleep when you're on

the train, Willow. You're not doing yourself any favors *going, going, going* the past three days. I'm afraid if I let you off the phone, you'll nod off and fall onto the tracks."

"I'm fine."

"You've arrived two hours early for a train you don't even want to be on."

"I took a nap yesterday." I ignore the urge to yawn. "And anyway, I just couldn't stand another minute staring at my ceiling. I needed to do something. I needed to *go*."

Which is true. Whereas I've always been jittery before flying out to Mom's, now I felt it more than ever. The day Jonas broke up with me, I just sort of stood there in a daze— wherever *there* happened to be. Well, and crying. Pretty much dehydrating myself as a constant leaky faucet. But yesterday morning, day two of my new life single, I woke up with a start, and my legs itched to jump up and go. As though my body was trying to compensate for the fact that my mind had become stuck in quicksand, and it had decided overnight it was going to handle all the movement from now on.

So, I got busy.

Shampooed every piece of fabric in the apartment.

Washed every towel and sheet we had.

Went on a grocery shopping spree and bought fifty-six lemons, then proceeded to make lemon meringue pie for every resident in our building.

Ate half a lemon meringue pie.

Spent way too long in front of a pet store, considering buying a cat.

Decided the cat was a bad idea before traveling, and instead decided it'd be brilliant to learn how to crochet for the train ride.

Watched a dozen videos on how to crochet for the train ride, went to the yarn store and bought supplies, realized it didn't really make much sense to give up two hundred dollars for the privilege of spending one hundred hours learning to crochet a subpar sweater when I could just pop down to Reminiscence consignment with a twenty-dollar bill, and hauled everything back to the store.

Packed.

Ate the other half of the lemon meringue pie.

Dressed to the nines in an explosion of Christmas cheer.

And now, here I am.

Ready for my two-week-long train ride across the country on The Christmas Express. And the only thing truly different about the reality of this moment versus what I'd dreamed it would look like all year is that, instead of holding one golden ticket to hand to some cheery conductor at precisely 7:12 a.m., I'm holding two. One for me. One for my boyfriend of seven years who met a waitress on the corner of 55th and 10th precisely three-and-a-half days ago and decided he was instantly in love. I don't know how, given the depth of their conversation couldn't have gone much further than, "Do you want your eggs sunny side up or scrambled?" but there it is.

So now, instead of traveling on the yuletide getaway I'd been dreaming about since I first clipped out the magazine ad about it four years ago, Jonas is driving down to the mountains of West Virginia, where his new love, *Be-cky*, and her family will share a holiday meal. While those in my family who haven't heard the news continue to run bets on where Jonas was going to propose (would it be under the tree Christmas morning? Or something terribly romantic on the train beforehand?), I get the joy of preparing how to convincingly converse with a flippant smile. "Actually, *and this is no big deal whatsoever*, we broke up after all. Yes, even though he bought the train tickets. No, Aunt Elda, I don't know what we should do with all the extra artichoke dip for the engagement party. I suppose, eat it."

As for me, I'm spending two weeks on a trip marketed by *Time* and *Leisure* as, "The Most Romantic Getaway of the Season." What *Parade* calls, "The Most Nostalgic Christmas Vacation You'll Ever Experience." Two weeks on a train full of doe-eyed couples—alone.

Because that's what you get when you have a nonrefundable ticket, a need to get home for Christmas, and a life on a tight budget. You get to be surrounded by couples mooning over heart-shaped marshmallows in their cocoa and ardently kissing under mistletoe. You get to be in purgatory.

"Well, at least you looked very nice this morning," Elodie says. "Frankly, I'm a bit surprised you decided to dress up."

"I'm trying to make up for the death I feel on the inside," I reply, raising my voice to be heard as another train slides up to the platform.

Elodie's right though. Aside from the dried tear streaks down both cheeks, I'm a far cry more pulled together today.

Instead of the bird's nest held together by grease and desperation that has accompanied me the past three days, my chestnut curls bounced buoyantly as I walked through town—as if they have tired of my emotional turmoil and have chosen to persist despite me. And I took extra pains with my mascara and liner this morning, which, at least before the great rat sighting, made my typically pale-green eyes sing in chorus with the blinking green bulbs of my Christmas sweater. And then, of course, there is the outfit: the cheery tree sweater, followed by a black corduroy skirt, black tights, and elf slippers.

"And I decided," I continue, "if I have to break the rules by going alone, I might as well follow the recommended dress code on the welcome packet."

"You didn't break the rules," Elodie counters. "Nobody is going to think that."

There's a long pause. I'm not going to argue with her. I know she's right. Still, I can't help feeling a bit guilty for being the train's unintentional third wheel.

"Can I be honest with you, Willow?"

My brows rise. In our five years together as roommates, I can't recall a moment where Elodie has been anything *aside* from honest.

"I find Jonas repulsive."

"Well, of course we find him repulsive," I shoot back. "That's been the group cheer the past three days. Your job is to keep me supplied with macarons while telling me he's a horrible person."

"And if you recall I did pat your head and stuff your sobby little ungrateful face with meticulously baked macarons, and I did ask where he was so I could hound him down. *But* what I mean is not just despising him now after everything. I'm saying he's repulsive. He's always been repulsive. And your taste in men is an appalling enigma."

A full minute passes in silence between us while a train whirs by, and all I can think to say when I speak again is, "How long have you thought this?"

"Five years."

I laugh in disbelief. "There's no way. You've hung out with him thousands of times over the past five years. *Thousands.* You threw us a surprise anniversary party last year. He asked you to be the godmother for our children one day, *and you hugged him and cried.* You can't be that good of a liar."

"It's chilling what I can achieve for the sake of my friends."

My eyes widen. Yes. Yes, it was.

"Annnyway," she says, her tone unnervingly brighter, "the point is, Jonas was selfish and weird about his stuff. You give to a fault. Jonas was boring. *You,* when you're not drowning in despair at least, are a delight."

I frown. "Thank you."

"And Jonas, quite frankly, was a jerk who always knew he wouldn't end up with you and strung you along far too long."

I shake my head. "No. He loved me."

"Yes, but he didn't love you *enough*. And he knew that. And he waited until he had somebody else in the wings to let you go."

"And lastly," Elodie rushes on before I can reply, "and most importantly, I don't think you really loved him enough either."

I feel slapped. "Elodie, you know that's not true. I would've married him."

"I absolutely agree. You'd have stuck through it with him just like you've stuck with everything else in your life. For better or for worse."

Hey now. "Not true."

"Tell me, how long exactly have you stood in front of every pet store in town, mulling over whether or not to get a cat but never do?"

"Jonas was allergic, you know that."

"He just didn't *like* them, and *you* know that. What do you eat every Friday night?"

I know where she's going. "Taste of Thai. But that's only because it's downstairs and they have the best egg rolls in the Village. That's a well-known fact."

"And where do you shop almost exclusively?"

We answer simultaneously, "Reminiscence consignment."

"And who is your best friend?"

"I'm not sure." I narrow my eyes. "I may be about to be in the market for a new one."

"There's a *but* here." Elodie ignores me. "*But* thankfully, you *are* my little *ma belle petite étoile*. You are my beautiful little star. You may not welcome new adventures without being thrust out by the boot, but now that this is where you've landed, you're only going to be the better for it. I believe it. I'm *certain*."

There are several more "buck ups" and "once you take off those Jonas blinders, you'll see how wonderful the world is" statements, followed by a fair share of demands like, "Now if you see this difficult-to-find cheese or that rare-and-authentic ingredient somewhere, make sure to buy three . . ." that all ends with a string of French expletives and a *click* when her baguettes start to burn.

As I pull the Bluetooth out of my ear, I take in my surroundings. The small platform between the trains is empty now, but for a single trash can beneath blue signs. Two empty trains wait silently on either side, making the space look suddenly quite lonely and forsaken. I hadn't intended to stay down here so long. Only enough to take a quick peek to be certain I had the train right and then move back upstairs to wait it out in the main hall.

I drop the old receipt in the trash can, and when I turn back toward my suitcases, stop.

A man is standing halfway down the stairs.

One hand resting on the silver railing, his back leg lingers on a step behind him as though having been busily on his way down when stopped abruptly. The look in his eyes confirms it. The thing that had stopped him was me. *Me.*

There's a light in his eyes, almost as bright as the shiny bronze bell at the end of his emerald-green hat. In fact, from his head to his toes he's in emerald green, save for the black leather slippers curling at the ends. Sandy-blond hair curlicues beneath his hat, and his cheeks, well, they look as ruddy and innocent as if he were a live-in-the-flesh elf himself.

While he stands there, smiling at me through his gingerbread-brown eyes, I can't help but feel a tingle run through my spine.

Although, to be fair, at the moment the reason is cut down the middle on whether this is because I may have run into a psychopath, or because . . . well, something much cozier.

"Excuse me," he says, and his voice is rich and deep as though he isn't in fact wearing an elf costume but instead is a dignified businessman in a trench coat who just had to stop and talk to the beautiful woman. He holds out a hand. "I just have to commend you. That is one of the most striking Arrival Day ensembles I've ever seen."

Then he beams at me. Actually beams, as though I fulfilled and exceeded every task.

For the first time in a long time, I feel a funny feeling on my cheeks as two warm, no doubt bright, spots form. "Why . . . thank you," I say, then wave at him, "And you . . . you have a lovely Arrival Day ensemble on too."

We smile at each other for one infinite moment.

He glances at the watch hidden beneath his gold-threaded cuff. "Say, we have a little while before the train comes. Want to grab a cup of coffee?"

And just like that, the Jonas blinders have flown off.

Chapter 2
ALL ABOARD!

"Ian's *amazing*," I whisper, ripping off a paper towel beneath the fluorescent lights of the station's restroom. Hastily, I drench it under cold water.

"Sweetie—"

"And so *sweet*." I lean in until I'm two inches away from the mirror for a full examination of my makeup.

"Now just hang on—"

"And we have *so much in common*. It's unbelievable, Elodie! He loves traveling. Talked for nearly twenty minutes about his absolute passion for all things planes, trains, or automobiles. And yes," I add, before she can protest, "I know I haven't exactly *traveled* a lot, but I've always *wanted to*. Oh! And his heart for animals"—I clutch the soggy paper towel to my chest in memory of the sweet conversation of his dog (or was it cat?), Chaucer, with whom he is so inseparable they not only share the bed but breakfast—"and *reading*." I swoon internally at one of my favorite reminders. "Ian says he doesn't even *own* a television. Says he's always preferred literature as the 'paramount form of entertainment for his mind.' Tell me, Elodie, when's the last time you've ever heard *any* man prefer a book to television?"

"*Willow,*" Elodie cuts in sharply. "When I gave you that little pep talk an hour and a half ago about finding other fish in the sea, I didn't mean to find the *literal* first human being you spot and reel him in."

"I know that." I blot at a mascara spot beneath my eye. "I know. It's just . . . he's perfect."

"Noooo." Elodie's voice slides on the word until it hits a note a full octave higher. "See, what you actually have is a grown man in an elf costume who bought you a crappy cup of coffee in a train station. And what I have on my hands right now is a sleep-deprived, emotionally unhinged roommate who's been so dispossessed of proper treatment in the relationship department that she's ready to hitch her wagon to the first guy she meets. Do *not* get yourself too entangled with this guy. Remember, you are rebounding, sweetie. *Rebounding.* You can't trust your instincts right now."

I frown at myself in the mirror as I begin swiping beneath the other eye. "This isn't rebounding."

"Honey, this is the *definition* of rebounding. If I were leading a class on the art of rebounding, you would be my example."

A janitor walks her yellow bucket and sopping mop into

the bathroom, and I lower my voice even further. "It is only rebounding if the man doesn't turn out to be *the one*."

A string of French curses ensues, followed by, "Willow Renee Fairbanks. Do I need to come down there *and get you*?"

This follows with one long lecture, along with whole sections of untranslated paragraphs I can only assume were repetitions she felt were so important they needed to be included in two languages. I'm fairly used to these ramblings at this point in my life, and while she carries on, I finish reapplying some mascara, do what I can to retwist some curls that are already coming undone, and give my cheeks a couple life-lifting slaps.

"Elodie, I love your concern for me, but I gotta go," I interject at last, slipping my purse over one shoulder and giving a parting smile to the janitor as I leave.

"Do *not* elope with this guy!" Elodie replies, as though sliding in that last-second warning just might save me from imminent disaster. "Or make any last-minute decisions of any kind. You hear me? *Do not make any big decisions of any kind*."

I finish the call and cross through the open exit, where Ian's face immediately comes into view. He's standing at a polite distance from the restroom, not so close that it's creepy, but just close enough that it's clear he's waiting for someone. *Me*. Guarding my suitcases, he holds both of our second cups of coffee.

As I move in, he grins widely and hands me mine.

"Just about time for the *big arrival*," he says, and his eyes positively dance. "Shall we?"

He takes the handle of one of the suitcases, which allows me to hold the second in one hand and my coffee in the other. And so, together, we move.

Like an adorable couple.

Bing Crosby's "Silver Bells" is playing over the speakers, and as we walk along, just two elves in a sea of black coats, I can't help glancing at him out of the corner of my eye. We've shared about our hobbies and habits, but I still am a bit afraid to bring up exactly how he ended up on this train like me. Alone. Or if there's not some elf girlfriend straggling behind.

After all, this is a *romantic* holiday getaway for two. And I can't help noticing, he isn't carrying any luggage.

And while he's been chummy and nothing short of delightful, at the same time, it'd be terribly embarrassing to assume what he's thinking. He did buy me coffee, yes. But that could just have been a friendly gesture with a fellow passenger. I *think* he pulled a chair out for me at the little coffee shop, but then there's a halfway decent chance he actually tripped on the leg of the chair and recovered with a little dance step after. He attentively listened and nodded almost nonstop with his ruddy cheeks and twinkling eyes, but it *could* be that he's just the friendliest elf alive.

Dash it. I'm going for it.

"So," I say, as we move underneath the sign directing us toward our train and follow its arrow toward the opening with its descending stairs, "I can't help but notice you're going stag on this little excursion for two."

"You know? I can't help but notice the same for you." He adjusts his grip on the suitcase, lifts it, and, together, we take our first step down.

Butterflies flutter in my stomach at his tone.

"Actually," he continues, slower now, "I was . . . wondering . . . as we're both going alone . . . maybe we could partner up on this trip. Traveling is always so much nicer when you have someone to enjoy it with."

"*Yes,*" I say immediately. Elodie's fists are pounding somewhere in the back of my cranium.

But this isn't a big decision. I'm just saying yes to partnering up for the next two weeks. Just two weeks. What's the alternative anyway? Doing everything alone? I smile up at Ian. "Yes. That'd be really nice. I've never been to . . ."

But as the platform comes into sight below, my words fade. Because standing there, smoke curling around its chimney, is our train.

I don't know what I had expected it to look like before; something akin to all the other mud-dusted silver bullets that have come in and out of the station. But *this*. This is something entirely different. Gleaming candy-apple red paint across the body, trimmed throughout in gold and green. A colossal wreath hangs on the front of the engine, the scent of pine needles already waging and winning the fight against the typical greasy air. And through the cab window sits a conductor in a dark-green coat and wide-crowned pershing hat, pulling a golden rope that leads to a large brass bell. The walls echo with its chime.

If there was still any question, letters fall across the body of the train in gold script.

The Christmas Express.

"Beautiful, isn't it?" Ian breathes with a sigh of near reverence. He looks practically giddy as his pace quickens down the stairs. "C'mon"—he turns behind him and, with my own heart momentarily faltering, winks—"partner."

Chapter 3
POLAR EXPRESS

A short, stout man in a red nutcracker suit stands at the opening to the train, taking tickets with one black-gloved hand while tipping his tall black hat in welcome with the other. Elves scurry this way and that at the nutcracker's command, relieving patrons of luggage and laptop bags and, in the case of one passenger, at least twenty gift bags overflowing with red and green tissue paper.

Ian ushers me forward with a gentle press on my lower back, I notice with flushing cheeks, and before I know it, I'm handing Mr. Nutcracker my ticket.

He slides it onto the top of the stack in his hand, and while he does so both he, and I, seem to notice mine is different than the others. Thicker. Whereas the others are coal black with a dignified red script, mine looks more like Willy Wonka's golden ticket.

Huh.

It clearly means something, because the man raises his bushy brows to give me a proper look, and next thing I know he's nodding over his shoulder—where an older man, dressed in what I'm fairly certain could only have come from a vintage shop full of old English butler's suits, materializes out of thin air.

"Welcome aboard The Christmas Express, Miss Fairbanks." The ticket taker takes my hand in his gloved one and glides me over the small opening between platform and train. He inclines his head toward the man. "Jenkins here will guide you to your suite and see to any needs. Would you like Miss Lacey, one of our lovely elves, to partake in your complimentary unpacking service while we bring you a beverage?"

"I—" I'm momentarily stumped for a response and cling tighter to the paper coffee cup in my hand. I don't know how much Jonas paid for our tickets, but it's *quite* clear he upgraded.

But of course he did. An old East Egg money boy, Jonas always upgraded whenever there was an option. Made amends for offenses the way his parents and grandparents and great-grandparents did—through gift giving. The greater the offense, the greater the reparation. And if I recall correctly, the particular evening he'd bought our tickets was after the funeral of a dear woman I took care of exclusively for two years.

When Jonas, hands on the steering wheel as we drove slowly in the procession line through the rain, mistook my grieving tears for tears of anxiety over my job loss, he said, "This is exactly why I said you shouldn't have taken this job,

Willow. You put all your eggs in one basket and now, look. The basket's dead. *Diversification.* If you are going to try and eke out a living at this, please start listening to me and *at least* practice diversification."

Yes. That explains the Golden Ticket.

Mr. Nutcracker looks at me expectantly.

"Oh no," I say. I can just imagine the horror on the elf's face upon seeing all the thrift store cardigans and holey jeans stuffed inside my suitcase. I'm certainly not the steam-my-pashminas-and-be-sure-to-color-coordinate-my-cashmere-neutrals material. "I can unpack myself. Thank you though."

To prove my point further, I reach for my suitcases, but when I turn around, Ian is no longer Charming Mystery Train Man turned Getaway Partner. No, now he's Helpful Elf, standing at attention with both of my suitcases, no coffee in sight.

"Ian?" I begin, and then the pieces begin to click together. "Ohhh . . . Ian. You're—"

"Assistant Head Elf Perkins, at your service." The heels of his elf shoes click together as he says so and my brow furrows, ever so slightly, as I hear the new pitch in his voice. Gone is the rich baritone, and in its place is a squeaky, childish tone a full octave higher.

"Right . . ." I say slowly, taking this in. "But we were just—"

"Taking a short break between stations." There's that familiar twinkle in his eye as his voice lowers. "Even elves have to have their coffee."

A group is gathering behind us in the aisle. I realize I'm starting to clog it up. "Oh of course. Right. That makes . . .

sense." I turn back toward my guide and muster up my voice to a cheery note, all the while trying to process the sudden shift in situation. "Terrific. I'll follow you then."

As I walk through the aisles in our little entourage, I take in the train. The aisle is lined with carpet in an intricately detailed weave of forest green. Rich red velvet chairs face one another in groups of four, each seat back embellished with a bell in golden thread. The air is thick with the smell of mulled cider and hot chocolate, which isn't surprising as nearly every one of the thirty or so couples I pass seems to be grinning childishly at one another while clutching a porcelain mug. An orchestra plays a resounding rendition of "Do You Hear What I Hear?" through the speakers. The hum of excitement and anticipation is impossible to ignore.

We pass aisle after aisle, and car after car, until just before walking through yet another velvet curtain, Jenkins stops.

He turns toward a door. Gives the knob such a subtle yet refined twist I realize I've been doing it all wrong before. The door glides open, and Jenkins puts out a hand. "Your suite, Miss Fairbanks."

I step inside. And gape.

Suite is an understatement; it's more like an empire. Whereas everyone else on the train is coupled in groups of four facing one another with just enough legroom to recline, this—*this*—is something entirely different.

To the right is a fire—an actual fire—with flames licking the glass of the small woodstove, whose black pipe drifts upward and through the ceiling. Two mason green-striped wingback chairs face it, a small, needlepoint ottoman of Santa on his sleigh on each side. The walls are of deep-maroon damask wallpaper, and as I turn, my knees nearly buckle at the sight of a Christmas tree standing beside a mahogany four-poster bed. Wall-to-wall windows spread across the length of the bed, with a red-and-green plaid couch laden with throw pillows and a stack of sheets, quilts, and soft wool blankets on the other side. Two butter-soft-looking robes hang from a closet door, with another door cracked open to what appears to be a bathroom beyond. At the foot of the door sits a basket overflowing with peppermint bath bombs, candles, and a card.

I walk to the tree, and both Jenkins and Ian, I'm vaguely aware, follow in identical formation.

"Are you quite sure this is mine?" I take in the scent of pine as I touch the string of cranberries. Sure enough they compress slightly at my squeeze. The real thing. All of this.

It's too good to be true.

"Quite, Miss Fairbanks," Jenkins says. "We arranged everything according to Mr. Yates's wishes. Even"—he nods to the couch—"with regard to the surplus bedding."

And blinking in the words, I realize. This wasn't the standard Jonas upgrade. This wasn't just the typical "Let's upgrade to first class" situation.

Here, this is when Jonas would've proposed. He'd love the pictures. He'd love the background of the wingback chairs and the crackling of the woodstove fire. Perhaps he had already enlisted Jenkins to videotape it.

I'm as certain I'm standing in the exact spot where I would've gone from girlfriend to fiancée as I know my own life.

Ah.

Well.

I purse my lips and pluck a pine needle from the Christmas tree. All the better.

All.

The.

Better.

Now I have a gorgeous suite to enjoy all to myself, and—I glance over to Ian, who at the moment is grinning a little too brightly—*and* a nice guy to sit next to beside that cozy fire. When he's off duty. And a human again.

Is he currently overworking his smile to force dimples in his cheeks like a true elf?

I turn back to Jenkins and clasp my hands together in front of me. "This is absolutely *beautiful*. Thank you. I guess I'll just . . . start unpacking then."

"As you wish." And to my surprise Jenkins seems relieved—as though passengers in the past have actually given him trouble about all *this*. "And how about your beverage?" Discreetly he's already slipped a paper out of his suit jacket and begins to read. "We have a number of options, Miss Fairbanks, all available with spirits upon request. Mulled cider. Mulled cider with a touch of cinnamon. Mulled cider with a sliver of orange peel. Hot cocoa. Hot cocoa with marshmallows. Hot cocoa with cinnamon marshmallows. Hot cocoa with—"

"A cocoa would be nice."

"Very good." Jenkins nods and slips the paper back in his breast pocket as though used to being interrupted around this point. "And for Mr. Yates?"

Out of the corner of my eye, I see Ian's dimples twitch.

For a long moment there's silence but for the quiet crackling of the fire.

"Mr. Yates has found himself otherwise occupied," I say, forcing an air of ease and a flicker Ian's way. "Permanently. It seems."

"Ah. I am . . . sorry." Jenkins's eyes drift down to my fingers, which I realize are betraying me by shredding the pine needle into a hundred tiny pieces in my hands. Then to the tree behind me. Then to the basket by the door. No doubt he's thinking of previous conversations with Jonas. When his gaze returns to me, they are full of compassion. "You know, I—I do believe our baker, Mrs. Byrd, has some fresh cookies coming out of the oven momentarily. Perhaps it'd be a nice complement to your cocoa." His eyes crinkle lightly as he attempts a smile, like a father trying to do his best to sew up an awkward situation he'd much prefer not to be in.

I nod. "That'd be perfect."

As they depart, Ian lingers just long enough to break the elf-act and give me a wink. "I'll see you soon," he whispers, and then he's gone.

Five minutes later, Jenkins shows up with a gold tray covered to the brim in gingerbread men and icing-laden sugar cookies in the shapes of snowflakes and Christmas trees and bells.

Poor Jenkins, I think, thanking him repeatedly as I take the tray from him. I overwhelmed the old fellow.

I send an update text to Elodie—who by now I know is knee-deep in the busyness of the bakery—unpack, toss the card while keeping the basket full of bath bombs, and settle into one wingback chair with my mug of hot chocolate just as the train begins to shudder and move.

And here we go. I watch the platform of the train station disappear from view. The cocoa smells deeply of nutmeg and cinnamon, and with the tray of cookies on the ottoman at my side, I watch the scenery change from concrete blocks and tunnel lights to gray skies and graffiti walls to, eventually, the snow-covered forests of Connecticut woodlands.

Two bundles of wood in the stove later, I'm just polishing off my fifth cookie when a knock sounds on the door. More specifically, to the tune of "We Wish You a Merry Christmas."

As I slide open the door, I'm greeted by an immediate new level of action. Staff are hastening through the aisle carrying clattering trays of this and that. "Let It Snow! Let It Snow! Let It Snow!" is playing over the speakers, and a hum of chatter resonates as the passengers have seemed to all awaken from the whispered revelry of that first golden hour. Before me stands a rather petite, rather cheerful, female elf.

"Your schedule, Miss Fairbanks." She hands me a thick card. "You'll find several elective activities down at the Mistletoe Room; lunch, unfortunately, is running a little behind but should be here soon; and of particular note is that we should be arriving at our evening destination tomorrow by four. We've included a suggested list for attire for your first activity . . ."

As my eyes scan the list, I can't help becoming distracted by one particularly surprising sound rising above the others. It's a baby. Or possibly a tortured coyote. It's hard at the moment to tell.

A baby? A baby on this train?

I look toward the source of the noise, and sure enough, two rows up stands one stressed-looking couple holding one very upset infant, and one stressed-looking Jenkins apparently trying to sort the situation out.

His face is as red as the velvet seats, perspiration glistening from his bald head. "But if, perhaps, you could possibly help to quiet the baby down from your quarters," he says, so gently you practically see his words trying to tiptoe over eggshells.

Clearly this wasn't the right thing to say, because the woman bouncing the baby in her arms looks at the point of explosion. "I've spent the past *two hours* hiding away in that closet. Surely nobody would expect me to jump back in there the second she cries."

"It's just . . . we have to be mindful of the other passengers . . ."

The infant arches backward and lets out an almighty cry.

Maybe "feral cat" is a better term to describe the baby. Or "derailing train with wheels screeching desperately." You know, there are a surprising number of metaphors.

The man checks over his shoulder at all the strained faces and looks on the point of caving, but the woman clutching the baby lifts her chin. "Look," she says, cheeks flaring, "I really am trying to be sensitive to everyone else here. It's just maybe if I try a new location, she'll calm down—"

"I understand. But . . . if we could discuss this in another location . . ."

And while she continues to stand her ground, it becomes a little clearer what is going on. The couple had purchased their tickets over a year ago, like nearly everyone on the train, but with the emergent placement of the infant as a kinship situation in their hands just five days ago, they found themselves suddenly in a tight corner.

The company had offered an exception to the rule in what sounds like a moment of sympathy, but the reality of the screaming infant—who apparently is both reacting to recent trauma and *severely* resistant to the overexposure of sights and sounds—is throwing a damp rag on the festive cheer of the passengers around them, and apparently the couple themselves.

Eventually, as Jenkins's soothing words and unyielding logic begin to tip the scales, the woman's defiance peters out. It's clear she is closer to tears than anyone.

Poor woman. Missing out on the trip they'd worked so hard for because of their own willingness to take their kin in. Clearly I wasn't the only one thrown by surprises on this grand getaway.

My phone rings on the wingback chair, no doubt Elodie too worked up by my texts to simply text back, and as I look inside my suite with its snapping fire and cozy bed, I see the room with fresh eyes.

Fresh, stinging eyes.

It must be done though.

It must.

With an almighty mental push, I clear my throat as I step quickly toward the group. "Mr. Jenkins . . . sir . . ."

Chapter 4
HERE WE COME A-WASSAILING

It takes a full fifteen minutes of standing awkwardly in the aisle, convincing first a very hesitant Jenkins, then the very hesitant interim guardian parents, but after repeating myself at least thirty times, they all finally take my offer. Plus, a few timely infant screams help move things along.

All during this time passengers openly looked on, which now that I was in the spotlight, helped me understand why exactly Jenkins had more than one bead of sweat trembling on his temples.

There was one passenger in particular whom Jenkins seemed particularly aware of through the exchange, to the point that I wanted to ask why. Why does Jenkins keep an eye on the older gentleman in the seat opposite the couples? Why does he care what the single passenger who keeps his own gaze out the window, hands resting on his cane, thinks? Of all the passengers who were irritated by the noise or looked like they were stringing up complaint emails in their minds, the older man looked the least concerned or offended by the situation—not to mention this suggested arrangement would benefit him most. So why does Jenkins dart his eyes continuously his way?

"And are you really sure, Miss Fairbanks?" Jenkins says one last time as the couple gathers up their belongings.

"*Really.*" Hoping to truly and finally convince him, I reach out and give his arm a light squeeze. "Really. The place was much too big for me anyway. Besides, the ambiance out here looks like a lot more fun."

And to some extent, I'm not just saying it to get him to stop saying, "But, Miss Fairbanks . . . the company truly will be unable to refund you . . ."

It really does look cheerier out here, among the hustle and bustle and mingling of a hundred jovial smells and words and songs. The suite was lovely, but to be perfectly honest, it already had started to feel a little isolating.

Perfect, I hope, for a baby and a celebrating couple. Not quite so perfect for the girl who gets a little too inside her own head when left alone for long periods.

"But, Miss Fairbanks—" Jenkins begins again.

"Henry," interjects the older gentleman in the corner, looking away from the window at last. He levels his gaze on Jenkins, his voice gentle but with quiet authority. "The young lady has graciously offered to give up her suite to the couple and the baby. Let the young lady partake in such seasonal goodwill."

This, at last, shuts Jenkins up.

And after several handshakes, and one surprising hug from the grateful couple, they are whisked off and all my belongings aside from luggage—which evidently will head to a new sleeping quarter somewhere else on the train—are brought to me.

"So, I guess I'll take one of these." I shuffle into my new little compartment where the older man sits. Of the two pairs of seats facing each other, it's just the two of us, and as I settle into a seat opposite him, I take him in.

He looks to be in his seventies, with puffs of cloud-white hair curling over his ears and down a trailing beard. Though the seats are roomy enough for me to sit crisscross should I choose, I notice he's filled his in, the buttons on his crimson sweater vest straining as they fight to stay closed. His eyes are baby blue. The only thing keeping me from calling him Santa right now is the fact that there is no rosy hue to his cheeks.

In fact, he looks downright pale.

From habit I glance down to his right hip and, sure enough, spot the bulge of the small black box tucked away.

"Hi." I lean forward in my seat with my hand extended. "I'm Willow. And . . . I couldn't help noticing how Mr. Jenkins wanted your approval back there."

The Almost Santa releases his cane to take my hand, and despite the paleness of his face, he gives a whisper of a smile. "Yes, Henry has always been a bit on the nervous side. You get the company into one lawsuit over chestnuts over an open fire ten years ago . . ." His words trail off, but in his face and eyes is a twinkle. "I'm Clarence."

I laugh, while at the same time noting the way his hand shakes ever so slightly as it leaves mine and returns to grip his cane. I want to ask more of this man who so obviously has a history here, but first things first.

"Would you like some almonds?" I say, all the while plopping my purse on the seat next to me and beginning to dig. It only takes a moment to find the Ziploc bag of snacks. I spot the containers of apple juice and reach for them. "Oh! I have an apple juice too," I say brightly, then hold it up for him to see.

As I do so, he regards me.

"Both would be greatly appreciated. Thank you."

"No problem." I hand them off.

I open a bag of trail mix of my own, not so much out of hunger after the last half-dozen cookies but to keep him company. For a few minutes we eat in silence, watching the icicle drips move nearer and nearer the coast out the window.

It's a snap decision, but already I sense I'm going to like him.

I tend to have two types of clients—ones who feel the need to discuss every little decision ten times over, and the ones, typically men, who would talk about the weather in the middle of a heart attack. I've always had a special spot in my heart for the latter.

"I am a little surprised." I note the time on my watch: 1:37. "I know they said they were running late, but it's getting up there and there aren't any trays in sight. We can't be the only hungry ones."

"They haven't brought you anything?" comes a man's voice over my shoulder, and I nearly toss my almonds in my startle.

He is far underdressed in comparison to the richly tasseled uniforms of nutcrackers and slippered elves, and yet there is an unmistakable sense of authority about him. Somewhere, I'd guess, on the southern end of his thirties. He wears a nutmeg cardigan, beneath which is a plaid button-up and matching tie. As he grips the back of my seat, I see the matching pair of snowflake-blue eyes as my Santa companion.

Ah. And here is his son.

"I'm fine," Clarence says, a couple almond crumbs lingering on his beard to prove the point. He gestures to me. "I know how busy you all are—"

"I told Ian to bring your meal an hour ago," the man protests, his frown between his brows deep. "He should have brought it to you *well* before the others." He stands and puts a hand on his hip. "I *knew* I should've done it myself—"

"Never mind, Oliver," Clarence breaks in. "I know my way to the kitchen. And even so, I didn't need to"—he nods to me—"thanks to my new companion here, who is admirably resourceful."

And sure enough, I do glow a little inside at the accolade, both because I've been a little starved for compliments these days and because it really is satisfying to see the pink returning to his cheeks.

Oliver shifts his gaze my way for the first time, as though he'd been so engulfed in concern for his father that he hadn't even seen anybody else in our section. He blinks and in that millisecond seems to register what is going on.

"Miss *Fairbanks*." He reaches quickly forward to shake my hand.

I take it, a little stunned at how quickly I've gone from the invisible person to one of importance.

"On behalf of The Christmas Express, I want to express our gratitude. Jenkins says the Patel family is settling in very nicely. Truly, I cannot thank you enough. For that," his eyes shift to his father, "and evidently, for this."

"It was nothing," I say, cheeks warming by all the fanfare of the last hour.

"It *was*." He levels his gaze, his eyes so deep blue they hold a wellful of sincerity. "In a day when a hundred things have gone wrong, you have saved me not just from one disaster, but two."

His gaze is so sincere and unyielding and his hand so warm in its grip of mine that I feel the temptation to giggle nervously like a schoolgirl. Almost.

"Now I wouldn't go so far as all that," grumbles Clarence from his perch, frowning as he looks out the window. "Now the derailment of '69, that was a disaster . . ."

I bite my lip to button a smile as I look back to his son and let go of his grip. "A derailing train? Yes. Well. That certainly would better fit the description of disaster."

"He exaggerates." Oliver rolls his eyes. "A two-hundred-pound deer on the track does *not* equal derailment, or even the threat of it."

"It was a *big* deer."

I laugh, which seems to please Oliver, and he shakes his head as if just realizing something. "I'm so sorry, I haven't introduced myself. Oliver Lodge, conductor in chief." He holds out his hand again, before he retracts it suddenly. "Ah. Sorry. Force of habit."

"We can shake again," I say, grinning broadly as I put out my own for a second time. "I'd hate to be responsible for breaking your routine. Nice to meet you, Oliver." I give his hand a hearty second shake. "I'm guessing you're following in your father's footsteps."

"Trying to. If we don't break down first." A distant clatter of a tray falling, from the sound of it, flows down the aisle, and Oliver sighs and checks over his shoulder. His shaking hand stalls but doesn't let go. "Listen." He looks back to me. "I would like to repay you for your kindness today—"

"Truly." I pull my hand away. It was time to put my foot down about this. To stop the commotion. "No need—"

"Have you ever driven a train?"

Oh. The surprising shift in question succeeds in derailing me momentarily from my stop-praising-me agenda. "Well . . . no."

"Would you like to?" A rather charming grin slips up one cheek. "Makes quite the story at dinner parties. You'll be a hit."

I pause, eyeing him suspiciously. "Well . . . I *would* like to be a hit."

His grin widens. "It's settled then." He claps his hands together. "Tomorrow after your excursion, I'll swing by and pick you up."

"That'd be . . . lovely." All of a sudden I feel acutely aware of his father sitting a foot away from the exchange, the elbow-jammed-in-the-rib sense that his choice of words sounded a whole lot like . . . well . . . a romantic gesture (although one could never be sure), and that the heat radiating off my cheeks could, at that very moment, fry an egg.

But one thing is sure.

I quite like the sound of it all, I admit to myself after Oliver strides back down the aisle and vanishes through the emerald curtain. I've never driven a train before. In fact, having lived in the city so long, I'm not even sure my driver's license is in good standing. But there it is. Me. Driving a train. With Oliver.

My stomach seizes up a little at the thought of it all, especially the last part. Which is absolutely ridiculous, because Jonas and I broke up a total of three days ago and I have jumped into a train relationship with Ian.

Ian.

I try not to grimace. Elodie really could write a lecture titled "How to Fail at Rebounding" from me.

"One cold glass of milk and cookies for Miss Fairbanks." I jump at the voice that manifested out of my thoughts, and my temples pulse as I turn to see Ian's bright, shiny face leaning over with a platter.

I need to move farther away to the window seat, where people can't keep startling me.

"Oh," I say, looking at the rather unappetizing platter of cookies before me.

"The one you—" Ian gives me a significant look before darting his eyes toward Clarence. "*Ordered.*"

Oh, dear. And here he is, trying to sneak in a sweet gesture.

"How . . . lovely." Begrudgingly, I take the platter in my lap.

I stare at the cookies. The beady eyes of the sugar-cookie snowmen are leering at me. Taunting me.

Ian waits expectantly, long enough that I am forced to pick up one of the angry little snowmen. I bite off a small piece of his head. "*Mmmmm.*" Honestly, if I have one more gram of sugar this morning, I'm going to throw up. "Delicious."

"Mrs. Byrd makes the best sugar cookies in all the land," Ian says.

I begin to put the cookie back on the plate, but his smile starts to fall. I put the cookie back to my lips, and his grin yo-yos up. Painfully, I force another small bite.

It's at this point I notice two rosy spots on his cheeks. They're actually rather inescapable to spot, shimmering slightly beneath the cabin lights. My eyes shift to two other elves standing nearby.

Does he . . . wear . . . blush? What . . . for his job?

For that matter I think, looking at the particularly light, cool pink with a touch of silvery shine, is he using the same blush *I* use? Am I potentially dating a man I could share blush with?

He notices me staring at his face and stiffens. I dart my eyes away, but it's too late.

I offer up a little laugh to emphasize the point that this is fine. It's all fine. "You know, I worked off set one summer in high school. I saw my fair share of guys putting on makeup for the job."

But to my surprise, Ian's shoulders hitch up even farther. In his octave-higher-than-normal voice, he says, "We elves get our glowing cheeks from our sugary diet."

He was offended. Not that I had questioned whether he was or wasn't wearing makeup, but because I was questioning his authenticity as an elf. An *elf*.

"Oh." For a moment, I'm at a loss for words. "Sure." I nod vigorously. "Of course."

A long pause sits between us.

"Anyway," he continues, more cautiously and at a near whisper, "today's swamped but I'll be off tomorrow sometime in the afternoon. I could borrow you for a minute. Give you a little tour of my collection," he adds a bit mischievously, as though it really is something to be quite proud of.

Collection? What kind of collection? Oh, yes, the books. His passion for literature. Ian's very handsome and charming passion for literature.

I smile widely. "I'd love that."

"Wonderful," Ian whispers, and gives me a heartfelt squeeze on the shoulder. A squeeze that feels a little like, *And I forgive you for what you said about my blush earlier.*

As Ian leaves, I turn back in my seat to find Clarence gazing out the window, hands folded on his lap, and I get the sense I'm not the only one in our compartment who can see through a situation.

But he doesn't say anything.

Instead, a minute later, Clarence reaches into his own bag. He flips a small tray table up from the armrest beside him, and sets a checkered board on it. As he places a wooden knight on a horse on the board, sword raised toward the sky, he says, "So. You're a shrewd girl. How do you feel about chess?"

Chapter 5
LAST CHRISTMAS

Oh y-yes, he's *wooooonderful!*" I stutter, my hands struggling to decide between staying frozen at my side and reaching for my throat. Now it's my turn for my voice to be an octave higher. "Chaucer is so . . . so . . . *friendly!*"

My fingers climb again toward my neck, where the five-foot ball python slithers slowly toward one arm. But every time I move my hands, the snake's head follows, intrigued by the movement.

"And you say you he sleeps *with you?*" I say, my voice jumping up to near screeching level as two beady black eyes suddenly turn to look me straight in the eye, inches from mine.

"Every night." Ian pats the cage at the head of his twin bunk bed. Right beside the train-themed pillowcase. And the rows and rows of model trains, planes, and automobiles lining the shelves—which, I discovered within ten minutes of my arrival, was what he'd actually meant when he said he loved all things, "trains, planes, and automobiles."

"Right here where he's safe and sound, though, of course," Ian adds, then lowers his voice. "After the news came out about the strangled man with his pet snake in Ohio, I felt I had to." His voice is boisterous as he stands again. "Not that that would ever happen with my Chaucer though." He practically coos at the snake as he gives it a rub beneath the head. "Chaucer's much too civilized for that. Aren't you, Chaucer?"

"*Okay,* I think he wants to get down," I say shrilly, as the snake slowly crosses my neck a second time. "Come and get him. Please. *Please.*"

The second I'm relieved of the snake, I move to the other side of the room. I'd press myself against the wall, except with all the cages hidden among the posters and books, there's half a chance I'd bump against some other "pet" I'd rather not meet.

When Ian said he loved animals, I didn't expect him to mean insects. And lizards. And snakes.

I hug my body tightly as Ian wraps the snake around his own neck. He takes a step toward me, and I swivel toward the wall as quickly as I can.

"So these are . . . your books," I say. "You really love . . ." I scan the wall consisting of, and only of, comics. "Books."

"How can anyone not?" He picks up a colorful comic book with a dozen flying, firing, bomb-throwing, fire-coming-out-of-their-eyes figures on the cover. "Television is so insufficient. It just can't *capture* the author's intention. It just can't *capture* the depths of their imagination."

There they were. So many pretty words. So insane in reality.

"You know," he says, picking up another one from among the stacks cluttering the floor. His lips upturn slightly as he looks back at me. "I was just thinking of you when I was reading this one. It kind of reminds me of . . . us."

He sees my half-in-shock, half-repulsed expression at the chesty, shield-wielding superhero on the cover and somehow, *somehow*, takes it the wrong way. "You know." He inches closer to me, snake waggling its black tongue. "I don't do this a lot, but . . . I could let you *borrow* it—"

Oh, good heavens! I eye the exit door behind him and his beady-eyed snake. I'm going to die here.

Suddenly, the door bursts open.

"There you are!" Oliver exclaims. "I've been looking all over for you, Miss Fairbanks. I was just about to give up on you."

And to my surprise, he actually does look as though he'd run the length of the train. His tie is as crooked as the short swoop of his disheveled brown hair above his left brow and cardigan. And the plaid button-up underneath is now rolled up to elbows.

It's quite a handsome look on him, I can't help noticing. And there's something about being wanted enough that someone would run across the train in earnest that awakens my already-overworked senses. But then, everything about the last hour has overworked my senses.

I open my mouth to ask what he's referring to—surely I

hadn't missed something?—when he answers for me. "You're about to miss the ringing."

"The ringing?" I say slowly.

Oliver's eyes tick from me to Ian meaningfully. "Yes. The ringing."

Ian, looking thoroughly confused himself, turns toward Oliver, snake swinging. "I—I thought elective activities ended an hour ago." He presses a hand to his plaid-green chest. "I was told we had a break. Believe me, Conductor. I would never, *never,* have encouraged Miss Fairbanks to retreat from an elective opportunity." He points a finger at me, loyalty flying out the window. "In fact, I tried persuading her to attend them multiple times yesterday. But she—"

"It's not an elective." Oliver raises a hand. "This is for the contest. Surely you remember the Christmas costume contest from our staff meeting."

Silence.

"And how the winner will be elected to ring the bell as we enter Rockhaven this evening."

"Ring the bell," Ian whispers, his eyes widening. He shifts his gaze back to me, holding the same reverence as when he explained the treasure of his 1956 *The Amazing Spider-Man* CGC 2.5 vintage classic comic find. "Willow, I'll—I'll save this for you." He pats the cover of the comic. Then looking at Oliver, he bites his lip. "You don't suppose I can—"

"Just a private ringing this time, I'm afraid." Oliver shrugs as though in apology. "Those were the rules."

Ian nods like this makes perfect sense, that no one—not

even the creator of the rules himself—can break them once they're put in place.

Ian steps aside, and in the sudden opening, I make my escape.

Once the door to Ian's room is shut behind us, Oliver and I move down the hall. I keep as close to him as possible as we walk through the employees' quarters and make our way past the Chestnut and Mistletoe cars, shouldering through the clusters gathered for game room and elective activities. I only realize how close I am when I nearly trip him up as he slows.

"Sorry," I say, giving one last look over my shoulder. Already my cheeks are starting to burn as anxiety over Ian's return lessens, and embarrassment over the whole situation I landed myself in, including this welcomed—but still humiliating—rescue mission I have no doubt Clarence initiated, settles in. I feel like a child.

A ridiculous child who got herself into a mess she was too much of a coward to get out of.

"So. I take it Ian's room tour wasn't your cup of tea."

"No. Not really." I put my hands to my cheeks to try and cool them. "Oh, this is so embarrassing."

"Don't let it be." He smiles. "Don't worry about it at all."

I shift the conversation as best I can away from Ian and his terrifying room. "I'm guessing you found me because . . ."

"Dad. He said he was, and I quote, 'on the cusp' of taking your queen and would very much like me to haul you back from Ian's room so you could stop evading defeat."

"*What*? My queen is thoroughly protected." I press my hand to my chest. "He doesn't have a chance and he *knows* it."

A bemused expression falls across Oliver's face, as though the whole competitive spirit between Clarence and me is quite adorable. But he hasn't been there for the past six games—three of which Clarence won, three which I claimed. And he hasn't seen how this seventh one is the *battle* to claim it all.

"Anyway," I brush an invisible speck of pride from my skirt, "I wasn't aware of any Christmas contest . . ."

Oliver holds open one of the curtains between the cars. "Yes. Congratulations. It's a great honor."

"And I'm the first to win such an honor, I'm guessing," I say, both pleased and embarrassed by the illustrative lie he's pulling off on my behalf.

I search for any clues in his face of frustration. After all, I don't know, maybe that's why Oliver came running, ignoring his obviously enormous duties on this busy day. Maybe Ian is notorious for luring unsuspecting girls to his room under the guise of wit and charm, only to throw man-eating pythons on them. And here I am, this season's dupe.

But my scan turns up with nothing—nothing but an easy expression like Oliver has all the time in the world.

"The very first," Oliver says, nodding solemnly. "No pressure, but if you don't get it right when you ring the bell, that'll be it for future generations."

My lips twitch a little. Every moment that passes eases the knot in my stomach. "It's not very kosher to admit as the inaugural champion, but I would've bet my money on that

candy-cane couple over in 12E. They even passed out candy
canes from bedazzled fanny packs. You can't get better than
that."

"The judges did consider them," Oliver says, quite seriously. "But, unfortunately, full range of motion in costume
was a requirement they just couldn't meet. And with the pool
noodle–canes situation out their backsides . . . Well. We hated
to disqualify them."

"We," I say, grinning at the image of Oliver standing in
some back cabin around half a dozen elves, arguing over our
costumes with score sheets. "Sure."

"But seriously now, if we're going to get to the ringing,
we'd better hurry." He leads the way as we pass several more
cars—including my own, where I pause long enough to shock
Clarence with a fabulous surprise attack with my pawn—and
as I glance out the windows, I see we are indeed slowing.

Frosted trees line one side of the train, and on the right
stands the rocky shore of the Atlantic Ocean, frothy waves
crashing against beaten sand. The landscape is dotted with
cedar-shingled saltbox houses and Victorians perched on
rocky cliffs, their steep gabled roofs standing watch over the
watery horizon. Lobster shacks with sailboats lie beached
alongside them, in no hurry to get back, and in the distance
stands a panoramic sunset of such watercolor oranges and
yellows, it looks like we've slipped off the page of a book.

Before I know it, I'm standing in the driver's cab. Walls,
gadgets, and ceilings are all painted in the same antique green,
the paint appearing as vintage as the dials themselves. Whereas

I wasn't sure before, now I'm certain. This train isn't some new replica straining to appear like ancient steam engines of old. It's the real deal, recovered in maroon velvet and golden tassels but never able to shed its true roots. Full of history. Full of life.

"How old is this train?" I take a step forward.

Oliver seems to appreciate the respect in my voice. "It's from 1953. Dad bought it when I was a kid. I spent my childhood running through these cabs. It got a complete remodel just two years ago—well, except for this. Wanted to keep this area just like the original." Oliver puts his hands on his hips as he admires his surroundings.

Geez, what is it with boys and trains?

"Wait. *Your family* owns this train?" I shake my head. "I can't even afford a studio in Queens."

"To be fair, I do hear the city is quite expensive. I've known my fair share of people who got out and are much the better for it."

I laugh. "Right. That's my problem. I'd have three trains and a plane if I could just get out of that darn city."

The train is inching along the tracks now, nothing but a few pedestrians hugging their coats on a platform outside and a few light poles with blinking electric snowflakes to welcome us into the tiny station. Oliver turns to me, then points toward the golden rope above his head. "You ready?"

I step tentatively into the already-crowded space and take a small breath to steady myself. A salty sea breeze sweeps in through the open window by the driver's seat, mingled with ashy coal from the billowing smoke rising from the steam engine ahead. I reach for the cord and see the flecks of a darker ultramarine circling his pupils as he grins down at me. Somewhere in the distance "All I Want for Christmas Is You" plays.

"Anytime now will do," the driver says, and I realize I've accidentally been pressing my hip against his shoulder.

"Oh. Sorry." I grab the cord and give the rope a pull. As the bell begins to ring, so do my thoughts. What is *wrong* with me? Jonas broke up with me four days ago and I'm ready to jump on board with anyone with a hint of testosterone. Am I really that desperate? Am I really that pathetic that I can't stand to be single for more than five minutes?

"Is that enough?" I ask, after the fourth bell ring.

"Enough to get everybody grabbing their coats. You ready?" Oliver's eyes are trained on mine, and in them I see it. An unmistakable twinkle.

No.

He couldn't possibly be attracted to me, too, after I'd made such a fool of myself like that.

He must just be excited to show off the first excursion. It's his life dream after all. And Elodie is absolutely right. I am just coming off an emotional shock and *cannot* trust myself right now. I can't trust my instincts. I can't trust those gut feelings that have steered me right before. I can't trust my thoughts. For the foreseeable future—a month? two?—I cannot make any decisions relationally. (I'll have to be sure to ask Elodie how long she thinks I'll be suspended from decision-making). I can just enjoy the ride, get home for Christmas, and *exist*.

And whenever I'm tempted to trust myself, I'll just remember the feeling of that python staring me in the eyes.

Faintly I hear the man in the nutcracker suit wishing passengers a nice evening through the window, and as people in my periphery begin spilling onto the platform, Oliver's gaze shifts over to the stream of passengers. A moment later the atmosphere has altered. It's time to get outside.

"Yes. I just need my coat." As an afterthought, in case Oliver was feeling torn between checking on his dad and getting himself out on the platform to lead the way for the group, I add, "I'll come with Clarence—that is, if he'll still talk to me after abandoning him halfway through the game."

"That'd be *great*." And as he walks after me out of the cab, Oliver looks genuinely relieved. Just as I begin to step against the current of passengers trying to head outside into the biting cold, someone touches my elbow and I turn. "Really, Willow," Oliver says, his eyes sincere. "Thank you. For everything."

Chapter 6
BABY, IT'S COLD OUTSIDE

The evening out on the little cliffside town was lovely. With Oliver leading the crowd through the cobbled streets, the group landed at a small inn so ancient, the roof with its moss-covered shingles slanted to one end and the heavy wooden door the tavernkeeper swung open like a piece of paper looked more like it belonged to a medieval castle. Rocks stacked upon one another to form deep wells of fireplaces dug into walls on either end, crackling away and lighting the old tavern with dozens of dripping wax candles. The smell of butter and mead and fish was thick upon each table laid out with oyster knives and cocktail forks and seafood crackers.

Clarence and I paired together without a word, and sure enough, the evening was one of harmony and laughter. With a life of travel he's gained more than his share of fascinating stories. Many of them included Oliver, naturally—the little boy whose life was spent on the tracks with his dear old mom and dad. Some of the stories made me laugh; others were so sweet my eyes wandered toward Oliver as he spoke. Overall, though, had I had any concerns about looking like a fish out of water before dinner, by the end, even the couples around us were leaning in to listen.

It was funny.

I was booked on the train with Jonas as my partner, then Ian in a madcap plan, but the reality was that I was going to be paired with a seventy-eight-year-old World War II veteran turned world adventurer with a bad hip and a bowl-full-of-jelly laugh that filled the room. And that was just fine with me.

Oliver, for his part, looked only more handsome as he took charge of the group, at ease in his position of authority as though he truly enjoyed mingling with each of the passengers. He stopped by our table a few times, but as couples finished their meals and trickled out to stroll the streets arm in arm, each guided to a particular spot or store by his advice, he was always left standing at the door. The whole evening, I'm not sure he sat once, let alone ate any of the lobster surrounding him.

I retired to my quarters when we returned, and the room, though smaller with a pair of bunk beds lining the wall instead of Christmas trees and wingback chairs, suited me well. The soft *Charlie Brown Christmas* sheets, thick red down comforter, and feather pillow were like slipping into a cloud, and for the second night, sleep on the softly rocking train came quickly and soundly, even with the soft whistle that came every few hours through the night.

As for the breakfast they carried out in the morning? Well, there were no words.

"Ready to switch?" I say, holding my section of the newspaper for Clarence with one hand while my other rests over the silver platter sitting on the pop-up table over my lap.

His frown deepens as he hands me the funnies and takes the world news, his eyes fixated on my gleaming platter.

I lift it, and immediately steam rises to tickle my cheeks. Three thick slabs of French toast fill up the plate, coated in confectioner's sugar and bathed with butter. A healthy serving of lush red strawberries, grapes, and mandarin oranges fill a small porcelain cup beside it, and three crispy pieces of bacon topped with crystal granules sparkle at me. I pick up one piece of bacon and take a bite, feeling the almost immediate need to close my eyes and sigh. "Brown sugar," I say, more to myself than to Clarence. "That's so clever."

"Hazel's recipe," Clarence replies. "Bake at four hundred and top with just a bit of brown sugar."

I open my eyes and see he's looking at his own bowl now. He prods the oatmeal with his spoon, and it wobbles in gelatin-like vibration in reply. He's told me about his late wife in conversation, passed ten years now, but I sense what is causing him to frown so deeply right now is most certainly food related more than memories of old.

From the looks of it, they didn't even add anything to the steel oats.

Just plain old oatmeal. Like his lunch yesterday that turned out to be a pitiful amount of cottage cheese and canned tuna.

I purse my lips.

"Clarence." I set my napkin on my lap. "Hold on a moment before eating that. I'm going to see if I can whip something up."

His eyebrows shoot to his receding hairline. "No, no, Willow. It's not that easy—"

I wave him off. "This is your train, isn't it? I'm just going to swing by *your* kitchen, do a little tinkering without getting in anyone's way, and come back with something you'll actually eat—that yes, is also good for you. Trust me. This is, quite literally, what I do. And frankly, I can't eat one more meal with you sitting across from me with those sad puppy eyes. It's killing my holiday spirit."

He hesitates, looking very seriously at his mash as if wondering if he could manage to choke it down after all. "Okay," he says at last. "But if Mrs. Byrd seems to have a fit, you get out of there. I mean it. Don't get yourself in trouble on my account."

I laugh. He practically sounds like a schoolboy. "Deal." I dig through my overhead suitcase for a few stowaway ingredients I'd wager my ticket they don't have on hand, slip them into a purse over my shoulder, and dash away, moving quickly through the cars before Clarence changes his mind. I have no doubt he'd rather have just about anything than that sludge, but at the same time, he's got that same giving spirit I saw in Oliver the night before, willing to put himself out for the sake of not inconveniencing others.

Thankfully, however, I'm not them. Not when it comes to others I care about at least. I once entirely stopped traffic just to save Miss Clark's gift-from-her-long-distance-daughter flyaway umbrella. I can certainly fix up a little breakfast for the train's owner.

The car dedicated to food isn't hard to find; I just follow the string of elves coming and going with breakfast platters. The kitchen is surprisingly as far as possible from the passenger area, and the closer I get, the more I understand why.

The closer I get, the clearer it becomes why Clarence was so hesitant as well.

He may own the train, but it's obvious Mrs. Byrd owns the kitchen.

"I don't *care* if you sprained your ankle tripping on your own feet. Quillet, get this coffee out to 3G *now*. Margaret, *I'm still waiting on that bacon!*"

The looks on the elves' faces as they push open the curtain and exit, laden with pushcarts and heavy trays, make it clear they are scrambling under her direction. I edge out of the aisle as much as I can to let them pass, and after a moment's hesitation, step inside.

The train kitchen is chaotic. Stainless-steel pans swing gently from their hanging posts on the ceiling, and an inordinate number of people are pushing against one another, reaching over and under one another's bodies in their quests for refill sugar packets and bundles of silverware for their particular guests. In the center of it all is an industrial-size oven where one of the tiniest women I've ever seen stands beside it. With both hands elbow-deep in oven mitts, she bellows at one of the elves while she yanks a pan full of steaming bacon out of the oven and tosses in a fresh one.

"Willow?" I turn as Oliver steps beside me, clipboard in hand. He's clearly surprised.

"Oliver, hi." I feel a little relief to see his face in the chaos. "I came for Clarence. Is there any space around here, by chance, for me to fix up something for him really quickly?"

Oliver's forehead crinkles. "Did something happen to his meal?" He raises a hand, getting the attention of an elf. "We can send off another one."

"No, no. It's just that . . . eggs are such a great way to slow down the glucose absorption, too, and given that he's partial to them over oatmeal—"

Despite how I've lowered my voice, the room halts.

At least a dozen heads turn.

Out of the corner of my eye, I see Mrs. Byrd snap the oven shut. She puts both oven-mitted fists on her hips, her pastry puff chef's hat tilting to one side. "What's this about my cooking?"

"Oh, nothing," I say quickly. "Nothing at all. Your cooking is phenomenal. It's the best thing here—"

Oliver raises a brow and I add quickly, "Except those excursions. And, wow." I scan the elves. "The service is just *great*." Time to move on. "But I was just telling Oliver"—I tread carefully—"since Clarence is on a dietary plan—"

"I'm aware of Mr. Lodge's dietary plan," Mrs. Byrd cuts in.

"Oh. Yes. Of course you are. Well, it's just . . . it seems like . . . as you are so busy here with everyone else, perhaps I could make something that is an alternative meal plan for him but still has the essence of what you are making for the others. So it's similar to the wonderful meals you provide, just . . ."

"Different?" Her pupils are the size of pinpricks. I notice at least one elf moves out of the line of fire between us.

Oh, dear. This isn't what I intended at all. I had imagined I'd sneak in, ask if I could whip Clarence up something, watch the employees stumble over themselves telling me to take absolutely anything for *the* Mr. Lodge Senior. Just as everyone has acted around Clarence so far. But as it turns out, Mrs. Byrd *isn't* everyone. No. She's quite the opposite.

"I have a kitchen in my cabin that'll be perfect for the job," Oliver says, breaking the silence. "What supplies did you have in mind, Willow?"

And while I shoot off ingredients from the top of my head and avoid Mrs. Byrd's gaze, Oliver looks purposefully oblivious to her shooting looks and fills his arms with the items from the fridge.

"C'mon," he says, and to my surprise, starts walking toward a swinging back door I hadn't noticed before.

My relief must've been visible, because the second we step through the swinging door, he says, "Sorry about that. Mrs. Byrd can be a little . . . touchy."

"Oh no." I wave it off quickly. "I came into her kitchen. The right is entirely hers."

We go through a narrow passageway lined on either side with food stock and through another door where we come to another little hall. A red door stands at the far end, with a brass lock and knob, and we pass it.

Oliver's phone rings, and he ignores it. "If it makes you feel any better, I think I've spent half my life being pushed out of the kitchen by her with a broom. Of course, back then I completely deserved it." He grins at me, and I grin back at the image of Oliver as a child, pockets stuffed with stolen cookies.

"I've heard some of the stories. So tell me, did you really try to strap yourself to the roof?"

"I went through a Clint Eastwood phase in high school."

"Including getting yourself killed on a train going 150 miles an hour? Nice. Very teen thinking of you."

"Well, what was I going to do? Run away and hop on a train?" A smile flits on Oliver's lips as he glances over his shoulder while adjusting the eggs in his arms. "But seriously, how much could you and Dad possibly have talked?"

"Oh"—I shrug, a mischievous smile lifting of my own— "just enough to be dangerous. If I were you, I'd consider throwing some extra marshmallows in my cocoa and arranging for some one-horse open sleigh lifts to excursions to keep me from talking to the other passengers—"

"Horse-drawn sleighs are what it takes to win you over, eh?" Oliver stops at another door, same red, same brass knob. He moves to reach for his pocket, no doubt for the keys, but with the bundle in his hands, he struggles.

I tingle at his words but quickly brush them aside.

"Here." I take the eggs and the green and red peppers and the mushrooms from his hands.

I must admit, it makes me feel a little special standing back here in the tiny hallway. No "Frosty the Snowman" playing over the speakers. No elaborate carpeting or golden tassels and elves rushing around with silver platters. Just the quiet rumble of the train moving underfoot, and the rush of a pale winter sunrise dancing on the walls. Handfuls of groceries. And just Oliver and me.

It's funny. As special as that suite was, this is even better.

I'm not sure what I expected out of Oliver's cabin, but the moment I step inside, I know it wasn't this. Whereas the suite was like a holiday page from a catalog, Oliver's room looks . . . normal. Beneath a row of large windows is a cognac-tan couch, well-worn but in the kind of way that invites sitting. A bookshelf and television sit next to the opposite wall, but instead of seeing a row of comic books and animals in cages, I'm looking at a healthy dose of westerns and travel books interspersed with a few board games with tattered edges and the evidence of group hangouts. A bed lies on the opposite wall with a crumpled gray comforter lying on top, not yet—or who knows? Perhaps never—made. A treadmill is pushed in the corner directly to my left. And straight across from me is a row of kitchen cabinets, a tiny stainless-steel sink, and an even tinier oven range so small it looks like an Easy-Bake Oven. We move toward it.

Oliver's phone rings again, and I fully expect him to check it, pull a face about whatever disaster was happening on board needing saving, drop the ingredients off on the small countertop, and wish me luck.

But he doesn't.

Subtly, he just silences it.

"So," I say, setting the peppers and eggs on the counter, "is this where you live all the time?"

"Oh no. I have a little place in San Francisco right now. We follow a two-week on, two-week off system, and I run a lot of tours from there. Plus, I like the sunshine."

I nod. "Yes, I've always wanted to visit San Francisco—especially on those twenty-degree days in February. It's on my bucket list."

"Too bad we'll miss it this time," Oliver says, and opens a drawer full of knives. "Knife?"

"Please." I select a serrated one. I begin to feel self-conscious and say, "Hey, if you want to leave me the key, I can be sure to lock up. After all, it's not like I can really escape if I turn out to be a klepto—"

But before I can even finish my sentence, he's selecting his own knife from the drawer and shutting it. As his now-silenced phone begins to hum as it vibrates in his pocket, he says, "I'd be a poor conductor if they couldn't do without me for thirty minutes. So. What are we making?"

Part of me feels selfish. Part of me knows I ought to press him, telling him I know how busy he is and how I can handle it. How I'm well aware of how he takes the brunt of the work leading excursions by night and managing the train's activities and general chaos of the day. Part of me knows this.

But another part of me . . .

Well, he's a grown man, isn't he? He can make his own decisions.

And as if to solidify the moment, my own phone rings.

I pull it out.

It's Jonas.

Jonas.

I stare at the name on the screen, incapacitated for one standstill second.

Then silence it.

As the phone slips back into my pocket, I smile. "How about you handle the dicing, and I'll make the cheese sauce for the omelet."

I reach in my purse and start taking out the bottle of lemon juice and canned coconut milk.

As he's running the peppers under tap water and his eyes gaze at me, his hands slow. When I pull out the bottle of nutritional yeast from my shoulder bag, he's openly amused. "So, you just keep nutritional yeast on hand, do you?"

"I have a particular fondness for nutritional yeast, actually, so yes," I reply without slowing. "It began when I started experimenting with cheese-alternative recipes for a lactose-intolerant client, and then when I discovered how tasty *and* healthy it actually was, I started using it for all my clients. I love it."

As I shake the bottle over a mixing bowl, he eyes the yellow flakes pouring into the bowl. "It looks like fish food."

"They all say that at first. You're just like every one of them."

"And how many of 'them' are there?" He moves the peppers to the cutting board. The kitchen counter is so small we stand practically hip to hip.

"Currently? I have three clients. Two I split between

mornings and afternoons, one I only stay with overnight when her son's out of town. I'm in home health."

"Do you like it?"

Well, if that wasn't a trigger question. "I went to school for hotel management. It was never the plan to be doing this so long."

"But do you like it?" he asks, undeterred.

I hesitate. "Yes. I've been doing it since I was sixteen. I get to be a professional friend maker. Frankly, I can't imagine doing anything else."

"Then why did you study hotel management?"

"Oh, Jonas thought it made more sense." The answer slips out quicker than I'd intended, and I hesitate afterward ever so slightly. "He thought it was wise to use my interest in hospitality in a way that was more financially advantageous. I just . . . never really got around to it."

"Ah. Mr. Yates. The one who I've heard had the misfortune of missing out?"

"On this trip? Yes."

"The trip, yes. And of course, more."

He gives a wry smile, not so much flirtatious but comforting. The kind of companionable smile that says, "He was a fool, wasn't he? But look how much better off you are already without him."

Oliver turns his gaze back onto the peppers as he continues to dice. "I've been there. Only, it was parent pressure instead of girlfriend, and I proved to be a little more stubborn than you and skipped the college degree altogether."

I raise my brows. "From the way your dad talks, I figured he wanted you to always take over the touring business."

"Oh, he did. He just thought I needed a plan B too. I felt otherwise."

"Well," I say, grinning, "it looks like it all worked out just as it should be."

"Same for you."

And to my surprise, the way he's looking at me while he says the words brings a rush of warmth to me. And not just because I can't help but admire the way he stands there, the tiniest five o'clock shadow across his cheeks, pepper in hand.

No, it's also because he's looking at me like, well, he thinks my chosen career isn't a disaster of a decision. Like it isn't absolutely pathetic to see a twenty-five-year-old woman living off thrift-store finds—despite the depths of her love of vintage wool threads—and holding off dentist appointments as long as possible, and living with a roommate, and eating more noodles and butter than is deemed acceptable, and making it all work for this job instead of taking one in management for three times the pay. Like I wasn't an idiot for getting a degree and not using it—as I've heard on so many occasions before.

No, what meant something to me was the way he looked at me like I was right where I was supposed to be. Am supposed to be.

And that look in this moment . . . well, I can't help but start to believe it.

Chapter 7
ONE-HORSE OPEN SLEIGH

Nearly two weeks pass, and the landscape has changed from sea breeze hills and snow-dusted gentle forests to the wild and soaring peaks of Montana. The time has both flown by and stood still. So much so that it's hard to imagine life off the train after it's become everything I've eaten and breathed and lived for so long.

True to promise the activities have abounded both inside the train and out, and before I know it, the messages that pass between Elodie and me are covered in dozens of pictures. Of Christmas symphonies in Chicago and ice skating in a tornado of flurries in Minnesota. Of eating things I've never tried before and dancing like I've never danced before and frankly just having the best time of my life. Every evening as I spy the train sitting in the station, smoke curling up toward the dark sky as it waits for my return, my heart warms.

I feel like I could live on this train forever. Truly.

It's so painful to imagine leaving that I've had to stop letting my thoughts drift there entirely.

"I don't like oatmeal." Clarence looks at the bowl on his tray, then at me as if I've betrayed him.

"Don't think of it as oatmeal." I pause midsip of coffee. "Think of it as overnight apple cinnamon rolls. You like cinnamon rolls."

He grumbles under his breath, but as I move my attention back to the paper, I see he's edging near it. This is how our days on the train have turned. When lunch arrived after that first successful breakfast cooked in Oliver's quarters, and Oliver dropped by to see Clarence's pained expression as he chomped slowly on the hard-boiled eggs sliced over what appeared to be sprouts, sans dressing, he leaned in and whispered in my ear, "Any chance you want to upgrade this?"

I jumped out of my chair faster than a speeding bullet. Clarence loved my stir fry noodles in tahini sauce, and every morning and lunch since, I've taken on the task of preparing his meals. Not because I have to, of course, but because I want to. I really want to, actually. While other passengers revel in the endless service and relaxation, the reality was that just wasn't me. My feet started itching the first day on the train for somewhere to help. Whereas Elodie and my mother and every propaganda on the train emphasized telling me to relax, relax, relax, I found it was much more relaxing to have something to do. Someway to help. And preparing Clarence's meals turned out to be a perfect outlet.

Plus, it was nice how much I ran into Oliver. How often he stayed to cook beside me—despite how often I could hear his phone vibrating—and the stories we shared back and forth about our lives and experiences. Eventually he asked about the elephant in the room (how exactly things didn't pan out with Jonas), and eventually he in turn shared about a woman named Phoebe in San Antonio who almost lured him away from his train life. We watched movies in the background as we cooked. Some of my favorite moments, in fact, were dicing and stirring in companionable silence.

And yet, he never pursued me beyond friendship. And despite the hundreds of times I've reminded myself that that was a good thing during this season, I couldn't help but end each night with a little disappointment.

Throw in the expanding list of missed calls I've successfully ignored from Jonas that began on day two of the trip, and the disappointment has grown.

Well. To be clear, I've successfully ignored them all after that first dreadful mistake of a pickup.

I was in the middle of a Santa's Workshop class one afternoon, my nose pressed to the hot glue gun in my hand as I took aim at the tiny wooden bead for a Scandinavian Wooden Snowflake elective I opted for before the evening outing. It was a small class that day, most opting for a foxtrot class in the Mistletoe Room instead. And most were long gone while their ornaments sat on the table in the corner drying. But that didn't mean I was alone.

"I have never, and I mean never, seen anyone take ornament making so seriously."

Oliver's elbows rested on the table as he sat, leaning forward in his seat, beside me. So close I could smell the pine-scented dish soap coming off his hands, which I'd become accustomed to in his kitchen. "You're going to miss dinner."

"No." I shook my head. "*We're* going to miss dinner if you stay here chastising me for making the perfect snowflake. Also, as I've said before, this glue gun is defective. It's not my fault."

Oliver smirked. "Right. Just like the first and second glue guns were defective too. Such a bizarre shame."

Right at that moment my phone on the table began ringing.

I paused on the trigger of the gun, gaze flitting over to the phone. It shook on the table, and I fully expected to see Elodie's name dancing on the screen. But it wasn't. It was Jonas.

From the corner of my eye, I could see Oliver glance at the name, then shift away.

I silenced it, turned it over, and returned my attention back to my ornament.

Oliver was silent through the hot gluing of two more beads on my snowflake.

"You don't answer his calls?"

"No," I said, picking up another small bead with my glue and transferring it to the ornament.

"Never? You haven't answered any of them?"

So he had noticed. "There isn't anything to say."

Long pause.

"Not even . . . stop calling? Take a hint and leave me alone?"

I could hear it in his voice. It bothered Oliver that Jonas was trying to contact me. And that caused the hint of a smile to rise to my lips.

I set the glue gun down. "Jonas and I have been through several breakups over the years. Probably half a dozen."

Oliver frowned.

"They've never lasted more than a week, month tops."

The frown in his blue eyes deepened, and I hurried on. "And I always let him come back. It's been three years without a breakup. I thought we had finally moved beyond the threat of one. I thought we had finally moved on to . . ." I hesitate, not wanting to say the word *marriage* or anything related to it. "To other things, but obviously that wasn't the case. And . . . maybe he hasn't moved on, but I have."

I lifted my chin, as Elodie almost nightly instructed me to during her evening TED Talk with me as the single audience member. The theme: *Why You Are Better than Jonas* and *How You Will Do Everything I Say to Get Him Rinsed Out of Your Life.* "So. I'm going to do things my way this time. And that includes letting Elodie act as my contact and mediator on my behalf."

The air visibly lifted with Elodie's name. Oliver had heard enough of Elodie by this time—even heard her over speakerphone a time or two in all her brassy glory—to like and trust her intrinsically. "And so what do you do?"

"My job," I raise my chin, "according to Elodie, is to silence my phone. Next week I'm supposed to move on to blocking the number, but . . . I'm just not quite there yet."

I felt cowardly as I said it. After all, what sort of idiot hung on to the threads of a bad relationship? Even if it was just a number you didn't ever want to answer?

"Ah. I see. Elodie does have it all figured out." But despite his tone, Oliver's eyes were warm. In them he seemed to be holding a well-ful of thoughts. "And really, it's wise not to rush," he said at last, then picked up the glue gun and held it out to me. "Sometimes, I think, just sitting with the reality of what you inevitably must do is enough."

That night, I blocked Jonas's number.

And, surprisingly, didn't feel that sense of remorse I had so dreaded. Surprisingly, I didn't feel anything at all.

I pause in my scanning of the newspaper and turn to the chessboard on the seat beside me. It's been an hour now, and I still haven't pressed the trigger on a move.

"He's going to go for the bishop," Clarence says, and I look over to see a heaping spoonful of oatmeal in his hand, the bowl half empty.

"I thought about that. But surely he wouldn't expose his castle this early in the game . . ."

I spend another minute mulling it over, then hasten when Clarence announces he spies Oliver coming down the aisle.

I knock over his pawn with my bishop a millisecond before I feel him standing over me. He pats my chair.

"Cutting it a little close, aren't you, Fairbanks? So. Have I stumped you?" Oliver stands above me, hand resting easily on the top of my chair, looking like a child who knows he's two moves away from undeniable victory.

"Like the last two times? Oh wait. Sorry, I get so confused between you and Clarence."

Clarence, who did in fact win the past two games, grins surreptitiously over his bowl.

It didn't take long for Oliver to go from being the interested bystander in our games to wanting a go of his own on the board. The only problem, of course, was that a single game tended to clog up an entire day with how busy he was running from game to business. So eventually at a stop outside Cleveland one night, we found a solution. Found another board, and now we keep two games running: one between Clarence and me, and one with Oliver. The only rule is that every time he passes by our compartment, a move *must* be made, and every time he stops at our seats, I must've made my own move or else I forfeit a piece.

This, as one might expect given how often he finds himself rushing from one car to another, often turns out to be quite humorous. Let's just say I've won (and lost) my share of queens by millisecond mistakes.

"Will you be coming out tonight?" I say to Clarence, who has chosen a quieter evening in his car the past two nights over the fray.

I see Clarence give his son a meaningful look, although why, I can't tell. "Plan on it. Going to help Mrs. Byrd out with a little inventory this afternoon first."

I shake my head. "You put the definition of retirement to shame, Clarence. I think you work more than most employed people here."

And it's true, although I've learned over the past two weeks that that's exactly how he likes it. Much like me, Clarence can't seem to completely cease work, and more often than not in the afternoons, I find him gone missing into the kitchen to help with some disaster. (According to Mrs. Byrd it's always a disaster, whereas to Clarence, pots could be flying past his head and he'd comment about the flock of Canadian geese out the window.) And the number of times staff have deferred to him . . . I have literally had to stop an elf from waking Clarence up over a question about restocking toilet paper. It seems that no matter what, when you've been in charge for so long, there's just no getting out of the words *conductor in chief.*

Which, to be fair, did save me. It was the afternoon after the fiasco of a room tour with Ian, and I was head deep into a book when Ian sidled up to me.

"Package delivery, Miss Fairbanks," he had said, his voice a near whisper as his eyes shifted from Clarence's sleeping face back to mine. There was a twinkle in his eye as he held the gold-and-green package in both hands. "Now I know it isn't Christmas yet, and we'll have to keep it in my room for a while, but as this came special from the North Pole . . ."

"Oh," I said as I looked at the box, trying to gauge what exactly those holes poking through the wrapping could be for. My arms didn't move. "Oh, Ian. You shouldn't have."

He practically kicked the aisle floor with his elf shoe in his bashful excitement. "If you're worrying about not having a gift for me yet, don't. You'll have plenty of time to find something for me by Christmas too." He winked. "Partner."

My hands were glued to my book. It wasn't that I *didn't* want to move to take the box. It was just that I was temporarily paralyzed. "What"—I felt my back pressing against the armrest—"is it?"

He waggled a finger at me. "Now, now, Miss Fairbanks. You know the rules. You have to open it yourself."

He looked so earnest, so innocent, that, with great effort, I managed to set my book down. I sealed my fate and took the box from him. It was heavy. Python-curled-in-the-center-of-the-box heavy. Carefully, I avoided touching any of the open air holes. "Is it . . . alive?"

At this point Clarence rounded out of a dead sleep and said, as if he'd been a part of the conversation all along, "Elf, where are you supposed to be at sixteen hundred?"

Ian stood immediately upright. "Working, sir. Here, sir."

"Is it true that you are partaking in unholiday behavior by displaying favoritism in gift giving while everyone else is left to be mere onlookers?"

Ian checked over both shoulders, suddenly self-conscious. Nobody was watching us. "No, sir. Well, yes, sir. It's just that, sir—"

Clarence leveled his gaze at him, and his bushy brows nearly covered his eyes. "And I *know* you wouldn't be soliciting the interests of single young ladies while in uniform. Because certainly you recall Section 22B of the contract referring to the imperative of staying in character."

"Oh, ye-ye-yes, sir." Ian looked down at his elf costume.

"And I would absolutely hate for us to lose such a fine employee as yourself due to lack of compliance with said contract."

At that, Ian snatched the package from my hands.

There was a long moment of silence, Ian looking absolutely terrified, Clarence gazing at him like a father trying to decide in a moment of discipline if he had sufficiently gotten across his point. At last he dismissed him. "I believe they need a hand with the caroling karaoke contest in the Mistletoe Room."

After Ian had zipped out, I turned to Clarence. "Do you really have a line about staying in character in your contract?"

"The question is"—Clarence tapped his cane to his temple—"will he be brave enough to come back and point that out?"

As it turns out, Ian wasn't brave enough.

In fact, had I not eventually given myself enough of a pep talk to seek him out and tell him the reality of the situation from my end—that I was sorry, but we just didn't seem like a good fit together—I don't think he ever would've shown his face in our car again.

On the bright side, he handled it well. Remarkably well, in fact, to the point that he admitted his own glowing attraction to me had faded since the moment I'd referred to dear Chaucer as "it." We parted on good terms.

"Your move," Oliver says, taking my bishop with his and,

sure enough, exposing his castle without qualm. "Hey, I'm going to assist with the wreath making at four. Were you planning on going?"

"Yes. I'd like to make one for my mom for Christmas." I check my watch and start to rise. "Which actually means I'd better go get changed now for tonight's activity. I'll see you there."

"I'll save you a 'properly working' glue gun." Oliver winks at me, and for my part, I can't help but feel my cheeks flush.

The next few hours pass in peace. By the time the wreath-making activity is over, my hands are sticky with pine sap and hot-gun glue, stray needles adorn my hair, and I'm fairly certain I'm going to smell of spruce for days. But I did manage to make a rather sweet wreath covered in both holly and silver bells, along with a little posted sign saying *Merry Christmas*. I know Mom will be pleased.

The evening activity is supposed to be a night out at something called *Dickens of a Christmas*. I know little about the specifics aside from the fact that we'll be located in a small town outside Glacier National Park. So I am sure to dress appropriately for the extreme weather I've experienced the past two days as we chugged along the northern border of North America. The previous afternoon I took part in a Christmas sweater embroidering workshop, which actually turned out so surprisingly lovely (thanks in great part to Mrs. Faris, a teacher with great insights regarding her embroidery machine), that I put it on for tonight's event. Instead of the loud Christmas knits I've seen and worn a hundred times over, this one is subtly in the spirit: a cream sweater dotted with embroidered firs and spruces in a variety of threaded shades of green, a dozen small snowflakes hanging overhead.

I've put on my warmest pair of wool socks (quite the treasured thrift find, a handknit pair with the words *Noel* across the ankles) I could find under my boots, and before I step off the train, I slip on my thickest pair of mittens.

My coat swirls around my jeans where the tops of my boots meet them, and the second I step out onto the platform and feel the mascara on my eyelashes start to freeze, I remember I've forgotten my hat and should turn around. Only, the very same moment I have this intuition, I see something very strange.

It's Clarence. Standing in the center of the huddled crowd of passengers clapping their sides and bouncing impatiently in their boots.

Clarence. In a Santa suit.

Clarence. Leading the group.

"Come on then, everyone! Stay close and follow me. *Ho ho ho!*" He heads in the direction of a small cluster of buildings ahead, holding to his cane, as usual, but on his other side is petite Mrs. Byrd, her arm wrapped firmly around his waist.

For stability?

Or theatrics? Is she playing the Mrs.?

Or . . . could that possibly be a real, live romantic gesture?

"What . . . ?" I begin walking toward the group, and as I do so, my head swivels around, looking for Oliver. Why hadn't Clarence mentioned this to me? The man's walked a sum total of a hundred steps back and forth for the past two weeks, going less than half a mile an hour *on carpet*. And then here he goes traipsing around town with two feet of snow blanketing every square inch not covered in salt, playing Santa for the train.

But no, no, don't mention the grandiose plan to me. Talk about your love of fish sticks you had in a particular diner outside Kansas City thirty years ago for half an hour, sure, but don't even think to mention—

My thoughts halt as Oliver comes into view. He's standing at the far end of the station's empty parking lot, lit only by a couple lampposts and the receding lights of a turning car.

When our eyes lock, his lips tilt slightly upward, and he beckons to me with one gloved hand.

The other holding firm to the reins. The reins.

Of a one-horse open sleigh.

I freeze.

Something inside me says, *he's not really meaning you,* and I check over my shoulder in both directions. But nobody is there. Nobody except a few of the staff watching from the windows who, when they spot me, dart behind the curtains.

He really means me. *Me.*

My boots crackle along the deeply salted sidewalk as I move toward him. The sleigh grows larger the closer I come, and when I finally have made my way across the parking lot and taken several knee-deep steps through the snow-blanketed field to the sleigh, I take it all in. The horse is larger than any breed I've ever seen, its black mane glistening beneath the moon of the cloudless night sky. Icicle clouds curl from its nostrils as it exhales and shakes off a thin layer of snow. The wooden red sleigh itself is small enough for two or three passengers in the cab, with a raised area another foot higher for the driver. Only Oliver is not sitting in the cab. He's alone, standing in the driver's area, waiting for me.

"Want a lift?" he says.

I raise a brow. "I don't know. Are you driving?"

He grins and takes my hand, steadying me as I put my foot on the wrought-iron step and pull myself up.

Icicle clouds form around my face as I exhale and look around. On the wooden seat is a wool blanket. To his left on the seat, a wicker basket.

He lets my marveling linger for a full minute, then explains. "I know a guy."

"What? Who lends you one-horse open sleighs on occasion and you lend him trains?"

At this Oliver's face breaks into a full and wide smile. "Something like that. Shall we?"

As we settle in together, side by side, and I feel his warm body against mine, I can't help but remember the question that had seemed so innocent days ago. *"Horse-drawn sleighs are what it takes to win you over, eh?"*

"I can't believe this." These are the words I find myself repeating as the horse clomps its way upward on the path between the trees. The moon trails along overhead, lighting the lean white bodies of the quaking aspen and the glittering mounds of snow at their feet. A long way off lies a cluster of pines at the base of the first of a collection of gargantuan mountains, all reaching toward the moon with sharp, needle-thin tops as though trying to pop it. Overhead hang a hundred thousand stars.

I turn and face Oliver. I'm so overwhelmed by it all, so afraid to really show how much it all means to me, that instead I say, "So this is how you treat people who beat you in chess, then? You treat them to one of their dream goals?"

"That's another thing I like about you, Willow," Oliver says, not baited by the jest. He gives a light shake on the reins when the horse slows. "Your dreams are so attainable."

I note the way he said *another* and pocket it quietly.

"Attainable?" I look at the scenery around me. "I'm sorry, but this? This is not easily attainable. My dreams are challenging to achieve, sir. *Challenging.*"

Oliver tilts his head toward me and raises a brow. "You told me in Lancaster that you achieved one of your deepest lifelong dreams by eating roasted chestnuts over an open fire."

"Because *how many people get to do that*?" I exclaim. "That *is* a legitimate goal."

"You said in Minnesota you met a lifelong goal by *ice skating.*"

"It was on a *frozen lake.* Frozen. It was dangerous, really. I could've fallen through and died."

"We drove onto the lake to get there in trucks, Willow. You wouldn't have fallen through while skating."

I suck in my breath. "That wasn't a *road*?"

Oliver snickers, his own breath blooming in thick plumes around his face.

The forest is silent, all except the horse's steps and the softly jingling bells along the sleigh's sides. The moon provides the only light, but it's more than sufficient in leaving the blue-tinted glittering of snow all around. It's so peaceful it feels as though we've stepped into a church, and for several minutes we sit in silence.

Oliver steers the horse left as we move into a clearing.

When we stop, he reaches for the basket.

"Coffee? Or cocoa?" He holds up two thermoses.

I choose the cocoa, he goes with coffee, and before long we've got the large wool plaid blanket draped over our legs and my mittens are toasty with the hot mug in my hands.

Our sleigh faces the mountains, which is breathtaking, but my eye catches the cluster of lights from the small town glow from below. The candy-cane-red train gleams in the moonlight. From the top of our small hill, I feel almost like the Grinch must've felt looking down at the inhabitants of Whoville. Only, instead of feeling lonely and bitter and anxious about the future, as I can so freely admit I felt mere weeks ago, I'm full.

I look at Oliver. The way his hand rests on the reins. The way he so peacefully gazes out at the mountain scape.

Yes, I'm happy. Happier than I've been in ages. Maybe ever.

"I got you something." Oliver reaches under his seat. "Nothing fancy. Just . . . a little something to commemorate the trip."

The rectangular box is wrapped in simple brown kraft paper, twine crisscrossing where a single candy cane lies attached to a bit of holly.

"Oh, Oliver, thank you. I—I got you something too," I say, stuttering as I take it from him. "A little Christmas present. It's in my room."

And it's true. After a Christmas musical one evening in Minneapolis, I slipped inside a convenience store and printed a candid photograph Jenkins took of the three of us one afternoon. It had been the chess game of our lives, and in the shot Clarence was leaning forward, bearded chin on his cane, as he watched me knock off Oliver's knight in my final, triumphant move. Oliver, cardigan long ago cast aside as the heat of the game progressed, was sitting opposite me, head in his hands. I grinned maniacally. Multiple passengers were hanging over our seats, arms raised in midcheer.

I had bought a little frame from the convenience store and framed it, but the longer I looked at it in my room that evening, the more my confidence waned.

It was my eyes.

The way they were only on him in the shot.

The way they gave me away.

But now . . .

Carefully I slip off the twine, candy cane, and holly, and tug at the tape on one end. I open the lid of the box, and inside sits a cardigan. Soft, I feel as my fingers rub the wool. I lift it out of the box.

The dye is of blue beryl, the color of Oliver's eyes, and

embroidered throughout is an ice-skating scene—swirling white and silver threads beneath an ice-skating couple, dotted snowflakes above. I touch the zipper, where a small felted ice skate serves as the pull.

My brow wrinkles as I look closer. There's an embroidered green truck in the distance, the same wreath on its front bumper as the one that evening. And the girl, she looks . . . She has my hair . . .

And the boy smiling beside her, his eyes . . .

I turn to Oliver. "Where did you get this?"

"I asked Mrs. Faris to make it the night after we went ice skating. She had me make up some drawings, which I admit I was pretty terrible at, but after a few rounds—"

"I *love* it," I breathe. "I can't believe you did this. I can't believe she did."

"I had to bribe her for it. Did you know the back wall of the Chestnut Car now sells her embroidery?" There's a pause. "But seriously, of course she did. She took a liking to you." The air crackles with a flurry of snowflakes and electricity as he hesitates. "We all have."

This is it.

My heartbeat quickens.

His gaze lingers on mine momentarily, but when I don't immediately reply, he carries on. "I know you've just gotten out of a serious relationship, Willow, and I have no intention of rushing you into anything. I've held back as long as I could these past two weeks. But . . . the reality is, you're getting off that train tomorrow in Seattle, and if I don't say something now, I'll regret it for the rest of my life. The thing is . . . I want to ask you if you might stay."

I raise my brow. This, of all things, was not what I was expecting. "Stay?"

"The next tour is leaving after the New Year, and I want you to join me. Join us."

I blink. "What about my job?" Slowly, I begin to shake my head. "I can't just become unemployed."

"No, that's the thing. I'm offering you a job," he says in a rush, as though he's thought this all the way through. "You've done so much for Dad. I want you to be his health companion. Help with his meals. I've already spoken with Mrs. Byrd about it all." My brow rises, but he presses on. "You could work with her to start creating meal plans for those on board with more restrictive diets. We could start becoming more tailored to those with allergies, lactose intolerances, paleo, keto, sugar-free diets. The sky's the limit. We could even start advertising with that new feature. In fact"—Oliver puts a hand on his chest—"if you don't want to pursue anything beyond friendship with me, that's fine, Willow. The offer still stands. Come on board with us. Come check off all those items on your bucket list. See San Francisco in February. Ride down the South Rim of the Grand Canyons by mule. If you're not interested in me, just consider the last two weeks the longest job interview of your life."

I hesitate, and my mouth upturns. "Why do I get the sense that you're lying about that last part?"

"Not lying. If I have to think about how to woo you under

the flag of friendship later on, so be it. The point is, it's going to be incredibly hard to win you over when you live a thousand miles away, and I feel like I deserve a fair shot."

I laugh at how he's turned this into a victimizing thing, all while my mind runs a hundred miles an hour. No words are coming to mind, just emotions, but I feel my mouth open to respond anyway. Forget what Elodie says. Forget the fact that I am technically in a period of emotional crisis and relationship jail. If there's one thing I've learned from my experience with Jonas, it's that love doesn't happen on our timeline, no matter how hard we try to force it. Sometimes we just have to take life by the horns and embrace the ride.

Elodie would understand.

And right now, even with all the triggering words of such a drastic decision flitting in and out through my mind, words like "rent" and "salary" and "When-you-tell-Elodie-you're-leaving-her-*and*-the-city-*and*-the-state-she-is-going-to-be-flinging-pans-and-French-obscenities-for-weeks," the reality is I want this. Of course, I do. *I want this.*

I'm about to say this, or more likely blurt something to the same effect, when my eyes spot a scene that's formed behind Oliver's head.

A taxi has entered the parking lot of the train station below, and out of the back door a man pops out. A tall man slipping on black driving gloves before he shuts the door. In a long black coat. And black boots. Black boots I'd know anywhere.

He shoves his hands in his pockets and moves briskly toward the waiting train.

A moment later, he steps away from it and looks straight up the hill. At me. His eyes lock on mine and there's no question about it. It's Jonas.

No. *No no no.* Not now, of all moments.

"And I was hoping . . ." Oliver says, searching my eyes, "you feel the same way."

"I"—I refocus my gaze on Oliver—"do." I take one of his gloved hands. "I really do. I think I've wanted this since we first met."

"Me too." Oliver exhales and laughs. "And I'll be frank, I'm pretty sure Dad wants this as much as I do."

I grin, all the while seeing Jonas in my periphery, trudging through the feet of snow up the hill. Determined.

And that's the thing, isn't it? He sees me sitting in a sleigh with another man, single, obviously having a moment, and doesn't have an inkling in his mind not to ruin it. He doesn't care that I look deliriously happy. He doesn't care that I'm going to have forever etched in my memory the picture of Oliver meticulously working out the details for this evening— the sleigh, the mountains, the question—and then like a big blot of ink stain over my beautiful new cardigan will forever be the reminder of Jonas, coming up this hill to interject himself into the moment.

I just want to capture Oliver and me and this hilltop moment like a snow globe, so that no matter how hard Jonas tries to pry himself in, all he'd succeed in doing is shaking up the globe and making a more enchanted, flurry-driven scene.

Jonas lifts his hands to his lips, preparing to call out,

when suddenly something lobs across the field and lands to his left. He stops. Looks at the round hole in the snow by his feet.

He takes another step and stops as another white blob comes lobbing through the air.

The third hits him squarely in the back, and he turns.

And there, at the bottom of the hill beside the big red train, is Ian, standing tall in his green elf suit, a bundle of snowballs in his hands.

The hero.

My mitten goes straight to my gaping mouth, and at last Oliver turns.

Jonas, seeing the crazy elf, starts back up the hill, but Ian starts lobbing them faster. Eventually a second elf joins in. Then a third. Even Mr. Jenkins, looking quite refined in his black suit, lands one on Jonas's shoulder.

"What on . . . ?" Oliver begins, but I cut him off.

"Kiss me," I urge, pulling his gaze away with my mittens on his cheeks. "I'd like you to kiss me now, before we have to go down and deal with Jonas and any of that down there."

"That's Jonas?" Oliver says, but then his eyes alight as he seems to catch what else I just said. Despite the growing war behind him, he pulls me in without a second's hesitation. I feel the press of his glove against the back of my head, and our cold lips mingle, offering each other warmth. Flurries land on my cheeks and closed lashes and fall softly on my hair. The horse gives a soft neigh and shakes its mane.

And suddenly it's just us, on the hilltop, ice-crystalline

branches leaning forward in anticipation, stars twinkling as they hold their breath above.

Our very own snow-globe moment in time.

And with that kiss, the surety that everything in my life just officially changed.

All because, despite my own fears and disappointments, I said yes in those coffee-stained, jingling slippers to whatever unknown adventures lay ahead, and took a step onto The Christmas Express.

Epilogue

CHRISTMAS DAY, THE FOLLOWING YEAR

*V**ous appelez ça un biscotti? J'ai fait de meilleurs biscottis dans mon sommeil.*"

I jab Elodie in the ribs as she mutters, no doubt related to the fact she's just whacked the biscotti against her cup and no doubt something about making better biscotti in her sleep. Mrs. Byrd shoots daggers with her eyes at us from the other side of the expansive table, and I press on Elodie's foot under the table with my heel until she takes a bite, rubs her belly, and murmurs an unconvincing, "Mmmm."

Mrs. Byrd resumes slapping mashed potatoes on Clarence's plate.

Clarence stands a few minutes later, and I pause in pressing the napkin over my lap for the blessing. It's Christmas morning. The passengers of our twelfth tour of the year have departed after many hugs and exchanging of contact information an hour earlier. We had several repeaters from the year prior, it was nice to see, but what was even more special were the several first timers. Elodie. My mother. And even one extra-special attendee we all have come to love: Seraphina, the girl Ian met in a computer game six months ago and hasn't shut up about since. She truly is his soul mate. We know this because she spends half her salary on cosplay costumes for Comic Cons, of which they attend many.

"Lord, we are thankful," Clarence begins, and I take a moment to peek around the table of the Mistletoe Room.

Mrs. Byrd squeezes Clarence's hand, in what I have come to recognize as a quiet love that started with help in grieving his wife's death and turned into a companionable comfort, different, but nonetheless as strong as anyone else's, including Oliver's and mine.

The seats are full of the people I've come to cherish as much as family over the last year—staff and employees who have turned out to be some of the best friends both day and night. Not that I am without my monthly fill of Elodie, who meets me every few weeks on the platform of Moynihan Train Hall station, making winding motions while glaring at the conductor to wrap it up so she can pull me off and get me up to date on all the things.

The past year has been the best of my life yet. I have so many things to be grateful for. And so much because I embarked, regardless of the fear that had me trembling, on that very first adventure.

I feel a squeeze of my hand and the warmth of a kiss on

my cheek. Opening my eyes, I realize the blessing has ended, and Oliver is gazing at me, his baby-blue eyes warm. Only, he's no longer sitting beside me, but in the silence had dropped to one knee.

For a long moment he seems to work to find his voice.

When he does at last, a slightly shaky speech unfolds from his lips, about how his life was changed the day I stepped on the train a year ago, about how he can't imagine one more day without me. I squeeze his hands as he speaks, my own throat burning as he ends with, "Merry Christmas, Willow. And I hope, if you'll have me, to many, many more."

Out of the corner of my eye, I see the faces of loved ones around the room, the gaping mouths as they open their eyes to discover the scene that's unfolding before them. Mom has her hands clutched to her chest. Elodie is openly weeping.

From another corner of my periphery, I register the twinkling ring propped up inside the open box in one of Oliver's hands.

But I'm not looking at either of those things. All I can see is Oliver's earnest face, the man who has traveled thousands of miles with me over the past 365 days, and who still wants to spend hundreds of thousands more.

And I want that too.

Of course I want that too.

My reply comes in my kiss, and as I feel his lips press against mine in return, and his arms eventually clasp around me and raise me up off my chair, toes dancing above the floor, I hear the round of claps and whoops and cheers and the tinkling of a dozen spoons and knives being clinked against glasses.

"Merry Christmas," I repeat, kissing Oliver on the stubble of his cheek and whispering in his ear. "And to many, many more."

A Perfectly Splendid Christmas

AMY CLIPSTON

For my two greatest gifts—Zac and
Matt—with lots of love and hugs

Chapter 1

Kacey Williams watched as her sister wrung her hands and glanced around the counter at the Morningside Bakery. "So, what am I forgetting?" Danielle Donahue asked, blowing out a puff of air and examining the cash register before turning toward Kacey. "You know how to work the register, right?"

"Yes, Dani. Don't you remember last summer when I came for a week and helped you out? I also know that the price list is right there." Kacey pointed to the laminated list beside the register while working to keep exasperation out of her tone.

After all, her older sister and her family were going through a tough time, and the last thing she needed was sarcasm from Kacey. Instead, she would do her best to support her.

Dani frowned. "Sorry. I'm just so stressed out. Without my part-time help, I would have had to close in the afternoons if you hadn't come back home to Splendid Lake and offered to help me. Travis's mother can only watch Kelly in the mornings, so I would have had to bring her here in the afternoon. And how could I possibly run a bakery with a four-year-old running around?"

Kacey rubbed her older sister's shoulder. "You know I'd do anything for you, Travis, and the girls. I'm just glad I'm teleworking right now, so I can be here to help you. I don't know how long it'll be before I find someone to split the rent with me in Charlotte, but I'll stay as long as I can."

Dani sniffed and cleared her throat. "I can't tell you how much I appreciate it. I've put my heart and soul into this place. When Travis got laid off, I never imagined it would take this long for him to find another job. I can't believe it's been almost four months. We've nearly run through our savings. Plus, we've borrowed money from Travis's parents, but I have no idea how we'll ever pay them back."

"Didn't you say he has an interview today?"

"Yes, but none of the interviews have worked out so far. I'm trying to stay positive, but I don't know what we're going to do. The bakery isn't enough to keep us afloat."

"Hey, it's okay." Kacey gave her sister's shoulder another squeeze. "Now that we're in November, you're going to have plenty of orders for Thanksgiving desserts and even more for Christmas parties. It's going to get busier." She smiled. "Soon you're going to be complaining that I'm not a good enough baker to help you with the orders. I'm sure one of the interviews will work out for Travis soon. In fact, one of these companies might offer him a job on the spot. In the meantime, I'm here for you."

"You're the best." Dani picked up a napkin from the counter and wiped at the tears flooding her pale-blue eyes. "I know I have to be strong, but sometimes it's all I can do to keep it together."

"I have the bakery under control. You go pick up Kelly. I'm sure all these shelves will be empty before I close at six." She gestured toward the glass-front case filled with delicious-looking and smelling treats—a variety of cupcakes, pies, cakes, tarts, and breads.

"Thank you." Dani untied her bright-blue apron and removed her matching baseball cap with the Morningside Bakery logo from her long, light-brown hair. She stepped into the back of the bakery, where a line of ovens, a sink, a large table, and lines of cabinets made up the kitchen. Beyond it was Dani's office, a walk-in freezer, a stockroom, and a restroom.

"Oh, and please don't forget that Riley is going to walk from school to the community center next door for the children's choir practice." Dani placed her apron and hat on the counter.

Kacey leaned on the doorway. "You're letting her walk from the school to downtown with her friends?"

"It's only a few blocks, and she'll be with a big group of kids. Their practice ends at six. She knows to come here after." She gathered up her purse and pulled out her keys, which jingled in her hand. "Do you mind giving her friend Colleen a ride home? She only lives a block away from me."

"Of course I don't mind. I remember where she lives.

They're starting practices now for the Christmas Tree Lighting Festival?"

"That's right."

"Halloween was only a few days ago. Isn't it a little early?"

"Not really. The festival is only a little over a month away, and they're practicing on Tuesdays and Thursdays after school. Today is the first session." Dani glanced at the clock on the wall above the industrial-size refrigerator. "Oh no. I have to run. Peggy will be late for work if I don't hurry. Thanks a million, baby sis. See you later!" With a wave of her hand she rushed out the back door to her waiting Honda Odyssey.

Kacey waved and then returned to the front of the bakery. She glanced around the store, taking in the sea of wooden tables and chairs where customers liked to enjoy their pastries and the photos of all kinds of goodies that adorned the baby-blue walls.

The bakery sat in the heart of downtown Splendid Lake on Main Street. The quaint little downtown shopping area was one of the many reasons she loved her hometown, even though she had chosen to stay in Charlotte after college.

Dani had always dreamed of owning a bakery on Main Street since she and Kacey had both grown up enjoying the town's seasonal festivals and loved visiting the little stores there.

Moving to the window, Kacey looked out toward the stores that had been the backdrop of her childhood memories. The Christmas Shop was open year-round, and there was the Warner—Splendid Lake's single-screen movie theater—the Flower Shoppe, the Coffee Bean, and Scoops, the local ice cream parlor. The town's longtime family restaurant, the Splendid Kitchen, was known for its delicious and versatile menu. Like all the shops, it was owned and operated by local residents. The town hall, library, fire station, and police station all encircled the town square.

She hugged her chest as memories of the times she'd spent downtown with her family flooded her mind. They had attended all the seasonal festivals together. She recalled sitting on her father's shoulders while watching the Fourth of July Parade and holding his hand and singing "Jingle Bells" during the Christmas Tree Lighting.

Her chest ached with missing him. A massive heart attack had stolen him from their family sixteen years ago when Kacey was ten and Dani was sixteen. Their lives were never the same.

Kacey turned her attention back to the bakery. After spotting a few crumbs on the floor, she grabbed a dustpan and broom and began sweeping the dining area.

She was so proud of her older sister when she made her lifelong dream come true and opened the bakery six years ago. For as long as Kacey could remember, Dani had always loved to bake. She recalled the hours Dani spent in the kitchen with their mother—baking cakes, cookies, breads, brownies, and pies. Although Dani frequently invited Kacey to join them in the kitchen, Kacey was more interested in drawing and playing with her dolls than creating delectable masterpieces. But baking seemed to be in Dani's blood, stamped on her DNA.

After high school, Dani went to work at a bakery located a few towns away from Splendid Lake where she learned everything she needed to know about opening her own bakery in her hometown. And Dani's bakery had been a success despite her family's recent financial troubles when her husband was laid off from his IT job at a nearby bank. Kacey hoped she could help her sister keep that dream going for many more years.

The bell above the door chimed, and Kacey looked up as a middle-aged couple came in, both dressed in heavy parkas and stocking caps and bringing with them a gust of crisp early November air.

"Welcome to Morningside Bakery." Kacey stowed the broom and dustpan before slipping behind the counter to wash her hands and pull on a pair of plastic gloves.

The couple smiled and greeted her as they approached the display case.

Kacey stood up straight and pushed her thick blonde braid off her shoulder. "Is there something in particular you'd like?"

The woman pointed to the cupcakes. "Those carrot cake cupcakes look divine."

"They're one of my favorites too."

"How about we make that two? Along with two cups of coffee," the man said as he pulled his wallet from his back pocket.

"Coming right up."

Kacey was busy serving a line of customers at four o'clock when she peeked toward the front windows and spotted her eight-year-old niece and her best friend waving. Kacey waved in response before Riley and Colleen hurried next door. Riley's light-brown braids fluttered behind her bright-pink backpack as the two girls disappeared from the window.

Kacey turned her attention back to her customers and rang up a pink sheet cake decorated with a colorful unicorn and the words "Happy Birthday, Corinne." She tucked it inside one of her sister's signature bright-blue boxes.

"Is this your sister's cake?" she asked the teenage boy who frowned as he held up his wallet.

"How could you tell?" the young man deadpanned as he gave her the money.

She shrugged. "Lucky guess." She handed him change and a receipt. "Tell your sister happy birthday for me."

He grunted before sauntering toward the exit, passing tables of customers drinking coffee and eating treats as the murmur of conversations wafted over Kacey.

She continued working her way down the line selling cookies, pastries, cakes, and breads that her sister had baked earlier that day.

Once the customers were served, she made her way around the dining area, wiping down empty tables. Then she headed to the kitchen and stowed the paper towels and cleaning spray.

After washing her hands, Kacey returned to the counter just as her phone vibrated in her pocket. She retrieved it from her back pocket and found a text message from her sister:

Stay for supper tonight. Mom is coming too.

Kacey quickly shot back a response: Sounds great. Thanks!

The bell above the door rang and a line of customers walked in just as a chorus of young voices belted out "Joy to the World," the sound reverberating through the wall from the community center next door.

"Welcome to Morningside Bakery," Kacey called above the children's chorus.

During the next two hours, she chatted with customers and filled orders as the children next door continued to sing sections of "Joy to the World" over and over again.

By the time she locked the bakery door at six, she was certain she'd have the hymn stuck in her head on repeat for the next week.

After cleaning up the dining area and the counters, she quickly packed up the few leftover goodies in a blue box, left her apron and hat on the counter, and then retrieved her coat, purse, and keys.

Kacey headed toward the front door, expecting to find Riley and Colleen waiting for her, but they weren't on the sidewalk. Perhaps Mrs. Hansen, the community choir director, had kept the kids late to share details about the Christmas Tree Lighting.

She slipped out the front door, locking it behind her, and then traipsed down the short length of sidewalk to the community center as the cold evening air nipped at her nose. Above her the sun had begun to set, sending a beautiful explosion of colors across the clear November sky.

Kacey nodded greetings to a few familiar faces passing by. As she approached the door, she recalled her mother telling her the building had once been home to a Blockbuster and then a children's clothing consignment shop. A few years later, the town council voted to buy the property and convert it into a small community center that offered a variety of classes from karate and art to yoga and dance.

Kacey pulled on the handle and stepped into the lobby, where a young woman sporting purple highlights in her blonde hair looked up from a desk while smacking her gum. "Hi. Where is the children's chorus?"

"Last room on the left." The woman pointed before blowing a pink bubble and then popping it with her tongue.

"Thanks." Kacey headed down the hallway, dodging kids running past clad in white karate uniforms.

When she reached the open doorway at the end of the hall, she slipped into the room, where kids and mothers were gathered in small groups talking, kids were playing, and adults were ferrying kids toward the door.

Kacey scanned the crowd in search of Riley and Colleen. When she found them standing at the far end of the room behind the piano, the girls were frowning as a man spoke to them with his back facing Kacey and the rest of the room. Concern filled Kacey and her eyes narrowed. The community children's choir was supposed to be fun, not a place for children to be reprimanded. And she couldn't imagine Riley doing anything to warrant a scolding.

She tried to keep her expression friendly as she wove

through the noisy crowd, nodding at familiar faces until she arrived at the piano.

When the girls glanced toward her, Riley grimaced, and Colleen looked down at her feet.

Kacey cleared her throat. "Excuse me. Is there a problem?" The choir director pivoted toward her, and when her gaze met his, Kacey gasped as she took in Drew Murphy, one of her best friends from school, standing in front of her. "Drew?"

"Kacey?" Drew let out a chuckle as his handsome face broke out into a smile.

Riley's nose scrunched, and she divided a look between Kacey and Drew. "You know my aunt Kacey?"

"We were friends a long time ago," Kacey said as she drank in the sight of him.

He looked good—*really* good. He was taller than she remembered, causing her to wonder if he'd had a growth spurt during college, and he looked more mature and possibly even handsomer too. His dark-brown hair was cut short and gone were the shaggy bangs that had once hung in his gorgeous green eyes. His angular jaw was clean-shaven and his wide chest and muscular arms filled his gray, long-sleeved collared shirt well.

She tried to stop the swell of memories that crashed through her mind like waves pounding against the shoreline— their laughter during study hall, sharing a banana split at Scoops, sitting on the pier at his parents' enormous lakefront house and watching the sunset, holding her breath and hoping that he'd finally kiss her while watching a movie. They'd become instant friends in middle school when they shared a table in art class, and deep in her heart, she'd always craved to be so much more.

But that was a long time ago, and they were older now.

"I thought you were in Charlotte." He tilted his head as his brow puckered.

"My roommate got married, so I had to give up my apartment until I can find a new roommate. I'm able to work remotely for a graphic design company for now." She held up the bakery box. "And I'm also working part-time at the bakery to help my sister out. I'm saving money for a down payment on a condo—unless I find another roommate first." She gestured around the room with her free hand. "I thought Mrs. Hansen was the children's community choir director."

Drew nodded. "Technically, she is. I'm filling in this year. Her mother had to have surgery last week, and she had to rush off to Florida to care for her. She called me last minute and asked me to fill in."

"I'm sorry to hear that." She studied him. "Are you still a music teacher?"

"Yes, at Splendid Lake Middle School."

"That's so amazing. I couldn't imagine standing in front of a classroom every day and teaching. I used to freeze up with stage fright just giving presentations and speeches in school. The idea of speaking in front of a group is just terrifying!" Kacey's eyes wandered down to his left hand, and she was surprised to find it naked. She had assumed that by now some beautiful young woman would have stolen his heart and convinced him to settle down. Although she and Drew had found each other on social media a few years ago and shared a few brief conversations, she wasn't good at keeping up with old friends.

And, if she were honest with herself, there was a part of her that still cared for him and couldn't bear the thought of watching his life through social media posts—falling in love, getting married, having kids.

She quickly tore her eyes away from his hand and back to his face, hoping he didn't notice where her stare was focused. "You were having a pretty intense conversation with Riley and Colleen when I walked in. Did they get in some sort of trouble?"

Drew's dark eyebrows rose as he looked at the girls. "What were we discussing when Riley's aunt walked over?"

Riley wound one of her long braids around her finger. "You were telling us not to talk during choir practice," she mumbled while Colleen gave a solemn nod.

"That's right." Drew turned his emerald eyes back to Kacey. "Riley and Colleen seemed to want to chat and giggle more than sing."

Kacey turned her best stern look onto her niece. "Is that true?"

Riley's cheeks blushed bright crimson as she nodded.

"You know better than that, Riley Jean," Kacey said, and her niece cast her eyes down toward the toes of her purple sneakers. "I'll talk to them in the car," she told Drew. "I do have a question for you."

"Okay . . ."

"So, the bakery is right on the other side of that wall," she said, pointing in that direction. "And it's so loud that I feel like I'm here at choir practice with you. Are you planning to sing more than just 'Joy to the World'? I think I'm going to have that song stuck in my head until at least June."

Drew's lips twitched. "Well, maybe you should come over and help us learn the song faster so we can move on to something else."

Kacey laughed, and Drew joined her. She hadn't realized till now how much she'd missed that sound.

"You really don't want me helping with choir practice." Kacey smiled and suddenly realized she was there for a reason. "Well, we better get going before Colleen's mom starts to worry." Kacey motioned toward the exit. "Get your backpacks and coats, girls."

The girls scurried across the room.

Kacey faced Drew, and more memories filled her mind. "It was good seeing you."

"You too. I'm sure I'll see you again soon."

Kacey nodded, and Riley and Colleen zipped toward the exit as if their backpacks were jet packs. "I better catch up with them."

"Take care, Kace."

As Kacey hurried after them, her heart danced at the idea of spending more time with Drew Murphy.

Chapter 2

Have a good night," Kacey called when Colleen climbed out of the back seat of her mint-green Prius.

Colleen waved. "Thank you, Miss Kacey. Bye, Riley!" The little girl bolted toward the front door of her house with her wavy black ponytail flowing behind her sparkly purple backpack and her yellow coat.

Kacey turned toward her niece. "So, how are you going to behave at choir next week?"

"I won't chat or giggle."

"Promise?"

Riley held up her pinky, and Kacey linked hers with it. "Pinky promise, Aunt Kacey."

"Perfect." Kacey smiled. "I'll make you a deal. If you behave, I won't tell your parents that Mr. Murphy had to talk to you and Colleen."

Her niece's expression brightened. "You promise?"

"Cross my heart." Kacey drew an *X* over her chest.

"Deal!" Riley shook Kacey's hand.

Kacey backed her car out of the Parker family's driveway and headed down the street.

"Was Mr. Murphy your boyfriend?"

Kacey gave her niece a sideways glance. "No. We were just friends." *Unfortunately.* "Why?"

"You seemed really happy to see each other."

Kacey stared out the windshield, pondering her niece's observation. At one point, she had been certain Drew cared for her in high school, and she was sure he'd ask her to prom. But he never asked her, and only a week before, his best friend, Bennett, asked, which seemed better than staying home or going alone. To her surprise, Bennett also asked her to be his girlfriend, and she said yes, even though her heart still belonged to Drew. Soon after, her friendship with Drew was strained, and they barely spoke until graduation when they said good-bye and wished each other luck at college.

"Aunt Kacey . . ." Riley sang. "Did you hear me?"

Kacey slowed to a stop at an intersection and faced her niece, who was studying her, her blue eyes narrowed with suspicion. "I'm sorry. What did you say?"

"I asked if you saved me any of those strawberry frosted cookies."

"Actually, yes, there were two left, so I brought them home for you." She reached back and touched Riley's nose.

"Thank you."

Kacey turned left onto Maple Avenue and then steered

her Prius into Dani's driveway, parking behind her mother's burgundy Subaru Outback. She gathered up her purse and the bakery box while Riley shouldered her backpack.

They walked up the short driveway to the front porch of her sister's modest, three-bedroom brick ranch home.

When they reached the door, Riley pulled it open and rushed inside, announcing, "I'm home!"

Kacey chuckled to herself while following her into the family room, where Travis sat on a recliner. The delicious aroma of garlic bread filled the room and her stomach growled with delight at the thought of her sister's scrumptious spaghetti and meatballs.

"Hi, Mommy! Hi, Daddy!" Riley yelled as she sprinted toward her room.

Dani appeared in the kitchen doorway. "Hi, Riley! I made your favorite."

"Yay!" Riley called before disappearing into her bedroom.

Travis shook his head and smiled at Kacey. "I wish I had half her energy."

"Me too. How was your day?" Kacey set her purse on the sofa.

Travis shrugged, his smile fading. "It was about the same as all the other days lately. Disappointing. The interview didn't go that great." He picked up a can of Coke from the end table beside him and took a long gulp.

"I'm sorry to hear that. What happened?" Kacey set the bakery box on the coffee table, shucked her teal coat, and set it on the sofa beside her purse.

He raked his hand through his short, light-brown hair. "I think I'm overqualified. Everyone is looking to fill entry-level positions that they can pay less for these days." He leaned forward and lowered his voice. "I know Dani is going crazy with worry, and I've been telling her it's going to work out. But honestly, I'm starting to lose hope. I just feel like such a failure. I've let her down."

"No, you haven't." Kacey walked over to him and sat on a love seat beside his recliner. "You're doing the best you can, and she knows that. It will work out. Until then I'll help you as much I can."

His smile was sad. "We're both so grateful."

Kacey's heart broke for her sister and brother-in-law and their situation. Travis had been a part of her life for as long she could remember.

Dani and Travis met their first year of high school when he and his parents moved to Splendid Lake, and they'd been inseparable since. They even weathered a long-distance relationship when he attended Appalachian State University, and then they married soon after he graduated.

Kacey was grateful her sister had married such a good man. He always worked hard for his family, and his love for his wife and daughters was apparent in the gleam of his hazel eyes when he gazed at them.

"How was your day?" he asked before taking another sip of his drink.

"Busy. Dani is going to have a lot of baking to do tomorrow morning."

"Well, at least there's some good news today."

"Auntie!" Kelly came romping down the hallway, her curly blonde pigtails bouncing and her arms up in the air, waving above her head.

Kacey's mother followed her younger granddaughter, grinning down at the little girl. "Slow down, Kelly. You're going to trip and go boom."

Mom's light-brown hair was threaded with gray, and her beautiful pale-blue eyes sparkled with love for her children and grandchildren. Mom seemed much younger than her true age of fifty-seven. Kacey had always thought Dani resembled a younger version of Mom since they shared the same eye and hair color, while Kacey's hair was blonde and her eyes a deeper shade of blue, like her father's.

Scooping her four-year-old niece into her arms, Kacey kissed her little head. "Hey, snuggle bug!" Then she smiled at her mother. "How were things at the elementary school today?"

"The front office was busy as usual," Mom said. "I heard you tell Travis that the bakery kept you hopping too."

"Kace," Dani called from the kitchen, "could you please help me?"

"Of course." Kacey handed Kelly to her mother and then slipped into the kitchen, where Dani stood at the sink, pouring a large pot of spaghetti into a colander. "Put me to work."

Dani shook the colander and then poured the pasta into a large bowl. "So the bakery was busy today?"

"I ran out of cupcakes, most of the cookies, and almost all the cakes." Kacey scrubbed her hands at the sink.

Dani handed her a large bowl of salad and the bowl of pasta. "Can you take these to the table?"

Kacey walked into the dining room, where Travis and the girls had gathered around the table. Then she returned to the kitchen and found Mom scooping meatballs and tomato sauce from a double boiler into a large serving bowl, and Dani standing at the refrigerator retrieving a can of Parmesan cheese.

Kacey leaned against the counter next to her sister. "Why didn't you tell me that Drew Murphy was the choir director?"

"Drew Murphy?" Mom spun toward her with her blue eyes wide.

Dani's brow puckered. "I thought Mrs. Hansen was the director."

"Apparently her mother had emergency surgery, and she had to go to Florida to take care of her," Kacey said, folding her arms over her waist. "Since Drew is the music teacher at the middle school, Mrs. Hansen asked him to fill in this year."

"Oh dear," Mom said. "I hope Dana's mother is okay."

Dani nodded. "Me too."

"I'm sure he's a wonderful teacher." Mom smiled. "I remember how talented he was. Couldn't he play several instruments?"

"That's right. He could figure out any song on the piano. Then he also learned how to play clarinet, trumpet, and

French horn. He was like a one-man band." Kacey pushed off the counter and picked up the basket of garlic bread. She couldn't help but wonder if he was single, but she shook off her curiosity. After all, she was planning to go back to her life in Charlotte, and he had built a life here.

Dani touched Kacey's arm, a smile lifting the corners of her mouth. "What did he say to you?"

"Not a whole lot." Kacey gave a brief overview of her conversation with Drew, leaving out the part about Riley and Colleen's behavior.

Mom's smile was wide. "I think he's still single."

"Ooooh," Dani sang. "That's right. You two were always so close. I'm surprised you never dated."

Me too. "That was a long time ago."

"But you're here now," her sister continued.

Kacey waved her off and carried the bread to the dining room, where she placed it in the center of the long oak table. "It would never work out between us. His life is here, and mine is in Charlotte."

"You don't have to go back to Charlotte." Mom set four bottles of salad dressing next to the salad. "You're teleworking here now. Why not continue to do it?"

"Exactly." Dani set the Parmesan cheese beside the bowl of meatballs and then took her usual spot across from Travis.

Kacey sank down on a chair beside Riley. "Because I love Charlotte."

"What's wrong with Splendid Lake?" Dani's expression matched her challenge.

Travis looked back and forth between his wife and Kacey. "What are we talking about?"

"There's nothing wrong with Splendid Lake," Kacey said. "I love it here, and it will always be my home. But I've always dreamed of owning a place in a city."

"Would someone please clue me in on what we're discussing?" Travis asked.

"Hang on. I need to make a point," Dani told Travis, and he blew out a puff of air. "But what if Drew is your future?"

"Drew who? Murphy?" Travis asked.

Mom wagged a finger. "Or your Christmas miracle."

"Christmas miracle?" Kacey snorted. "Seriously, Mom? My love life is so pathetic that I need a miracle? Thanks so much."

Riley yanked the sleeve of Kacey's long-sleeved white blouse. "May I please have a piece of bread and some spaghetti and meatballs?"

"Bread, peeease!" Kelly announced from her booster seat beside Mom.

Kacey lifted Riley's plate and added a small pile of spaghetti, a couple of meatballs and sauce, and a piece of garlic bread to it before handing it back to her. "Here you go."

"Thank you." Riley smiled up at her.

Across the table, Mom made a small plate for Kelly.

Dani added some salad to a bowl and then passed it Kacey. "Well, you're going to be seeing Drew on Tuesdays and Thursdays after Riley's choir practice." Her expression was smug.

"So Drew is the choir director?" Travis began putting the

pieces of the conversation together. "And he's the same Drew that Kacey was friends with in school."

Kacey forked some salad into a bowl before passing it to her mother. "Yes. Now let's change the subject. Riley needs to tell you about choir practice."

Her niece shot her a panicked expression.

"Tell them what song you sang," Kacey said, her words measured.

"Oh." Riley's expression relaxed. "'Joy to the World.'"

Kacey shook her head. "Yes, over and over again. I heard every word in the bakery."

"Oh, I know what you mean." Dani swirled her fork in the air. "You should have been there when the Zumba class was going on last spring. I was dancing around the bakery along with the pop music."

Travis snickered. "I'm sorry I missed that."

All the adults laughed, and Kacey glanced around the table as her heart warmed. She simply adored her family.

"So you like choir?" Mom asked.

Riley nodded while eating a meatball. "It's fun."

"I can't believe the Christmas Tree Lighting Festival is only a month away," Mom said. "Before you know it Christmas will be here. Where has the year gone?"

"That means Santa will be coming soon, Kelly." Riley grinned at her baby sister.

"I like Santa," Kelly announced, and everyone laughed.

Dani lifted her glass of water. "Thanksgiving is three weeks from today."

"That's right," Kacey said, forking more salad. "I feel like we were just at church for Easter."

Dani looked at Mom. "Are we going to your house for Thanksgiving again this year?"

Mom nodded. "Sure."

"I'll help cook," Kacey volunteered.

"Oh, don't do us any favors." Travis held his hands up in mock horror.

Kacey pointed her fork at her brother-in-law. "That's not nice."

"But it's true," Mom said as everyone laughed.

Kacey settled back in her chair and laughed along with them.

Yes, it was great to be back in Splendid Lake.

Later, Kacey parked behind her mother's Subaru at the small house her mother had purchased shortly after her father passed away. While it was painful for Mom, Dani, and Kacey to say good-bye to the four-bedroom, two-story home closer to the lake, Mom had explained that they needed to downsize so she could manage the bills without Dad's income.

Located a few blocks from Dani's home, the house had a similar floor plan to her sister's house with its moderate-size primary bedroom, two small bedrooms, two bathrooms, and small kitchen, family room, and dining room.

Once inside, Mom went to take a shower while Kacey retired to the guest bedroom, which had once been Dani's bedroom since Kacey's bedroom was now Mom's craft and sewing room.

Kacey sat at the desk, powered up her computer, and perused her work email. She clicked through messages from her supervisor, coworkers, and customers, responding when necessary. Then she checked her calendar and created a list of projects she needed to address tomorrow.

While she worked, her mind replayed her brief conversation with Drew, and his face filled her mind. She pondered what her mother and sister had said about her and Drew—that perhaps their time together would happen now, so many years after they'd last spoken in person. Yet, it seemed impossible that Drew would suddenly be interested after so many years. If he hadn't liked her as more than a friend back in high school, it seemed preposterous that he would now.

Against her better judgment, Kacey popped over to Facebook and found his profile. She browsed photos of him conducting the middle school band in the auditorium, smiling with students holding their instruments, laughing with friends, and then photos of two cats—one fat orange tabby and a gray cat that seemed to always have a look of disdain.

Her eyes flitted to where he'd listed himself as single, and her pulse fluttered.

She dropped her head into her hands and groaned. Who was she kidding? Drew Murphy was handsome, single, outgoing, friendly, and funny. There was no way he'd ever want to get involved with Kacey, his buddy from school. If they hadn't had a spark back then, why would they have one now?

But they had both grown and matured. Things might be different. What if Drew's feelings for her changed? What would she do about it when her life and her career were back in Charlotte?

Chapter 3

Drew set two bowls of wet, stinky, tuna-flavored cat food on the kitchen floor in front of his two yowling cats. "It smells horrendous, guys. Bon appétit."

He leaned against the counter and shook his head as Thor, his large orange tabby, and Loki, his gray-and-white feline, scarfed up the food as if they hadn't eaten in a week. Then he crossed to the kitchen table and sifted through the pile of mail he'd carried in from the box at the street, finding a couple of bills, a catalog, and a few advertisements.

After opening his refrigerator and studying the contents for a few moments, Drew pulled out a container of leftover chili he had cooked over the weekend, and he sighed.

"Chili again," he mumbled before pulling out a piece of wax paper, covering the container, and slipping it into the microwave. He pushed a few buttons on the microwave and it hummed to life.

Drew retrieved a bowl, spoon, and a bag of shredded cheese

while contemplating his day. It had started out ordinary, with a typical day at school before rushing to the community center for the first choir practice. And the first practice was also typical, with a mix of serious students and a few chatty students, but then his day took an unexpected turn when Kacey Williams popped in out of nowhere.

Kacey Williams.

Never in a million years had he expected to see Kacey again. He smiled as he envisioned her. She was still one of the most beautiful women he'd ever known with her hair the color of sunshine, deep-blue eyes that reminded him of the ocean, high cheekbones, pink lips, a long neck, and that smile and laugh that seemed to always go straight to his heart.

That familiar longing and regret that had followed him around since his senior year in high school welled up inside of him. Drew felt himself falling for Kacey when they were in middle school, but fear of losing her friendship had kept him from asking her to be his girlfriend.

Then in high school they grew even closer, and he was certain he loved her. As senior year approached, he'd planned to ask her to prom and declare his feelings for her. Then his nerves caused him to wait too long, and his so-called best friend, Bennett Clark, beat him to it and asked her first. To make matters worse, Bennett not only asked her to prom but also asked her out, and she accepted. Her relationship with Bennett not only shattered Drew's heart, but it also came between them, leaving their friendship awkward and strained, which was a clear sign she'd chosen Bennett over him.

If only he'd found the courage to be honest with her about his feelings, then maybe they could have been more than friends.

The beeping microwave pierced through his thoughts, and he fetched two pot holders before carrying the container to the table. The cats, who had both licked their plates clean, sauntered toward his small family room, where Drew was certain they would return to their favorite spots on the sofa and sleep away the evening.

Drew scooped chili into his bowl, added shredded cheese, and then began to eat while his mind continued to swirl with thoughts of Kacey.

A few years ago, he looked her up on social media and was shocked to find that she was still single. He had always imagined that she'd followed her dreams to Charlotte, settled down, and started a family. They shared a few short messages and then their communication stopped when it seemed they had each run out of things to say.

And now Kacey was back in Splendid Lake. He noticed her left hand was free of jewelry, and he couldn't stop the what-ifs from rolling through his mind.

At the same time, Kacey had made it clear that she planned to go back to Charlotte. Still, renewing a friendship with her would be a gift. In fact, just having her as a part of his life would be a blessing.

Drew's phone buzzed, and he pulled it from his pocket and found a message from his coworker, Garrett Douglas.

How was choir practice?

Instead of typing a response, Drew dialed Garrett's number, and he answered on the first ring.

"Was it that bad?" Garrett asked. Children's voices sounded behind him, and Drew imagined Garrett's wife wrangling their two- and four-year-old toward the bathtub.

Drew chuckled. "No, it was fine. I thought it would be easier to talk instead of typing. I had a full room. It was the usual mix of serious singers and kids who were more interested in their own conversations."

"Sounds like my math classes," Garrett joked. "Did you apply for that music department head job in Newton?"

Drew scrubbed his hand down his face. "I'm considering it."

"You should do it."

"Are you trying to get rid of me?"

"You know I'm not, but it's a great opportunity. You should give it a try and see what happens. It's a nice pay raise."

"I'll check out the job post again."

"Good. You're a great candidate." A voice sounded behind Garrett. "I'd better go. Duty calls."

"See you tomorrow." Drew disconnected the call.

After cleaning up the kitchen, he moved through the small family room, where his two fat cats snored on the sofa, and continued down the short hallway past the one bathroom and toward the two bedrooms. While his little cottage could fit into the four-car garage attached to his parents' sprawling colonial, this little house was his. Well, technically it belonged to the bank until he paid off the mortgage, but Drew had earned this home himself without his father's help.

He stepped into the first bedroom, which he had converted into his office, and sat at the desk before powering up his laptop. He clicked on the link he'd saved for the job and settled back in his chair as he folded his arms over his chest.

His mind spun as he perused the job post. Newton was nearly two hours away from Splendid Lake, so he would have to sell his little cottage and move there. And by doubling his salary, it would give him the opportunity to buy a larger home—not that it was important to him.

Drew rubbed the stubble on his chin. Applying for a job wasn't necessarily a commitment. There were no guarantees he'd even be considered for the position. So, it really couldn't hurt to try.

He began searching through his files for his résumé. Garrett was right. He should at least apply and see how it turned out.

———

Saturday morning Kacey pushed open the door to the Coffee Bean, which was located across the street from the bakery, the bell above her announcing her presence. While she enjoyed the coffee offered at the bakery, her sister only sold regular and decaf. This morning she was in the mood for a vanilla latte, and she offered to pick them up for her mother, sister, and herself.

The shop was buzzing with activity as customers sat at

the tables or in booths enjoying their coffee and pastries. A few others stood in line at the counter, where the sisters and co-owners, Ava Burns and Brooklyn Waller, took and filled their orders.

Kacey stood in line behind a group of women who looked to be in their midtwenties and then slipped her phone and keys into the pockets of her coat.

She took in the sisters working behind the counter and couldn't help but think that they looked exactly the same as they did when they were all in high school together. Brooklyn was twenty-three to Ava's twenty-six, and although they had physical similarities, those were hard to spot at first glance. They shared the same petite frame, warm smile, and friendly personality, yet Brooklyn had her mother's dirty-blonde hair and baby-blue eyes and Ava had her father's wavy, dark-brown hair and coffee-brown eyes.

Ava had married her high school sweetheart, Dylan Burns, who owned Burns Auto Repair with his brother. Kacey recalled seeing Ava and Dylan walking arm-in-arm around high school, and it didn't surprise her when she heard they had married.

When it was Kacey's turn, she moved up to the counter and Ava grinned at her.

"Kacey!" she exclaimed. "I thought that was you. Are you home for the holidays?"

"I'm teleworking and staying with my mom for a while."

"How fun! What can I get you?"

"Three vanilla lattes to go, please."

"Coming right up." Ava repeated the order to her sister and then told Kacey the total. "How's your mom doing?"

"Great," Kacey said as Ava ran her credit card. "She's still working at the elementary school."

Ava handed her the receipt. "I'm glad to hear it. It was good to see you! Have a great day."

"You too." Kacey moved to the end of the counter while Ava turned her attention to the next customer in line. She pulled her phone out from the back pocket of her jeans and scrolled through her messages. When she heard someone call her name, she spun as Drew approached her with a wide smile lighting up his handsome face.

"Drew. Hi." She pocketed her phone and pushed a lock of hair behind her ear.

Drew nodded toward the menu. "Let me guess. You ordered a vanilla latte."

"How'd you know?"

He scoffed. "Well, it wasn't all that long ago when we'd hop in my mom's old Beamer and go to that coffee shop over on Lincoln Avenue. And you ordered the same thing every time."

"You remember that." She gave a little laugh as she took in the sparkle in his lush, green eyes. They always reminded her of the grass in spring.

He lifted a dark eyebrow. "How could I forget?"

"Kacey?"

She pivoted toward the counter, where Brooklyn held a to-go container with three coffee cups. "Thank you so much."

"Come back and see us," Brooklyn said before fluttering off to fill the next order.

Kacey turned back to Drew. "I need to get to the bakery. My mom and I are helping Dani out today."

She turned to leave when she felt his hand touch her elbow and gently turn her back around.

"Do you have plans tonight?"

Her heart stopped. "No, I don't think so."

"Would you like to have dinner?"

"Yes, I would," she managed to say.

"Great." He exhaled, sounding relieved. "What time will you get off work?"

"Six o'clock."

"I'll meet you at the bakery then." He smiled, and headed for the line to order his coffee.

"Perfect. See you then."

She felt a spring in her step as she carried the coffees out into the chilly morning and across the street to the bakery, where she was greeted by the bell ringing above the door and the scrumptious smells of her sister's morning baking. Had that actually happened? Did she just agree to go on a date with Drew? She felt the smile on her face widen even more. But just as quickly, she tamped down her excitement. It was probably just dinner between two friends who needed to catch up on each other's lives. Nothing to get excited about.

Mom stood at the counter, cleaning the glass case.

"I have coffee!" Kacey sang before handing her a cup.

Mom breathed in the aroma. "Oh my! It smells divine."

Dani appeared from the kitchen with a tray of colorful iced cookies. "I was wondering if you got lost." She set the tray of cookies in the display case.

"There was a line at the Coffee Bean and I ran into Drew." Kacey gave her a cup.

Dani grinned. "Is that right?"

"And what did Drew have to say?" Mom asked.

Kacey shrugged, trying her best to not make a big deal about it. "He asked me to go to dinner tonight."

"He asked you out?" Dani pushed on Kacey's shoulder. "I knew he always had the hots for you!"

"Yeah, right. That's why he never asked me out. We were only friends, Dani."

"I think he was too nervous to ask you out," Mom said.

Kacey shook her head. "Why would he be nervous? We were best friends. He knew me better than anyone."

"He probably didn't want to ruin the friendship."

"Well, we're just friends now, and that's fine. It will be fun to go out for dinner and get caught up."

"But things are different now, Kacey," Mom said. "You're not kids anymore."

"And I'm also going back to Charlotte. He's made a life here."

"You never know what might happen," Dani sang before drifting back toward the kitchen. "Are you going to help me with these cookies, Kacey? Or are you going to stand there and talk about Drew all day?"

Mom shrugged. "She's the boss."

"She's always been bossy," Kacey joked as she made her way toward the kitchen.

As she set her coffee cup on the counter and turned toward her sister, Kacey found herself wondering if they might be right about Drew and the possibility of rekindling their friendship and maybe even something more.

Chapter 4

Drew peered through the glass door of Morningside Bakery shortly after six that evening and saw Kacey wiping down the tables while her mother cleaned the counter. Kacey looked beautiful with her blonde hair pulled up in a long, thick ponytail with wisps falling around her face. Excitement coursed through him at the thought of spending the evening with her, talking and laughing like old times.

When he yanked on the door, he found it locked. He rapped on the glass, and her gaze darted to his. Her pink lips turned up in a grin, and she waved as she hurried over. The lock clicked and then she opened the door wide.

"I was just finishing up. I'll only need a few more minutes."

He stepped into the store and inhaled the heavenly scents of the baked goods. "Take your time."

"Drew!" Mrs. Williams hurried over. "It's so good to see you. How are your folks doing?"

"They're doing just fine, Mrs. Williams."

She swatted his arm. "You and Kacey are twenty-six years old. It's time you called me Monica."

"That will take some getting used to," he said, and they both chuckled.

Kacey flitted behind the counter and then returned with a bright-blue bakery box. "I have a gift for you." She held out the box to him.

He opened it and found it half-full of chocolate chip cookies.

"Your favorite," she declared, beaming.

Warmth swirled in his chest as he closed the box. "You remembered."

"Of course!"

"Thank you." He balanced the box in one hand and pulled his wallet from the back pocket of his jeans. "How much do I owe you?"

"Oh please. I told you it's a gift." She waved him off. Then she glanced down at her blue apron, which was splattered with strawberry icing, sparkles, and flour. "I'm a mess. I wish I had a change of clothes here."

He shook his head. "You look great, Kace." And she did. She was even more beautiful than he recalled.

"Let me freshen up. I'll be quick." She took off toward the back of the bakery, through the doorway that led to the kitchen.

Drew set the box on a nearby table and then nodded at Monica. "How are things at the elementary school?"

"The kids are getting excited about the holidays. I overhear quite a few discussions about making a list for Santa, and it's not even Thanksgiving yet."

"The middle school kids are just as excited."

"Hey there!" Dani walked out from the kitchen. Her blue apron was dotted with even more colorful spills and splatters than Kacey's, evidence she was the baker. "I hear you're directing the community choir. How do you like it so far?"

"It's even more fun than I expected."

"That's great. Riley didn't say much about choir practice, except that she liked it." Dani wiped her hands on a paper towel. "Thank you for taking over for Mrs. Hansen."

"You're welcome, but I'm just grateful that she thought of me."

Monica's smile seemed nostalgic as she turned toward her older daughter. "I love the Christmas Tree Lighting Festival. I remember all those times we went when you were little and you sat on your father's shoulders so you could see the choir. Then when Kacey was old enough, she took her turn on your dad's shoulders. There's just something magical when the mayor flips the switch and the giant tree lights up Main Street and all the decorations are glowing on the light poles and the storefronts. It truly feels like the Christmas season is here."

"I agree." Dani pointed to the windows at the front of the store. "I'm planning to decorate and give out hot chocolate."

"Well, I'll help after I see Riley sing with the choir," Monica said.

Drew smiled. "I think it's going to be a magical night like it always is."

Kacey hurried out from the back room with her purse and coat slung over her arm. Her shiny blonde hair was down, cascading over her shoulders, and her makeup seemed to be refreshed, making her eyes look even bluer than usual. "Well, this is the best I can do. Thank goodness you keep some makeup here, Dani."

Dani scoffed. "As if you even need it, Kace."

"You look great," Drew agreed with Dani, but he kept the rest of his thoughts to himself.

Kacey blushed. "Thanks." She set her purse on a chair and then pulled on her coat over her blue T-shirt featuring the bakery's logo. "I'll see you all later." She looked up at Drew. "Will you drop me off on your way home?"

"Nah. You can walk," he teased with a wink.

She laughed.

He'd missed that sweet lilt!

"Good seeing you," Drew told Kacey's mother and sister.

They both grinned and waved.

"Have fun," Dani sang, and he noticed a look pass between the sisters.

He pushed open the door and held it for Kacey as she slipped through. "Would you like to eat here in town or go somewhere else?"

"Why would we go anywhere else when we're here?" Kacey spun on the sidewalk with her arms outstretched. "Let's eat at the Splendid Kitchen." She pointed to the family restaurant halfway down the block and across the street. "They have the best fried chicken."

"Sounds like a plan."

Drew felt as if he'd stepped back in time as they walked together down the street. He breathed in the cool November air and glanced around at couples and families also enjoying the evening.

Above them, the sun had begun to set, bringing with it its daily explosion of colors. He glanced over at his beautiful date, and a warm glow moved through him. He'd never expected to have Kacey back in his life. This time he hoped he could find a way to keep her there.

"So, tell me everything that's happened to you since high school graduation. Go!" Kacey said after they'd ordered dinner.

She and Drew sat in a corner booth at the busy restaurant. Servers dressed in jeans and Splendid Kitchen T-shirts wove through the tables and booths while murmurs of conversations floated around them. The delicious smells of home-cooked meat loaf, chicken, and beef, mixed with pies, wafted over Kacey.

The family-owned restaurant had been in business for as long as Kacey could remember and it was a favorite among locals and visitors.

Drew lifted a dark eyebrow. "*Everything* since high school graduation?"

"Yup."

"Huh." He rubbed his angular jaw. "You know I went to Appalachian State and studied music. And I earned my teaching certificate."

She picked up her glass of Diet Coke and took a long drink.

"Then I came back home and started teaching. That's pretty much it."

She traced the condensation on her glass and studied him. He was handsome, but it wasn't just his rugged good looks. There was something about him tonight.

"You're staring at me." He leaned forward. "What are you thinking about?"

Uh-oh! Heat crawled up her neck. "What do you mean?"

"You have this strange look on your face."

"I was just thinking about middle school," she said quickly. "Remember that Halloween when we had a party in your parents' enormous basement?"

"Eighth grade."

"Right! I dressed up like Wilma Flintstone, and you were Fred."

He chuckled. "Yes. And then those popular kids crashed our little party, and the food fight started."

"Oh yes!" Kacey groaned. "And we were up almost all night cleaning up the mess."

"You were the only one who stayed to help. Everyone else left."

"I can still smell that carpet cleaner we used trying to scrub the soda and dip out of the carpet."

"My mom wound up replacing it." He lifted his glass of Coke. "And my dad never let me forget that."

"He still blames you for what those idiots did?"

He took a long draw from the glass and shrugged. "Of course he does."

"Those guys who started throwing the food weren't even our friends."

"But it was my idea to have the party."

"No, it wasn't." She pointed to her chest. "It was *my* idea. I suggested we have a party with just our friends, but my house was too small." She clucked her tongue as guilt washed over her. "I'm so sorry."

He shook his head. "Kace, that was a million years ago."

"Yeah, but I still feel responsible." She took another drink. "At least I wasn't the one who suggested we go hiking without a map during that one camping trip! Was that Jake or Wanda?"

"Oh yeah! That was definitely Jake's idea. We were lost for four hours before we finally found our campsite."

The two of them laughed at the memory.

He wiped his eyes and hooted. "I'd never been so hungry in my life."

"Me neither!" She shook her head.

Drew pointed at her. "But you were the culprit for why we were stranded in Charlotte after that concert."

"You're right about that one." Kacey shook her head. "My mom didn't want me to go because it was more than three hours away, but she agreed because you were taking me." She smiled. "But then Mallory and Bennett backed out because they both got food poisoning from that sushi place where they ate the night before." She grimaced. "Ugh."

"And we got stuck in line at the T-shirt stand after the concert so by the time we got out to the parking lot it was nearly empty. Which was the prime opportunity for my car to not start because *someone* had to check her makeup before we went into the arena and *someone* had left the dome light on."

Kacey held her hand up. "Guilty as charged."

"Didn't it take, like, three hours for the roadside service to show up?"

"Yeah. But we had fun sitting on the hood of your car, looking at the stars." She smiled recalling how romantic it was. Then she frowned. "Gosh, Mom was frantic with worry, even though I called her and told her we were safe."

"But she forgave you. My dad, however, decided to ground me for a month."

Kacey blew out a puff of air. "Once again, *my* fault."

He opened his mouth to respond just as the server appeared with their meals.

"Fried chicken, loaded baked potato, and mixed vegetables for you, ma'am." The young woman set the plate in front of Kacey.

"Thank you." Kacey inhaled the mouthwatering fragrance of her supper.

"And then steak and fries for you, sir." The woman gave Drew his meal.

"That's right. Thank you."

The woman looked back and forth between them. "Do you need anything else?"

Kacey and Drew both shook their heads, and the server disappeared.

"This looks delicious." Kacey lifted her fork.

Drew retrieved the A.1. sauce at the end of the table and began pouring it over his steak. "I agree."

They were silent while they both started eating, and contentment settled over Kacey. She remembered their senior year and how their close friendship had suddenly fractured. It felt good to pick up right where they left off before things changed for the worse. Talking with Drew had always been easy. She forked a bit of chicken, and when she looked up, she found Drew watching her with an intensity that sent goose bumps trailing up her arms.

"Whatever happened to Bennett?" she asked, wondering why she decided to bring him up in that moment.

Drew hesitated. "Last I heard he was married and living in Atlanta."

"You don't keep up with him?"

He shook his head. "I guess you lost touch with him?"

"We lost touch in college. After all, I went to UNC Charlotte, and he went to Chapel Hill. Long distance never works, and we were so young. I never felt like we really clicked anyway." She began cutting up her potato. "How do you like teaching?"

His green eyes sparkled in the light of the colorful Tiffany lamp hanging above their booth. "I love it. There's something magical about watching the children learn how to play their instruments. It's a gift, really. I feel like the luckiest guy on the planet."

"That's amazing, and it's so you." She smiled with renewed admiration for him.

"It's so me?" He almost looked offended. "What does that mean?"

"You've always been so giving and thoughtful. I can remember countless times when you rearranged your schedule to drive me here or there because I didn't have a car. You always put other people before you."

He ate a fry and pushed his plate toward her. "Want one?"

"Thanks." She chose a fry and dipped it in his ketchup.

"What about you? I know you're a graphic designer, but do you like your work?"

She nodded. "I love designing websites, logos, and promotional material. I can really work anywhere."

"So why don't you stay here?"

She felt her eyebrow lift.

"I'm sure your mom and sister would love to have you here instead of three hours away." His words came out at a quick clip. "You said you're helping your sister, right?"

"That's true, and I love it here. But I've always wanted to live in a city. I'm sure you remember how I used to collect postcards from big cities."

"Oh yeah! You had an entire wall dedicated to postcards." He cut up more steak. "What happened to those?"

"They were tossed into a box and shoved in the attic when

Mom decided to transform my room into a craft and sewing room."

"Oh."

They ate in silence for a few moments.

"So, Travis lost his job?" Drew asked.

She nodded and wiped her mouth with a napkin. "Yes, he was laid off about three months ago. He was working in IT at a bank. He's been on a few interviews, but nothing has worked out yet."

Drew pushed a fry through the ketchup, creating a swirly pattern. "I'm sorry to hear that. I'll ask around at work."

"That would be great, thank you." She spooned the vegetables. "So, where are you living? Do you rent one of those condos on the north side of town?"

"Do you remember that little yellow house on Zimmer Avenue?"

She tilted her head. "The one with the purple shutters?"

"That's the one." He grinned.

She gasped. "You bought that place?"

"I sure did."

"Are you kidding me?" she asked and he shook his head. "Tell me you kept the purple shutters."

"Sadly, no. I painted the house gray, and the shutters are white."

"Oh, well." She laughed. "I never expected you to buy that place."

He shrugged. "The little old lady who owned it passed away, and it happened to be in my price range."

"That's so cool. I have to see it."

"Well, then you'll have to come for supper one night."

"It's a date." She lifted her glass, and her nerves began humming when she realized what she'd said.

"It's nothing compared to my parents' mansion on the lake though."

"You know I always loved that cute little house, and now it's yours."

"That's right, and it's just enough space for me and my two cats."

Questions filtered through her mind as she imagined him in his own little house, and she thought about his relationship status on Facebook. How could Drew actually be single? He was such a great catch! "Your cats are too cute."

He leaned forward. "Have you been stalking my social media?"

"Maybe?" She gave her best coy smile, along with a palms up, and he laughed. "How are your folks?"

"The same. My dad still makes comments about how I could make some 'real money' if I gave up teaching and joined his financial planning firm." He rolled his eyes. "Everything with him is about money, and he thinks I don't make enough."

Kacey set her fork down and studied him. "Your father isn't proud of you for being a teacher?"

"He says it's a noble profession, but he wants to leave the financial planning firm to me since I'm an only child. I have no interest in that." He shrugged. "It's no big deal. I just ignore him." He picked up his drink once again. "I applied for a job as the music department head for Catawba County. The office is in Newton, but it's a big pay raise."

"Oh wow. Would you have to sell the house?"

"Yeah, but I doubt I'll even get the job."

The server appeared. "Do you need anything else tonight?"

Drew leaned forward. "Share a molten lava cake with me for old time's sake."

She hesitated, and he gave her his best puppy dog look. "That's no fair, Drew Murphy. You know I can't resist that expression."

"It always works." He turned toward the server. "We'll split a molten lava cake."

"Coming right up," she said.

Chapter 5

After splitting an enormous piece of warm chocolate cake smothered in chocolate sauce and vanilla ice cream, Drew paid the check before he and Kacey walked outside. She was certain she wouldn't eat another bite of food for at least a week.

The dark sky sparkled with bright stars, and the air was crisp. Kacey breathed in the scent of a nearby woodburning fireplace.

Drew nodded down the street. "I parked at the end of the block."

"Do you still have that old Beamer?"

"No." He chuckled. "I got rid of it after I graduated from college and got my first teaching job."

"What a shame. It was a classic," she said as they started down the street together, passing the Warner movie theater, heading toward Scoops, the ice cream parlor.

"More like a money pit." He smiled at her. "I got myself a practical Honda Accord."

"How grown-up of you." She bumped his arm with hers. They walked in comfortable silence for a moment, and Kacey soaked in her company and their surroundings. "Pretty soon all the light poles will be decorated with candy canes. I love when they decorate downtown for Christmas." She looked up at him. "So are you going to have the choir practice something other than 'Joy to the World'?"

"No, I figured we'd just sing that a dozen times for you next Tuesday and Thursday." This time he bumped her arm as she laughed. "We're planning to sing the usual Christmas favorites."

"I look forward to the variety. I did talk to Riley and Colleen, and they promise to be quiet."

"I got the impression that you didn't tell Dani about my conversation with the two chatterboxes."

"No, I didn't. I promised Riley I wouldn't tell her as long as she and Colleen behaved next week."

"That's a good plan," he said as they walked past the Christmas Shop.

When they reached the end of the street, he pointed to a black Honda Accord. "Well, here it is."

She ran her finger over the door. "Very pretty."

"What do you drive?"

"A mint-green Prius."

"Very practical and eco-friendly."

She shrugged. "It was a great price, and I appreciate the gas mileage."

He pushed a button on his key fob and the locks popped.

Then he opened the passenger side door for her. "After you."

"Wow. You have such nice manners." She climbed into the seat and he closed the door for her. Then she fastened her seat belt while he jogged around the front of the car. "This car is lovely, but don't you miss the Beamer breaking down every day?"

He shook his head and laughed. "I do miss the adventures we had, but I don't miss paying a mechanic all the time."

She relaxed in the seat as he headed down Main Street and then turned left onto Rosemont. "This was fun."

"It was." He peered over at her. "We should do it again."

"Definitely. I really want to see your house. I always wondered what the inside of that place looked like."

"You won't be impressed."

"Sure I will. After all, I need to meet those cats." She looked at him. "Does the gray cat always look annoyed?"

He laughed. "Yes, Loki is marked that way. He has a permanent scowl."

"Interesting."

When Drew steered down her street, Kacey felt her smile wobble. Their wonderful evening together was coming to an end.

He turned his car into her driveway and slipped it in Park before turning toward her. "Hand me your cell phone?"

"Of course." She fished her phone from her pocket, unlocked it, and gave it to him.

Drew typed on her phone and then his phone dinged. He

pulled his out of his pocket and typed on it next. Then he handed hers back to her. "We have each other's numbers now."

"Perfect." She slipped her phone into her coat pocket. "Thank you for a wonderful evening."

"No, thank you." His smile lingered on Kacey's face a beat longer than necessary. "I'll be in touch soon."

She pushed open the passenger side door and climbed out of the car. She closed the door and hurried up the front steps of the house. When she turned and waved, Drew's horn tooted before he backed his car out of the driveway.

Happiness blossomed in her chest as she unlocked the front door and stepped into the family room, where Mom sat on the sofa watching *Last Christmas*.

Mom's expression lit up, and she pressed Pause on the remote. "How was your date?"

"It wasn't a real date, Mom." Kacey flopped down on the sofa across from her mother. "It was fun to get caught up. We reminisced, ate too much, and laughed a lot."

"That smile on your face makes me think it *was* a real date, Kacey."

She shook her head. "We're just friends, Mom. Plus, he applied for a job in Newton, and I'm going back to Charlotte eventually."

"I always thought you two should have dated. You got along so well. And he's so good-looking."

Kacey laughed and pointed to the television. "I love this movie. I'll watch the rest of it with you."

As the movie came back to life, Kacey pulled off her coat,

settled on the sofa, and pondered what it would feel like to have Drew in her life permanently.

———

"All right, everyone." Drew addressed the choir the following Thursday afternoon while he sat at the piano at the front of the room. "Let's take it from the top. Ready?" He began playing the introduction and then held up his hand for the children to start singing. "Jingle bells, jingle bells, jingle all the way . . ."

While they sang, his mind wandered through the past week. Kacey had lingered in his thoughts since their dinner last Saturday night. They'd been texting, but they hadn't connected in person, since she said she had a big project to finish for one of her clients.

He had hoped to catch her after choir practice on Tuesday, but when the session ended, Riley and Colleen hurried out of the classroom. By the time Drew left, the bakery was dark.

Although he enjoyed their banter over text, he couldn't help but wonder if she had used her job as a reason to avoid him. Perhaps she wanted to keep her distance, since she planned to go back to Charlotte. Or maybe she had a boyfriend waiting for her there.

Still, he knew she'd had a good time Saturday night, and he longed to see her again. He hoped today she would come to the choir room to fetch the girls instead of them rushing off to the bakery to meet her.

When giggles erupted from the back row, Drew scanned the choir until he found Riley and Colleen with their heads bent. He sighed. It was time to separate those two.

Drew stopped playing and clapped his hands. "All right. Let's take a break." He stood and nodded to the back row. "Riley," he called, and her head popped up, her eyes wide. "I'd like you to come and sit in the front row, please."

"I-I'm sorry, Mr. Murphy." She blinked, her cheeks flushing bright pink.

He nodded. "Just come sit up front where you won't be so disruptive."

"Okay." Riley glanced at Colleen, who looked equally embarrassed, and then with her eyes cast down, she shuffled to the front row and sat on a metal folding chair beside a first-grade boy. She looked down, studying her purple jeans.

Drew returned to the piano. "Let's take it from the top now."

After a few more run-throughs of the song, he noticed parents had gathered at the back of the room. He spotted Kacey leaning against the wall, grinning and holding a bakery box, and his heart lifted.

When the song ended, the adults clapped.

"Great job today," Drew called to the kids, who were busy stowing their music and gathering up their coats and backpacks. "See you next Tuesday. Practice the songs at home so you learn the words."

He closed his music folder and slipped it into his backpack as the mother of one of the fourth graders approached with her redheaded daughter in tow who was fiddling with colorful beaded bracelets on her wrist. "Hi, Mrs. Wagoner."

"I wanted to let you know that Patti is going to miss practice next Tuesday. She has a consultation with an orthodontist."

"That's fine. Thanks for letting me know." He looked at Patti. "I hope your consultation goes well. You know, I had braces."

The little girl's hazel eyes rounded. "You did?" Her face pinched. "Did they hurt?"

"My teeth were a little sore, but the cool part was being able to pick what colors I wanted for my rubber bands when I went for my checkups. The orthodontist has so many colors."

"Did they have purple?"

"They sure did." Drew met Patti's mom's gaze, and she gave him an appreciative smile. "You'll do great."

"Thank you," Patti said.

"See you next Thursday," Drew told them. He turned to the next mother waiting to speak to him and realized he had a line. His hope to talk to Kacey deflated.

After speaking to two more mothers about their children's schedules and answering a father's question about logistics on the day of the Christmas Tree Lighting, he faced the back of the room and was surprised to find Kacey still there, smiling as Riley gestured widely while talking.

Drew shouldered his backpack and approached them.

Kacey smirked at him. "I was happy to hear a different song today."

"Well, I chose the song with you in mind."

"I thought so. This is for you." She held the bakery box out to him.

"Wow. Thank you," he said, taking the box. Then he nodded toward the door. "How about I walk you to your car?"

"I'd love that." When the girls scampered toward the exit, she called, "Slow down, girls! No running!"

The girls, however, continued past the people milling about the hallway and out the front door to the sidewalk.

Kacey shook her head. "They listen so well, don't they?"

"Yeah." He chuckled. "They know where you park, right?"

She nodded as he held the door open for her. "My car is behind the bakery." She looked up at him as they stepped out into the cold evening air. "How did Riley and Colleen do today at practice?"

He grimaced, and she groaned. "It's all right. I moved Riley to the front of the room."

"Separating them is the only solution. I'll talk to her again."

"Don't worry about it. I'll just keep them separated. It's an exciting time of year for the kids." He lifted the box lid, and his mouth watered as he took in the assorted cookies. "These look amazing. You're going to send me into a sugar crash if you keep feeding me your delicious treats!"

"We had some leftovers today. Dani will bake more in the morning."

"How did your work project go?" he asked as they followed the girls through the alley between the bakery and the gift shop next door toward the parking lot.

She rubbed her hands together. "I turned it in last night, and my boss was really happy. I heard from her this morning."

"That's fantastic."

The girls rushed over to the mint-green Prius and grabbed the door handle.

"I won!" Riley announced.

Colleen shook her head, and her long black braids swished back and forth. "No, I did!"

"You both did," Kacey announced. Then she spun to face Drew. "Do you have plans tonight?"

"No, I don't."

"If you don't mind a noisy family, you're welcome to join me at my sister's house. Tonight is game night." She held her hand up. "I mean it when I say it's noisy."

He rubbed his chin. "Well, I am a teacher, so I'm used to noise."

"That's right! How could I forget?" She chuckled, then shared the address. "It's just a couple of blocks away from my mom's house."

He pointed to his car parked a half-dozen spaces away from hers. "I'll follow you."

"Perfect. I just have to drop Colleen off first."

Excitement filled Drew as he hurried to his car.

Chapter 6

Later that evening, Kacey glanced around her sister's dining table while Drew shared a story about when he taught a music class at a day camp.

"Most of the kids were more interested in swimming in the lake, but I had a few that actually listened," Drew said, and everyone laughed.

"Mr. Murphy," Riley began, "what's your favorite instrument to play?"

Drew rubbed his chin. "Hmm. That's a tough question. I'd have to say the guitar, since it was the first instrument I learned when I was about your age."

Kacey shared a smile with her mother. She was grateful when she texted her sister to tell her that she had invited Drew and Dani told her she'd made plenty of stew to share. They spent supper laughing and sharing stories while Drew sat beside her. He seemed to fit right in with her family. It was as if he belonged there. Her heart turned over in her chest at that thought.

Dani tapped Kacey's arm. "Why don't we clean this up and bring out that lemon cake I baked yesterday and make some coffee? Then we can play a game."

"Great idea."

Kacey and Dani carried the dishes into the kitchen and set them on the counter.

"He's totally into you," Dani whispered.

Kacey shushed her and peeked into the dining room, where Drew and Travis were engrossed in a conversation about IT jobs in the area. "We're just friends. You know that."

"I think he would like to be more than that. Haven't you noticed how he looks at you?"

"You're imagining things. Let's get the cake and go back in there." Kacey began filling the coffee carafe with water.

Dani placed her hand on Kacey's back. "Trust me, Kace. He's going to ask you out."

"And I'll have to tell him no because I'm not staying in town forever." Her heart sank at the thought of saying good-bye to Drew again, but her plan all along had been to go back to Charlotte.

Later, after half of the cake was gone, their coffee mugs were empty, and they had played a rousing game of Candy Land, Kacey and Dani filled the dishwasher before Kacey gathered up her coat and purse. She kissed her nieces good night, said good-bye to Dani and Travis, and then walked with Drew out to his car.

The air was crisp, and she could see her breath. Above her, the stars had begun to appear in the sky, and she inhaled the aroma of the lake in the distance mixed with the smell of wood fireplaces.

"I had a great time with your family." Drew leaned back on his car and smiled down at her.

Kacey shivered and shoved her hands into her pockets. "I'm glad you could join us."

He smiled. "You're freezing. You need to get in your car and turn on the heat."

"I will." She touched his arm. "Talk soon, okay?"

"I plan on it, Kacey. Good night." He opened his car door.

"Good night." Her pulse was racing as she jogged over to her car and unlocked it. She hoped to see him again very soon.

Garrett leaned in the doorway of the band room the following afternoon. "What are your plans for the weekend?"

"I was hoping to catch up with an old friend who's in town temporarily." Drew walked over from his desk in the far corner of the large room equipped with risers and music stands for the middle school band. "That reminds me. Her brother-in-law is looking for a job. Have you heard about any IT jobs with the school system?"

"I'll ask around. Who's the old friend?"

"Her name is Kacey. We were close from middle school until just before graduation."

"Did you date her?" Garrett's dark eyebrows lifted.

Drew sank down onto a chair by the door. "No, because I was too chicken to ask her out back then."

"Is she married?"

"No."

"Is she dating anyone?"

"Not that I know of."

"Do you have feelings for her?"

"Absolutely."

"So what are you waiting for?" Garrett said. "Go after her."

"She's not planning to stay here. Once she finds a new roommate, she's heading back to Charlotte."

"But she's here now. You need to find a way to convince her to stay."

Drew folded his arms over his chest and smiled. "You're right." A plan was beginning to form in his mind.

***

Friday afternoon, Kacey stood at the cash register in the bakery and rang up an order for a middle-aged woman she'd known nearly all her life. "May I get you anything else, Mrs. Dixon?"

"No, thank you. I believe those boxes of assorted cookies are perfect for the ladies' social at church tomorrow." She handed Kacey her card.

"I agree." Kacey ran the card and then handed it back with the receipt before placing the two boxes in a shopping bag sporting the bakery's logo.

Mom stepped out from the kitchen. "Loretta. So nice to see you."

"You, too, Monica," Mrs. Dixon said as she picked up her bag. "I can't believe Thanksgiving is only two weeks away."

"Where has the year gone?" Mom asked.

"I was just thinking on the way over here that I need to start on my Christmas cards. I always mail them out the day after Thanksgiving."

Kacey leaned forward on the counter. "You're very organized, Mrs. Dixon."

"Well, Kacey doesn't know it yet, but I plan to enlist her to help me with Christmas cards this year." Mom looped her arm around Kacey's shoulder.

"Is that right?" Kacey asked. "I'll add that to my list of duties while I'm home. You do know I'm a graphic designer. How about I design a beautiful Christmas card with our names already signed on it? Then all we'll need to do is print out address labels."

Mrs. Dixon shook her head. "No, no, no, Kacey. You need that personal touch with real signatures."

"I agree. Not only do we need to design our Christmas cards and handwrite our signatures, but we also need to go shopping," Mom added.

Kacey pointed at her. "I'm happy to help with shopping anytime."

Mom and Mrs. Dixon chuckled.

"You two enjoy the rest of your afternoon." Mrs. Dixon waved and then headed for the door.

"Come back to see us soon," Mom called after her.

Kacey looked out over the dining area, where a few couples sat enjoying their snacks and drinking coffee. When her phone buzzed with a text message, she pulled it from her back pocket. Her heartbeat gave a little kick when she saw who sent it.

"What's that?" Mom asked.

She opened the message and grinned. "A message from Drew."

Do you still love lasagna?

She fired back: Is this a trick question?

Maybe.

She laughed. Why?

Come over tonight and I'll cook for you.

What can I bring?

You work in a bakery. You'll think of something.

I'll be there after I go home and change.

Perfect.

Her heart flopped around like a fish. *Another date with Drew!* Then she shook her head. *It's not a date. We're friends!*

"Well?" Mom asked, bringing her back to the present. "What did he say? From the looks of it, it was good."

"He's going to cook for me tonight."

Dani appeared in the doorway. "Who? Drew?"

"Were you spying on me, Dani?" Kacey asked.

Dani shrugged. "Mom is going to tell me anyway, so you might as well spill it."

"Drew is going to cook for her tonight," Mom said.

Dani clapped her hands. "How romantic!"

Kacey couldn't hide her smile.

"I always knew you two would wind up together." Mom wagged a finger at her.

Kacey rolled her eyes. "He never liked me that way."

"That might have been true then, but I'm sure he does now," Dani said, and Mom nodded.

Kacey was grateful when the bell above the door rang and a group of teenage girls headed toward the counter. "Welcome to Morningside Bakery. How may I help you?" she asked, but her hands trembled with the idea that Drew might possibly care for her.

———

Later that evening Drew glanced over the table and rubbed his hands together. The table was set with candles, along with a bowl of salad. The lasagna and garlic bread sat on the kitchen counter ready to be served, and their delicious scents permeated his little cottage. Now he just needed his guest of honor.

When the doorbell rang, he brushed his hands down his green button-down shirt and his best pair of chinos before heading toward the door. He pulled it open, and Kacey stood on the porch holding a bakery box.

She looked beautiful with her thick blonde hair cascading past her shoulders in waves, her blue eyes accentuated by makeup. Her bright smile reminded him of the summer sun. "Hi," she said, sounding almost shy. Did she seem different tonight?

"Come in," he said, opening the door wide. "You're right on time."

She stepped past him into the house. "It smells heavenly in here."

"Thank you. Let me take your coat."

She set the bakery box on a nearby chair and shucked her coat. "This place is amazing! I told you, I always wondered what it looked like inside. Could I have the twenty-five-cent tour before we eat?"

"Of course." He opened the coat closet and hung up her jacket before motioning behind her. "This is the tiny family room."

"It's so cozy!" She walked over to the sofa. "Oh! Here are the kitties."

"That's pretty much where they stay too—unless they're begging for food." He pointed to his portly orange tabby. "This is Thor." Then he touched his gray cat. "And this is Loki."

She gave Thor a head rub, and he opened one eye before rolling over onto his side, facing away from her. "I guess they just want to sleep."

"Don't take it personally."

She laughed. "I won't." When she rubbed Loki's chin, he began to purr. "It's so nice to meet you both."

Drew pointed to the kitchen. "Over here is the tiny kitchen, where the table hardly fits."

"I think it's adorable." She set the bakery box on the counter and peered down at the lasagna. "Oh my. This looks amazing." She spun to face him. "Show me the rest of the house before we eat this incredible meal."

"It won't take but a minute."

She followed him down the short hallway.

He pointed to the right. "The bathroom is here." Then he opened a door beside it. "Tiny linen closet here."

She peered into the bathroom. "It's perfect."

He pushed on the next door, revealing a desk, bookshelves, and his console piano. "This is my office, music room, and everything else room."

"Wow." She stepped into the room and turned, as if taking in every detail. "So nice." She touched the bookshelves. "You still like to read?"

"I do, but I don't read as much as I used to."

"I remember when you always had a novel in your backpack." Kacey walked past him and he caught a whiff of her sweet perfume, which made his mouth dry. "And this must be your bedroom." She gripped the doorknob and then craned over her shoulder to look up at him. "Is it okay if I look inside?"

"Of course."

She pushed open the door and stepped inside his modest bedroom.

He stood in the doorway as she walked around his bed, looking at his dressers, and then spinning to face him.

"I love your house."

He lifted an eyebrow. "You're easily impressed."

"It's perfect, and since I don't have a house of my own, I think it's fantastic."

She moved closer to where he stood, and he touched her arm as he guided her out and toward the kitchen. "Let's go enjoy our meal before it gets cold."

They sat down across from each other at the table and began to eat their salad. While they ate, they discussed the Christmas Tree Lighting Festival and reminisced. Soon their salad, garlic bread, and lasagna were finished, and she helped him carry their dishes to the counter.

"I have a surprise for you."

"Oh?" She rubbed her hands together. "I love surprises! What is it?"

"I'm working on a song, and I'd like to share it with you."

"I'd love to hear it."

His hands began to sweat as she followed him toward his office, where he sat down at the piano, and she stood beside him.

Closing his eyes, he began to play the song, which had been inspired when he first reconnected with Kacey. His fingers flew over the piano as the melodious sound filled the room and a vision of her beautiful face filled his mind. When he finished, he opened his eyes and found her watching him, her eyes shining.

"Drew," she whispered, her voice sounding reverent, "that's beautiful."

No, you are. "Thank you."

"Are you going to write lyrics for it?"

"Eventually." He swallowed. "The music just came to me the other night. You're the first person I've shared it with."

"I'm so honored."

They stared at each other for a moment, and the urge to kiss her nearly overwhelmed him. But he couldn't give in to that longing just yet. Instead he pushed back from the piano and stood. "How about some dessert?"

"Oh yes. I brought a chocolate cake."

"Wonderful. I'll put on some coffee."

Soon they were sitting at the table sipping coffee and eating slices of the best cake he'd ever eaten.

"Do you remember when we used to sit on your parents' pier and stargaze?" She rested her elbow on the table and her chin on her palm as her expression became nostalgic. "We would stretch out on the pier and stare up at the sky for hours, talking about everything and pretending to pick out constellations."

Drew set his fork down. "Let's go do it."

"Right now?" Her brow puckered.

He pushed his chair back and stood. "Yes. Right now."

"Okay." She laughed as she stood too.

Chapter 7

Kacey smiled over at Drew as he drove his Honda down Splendid Lake Loop toward his parents' lakefront home. She folded her arms over her middle and settled back in the seat as she contemplated how much fun she'd already had this evening. She didn't want it to end.

"What are you smiling about?" Drew asked.

Heat infused her cheeks as she turned toward him. "I was just thinking about that time we took your dad's boat out without asking, lost track of time, and then got in trouble when we brought it back."

Drew snorted. "I remember that clearly."

"I still don't understand why you were in trouble though. We didn't damage the boat."

"It was because I didn't ask first."

"And that was my fault because it was my idea. Again."

He gave her a sideways glance. "You didn't force me, Kace."

"No, but I seemed to always get you into trouble."

His expression became intense, and her throat suddenly felt dry.

"It was always worth it." His features softened with the admission.

Drew steered his car onto the long, winding driveway that led to his parents' sprawling, two-story brick colonial home that sat on at least five acres of lakefront land. This was where Drew had grown up and where Kacey had spent countless hours with him. Memories poured over her as Drew drove halfway up the driveway and flipped off the headlights.

"What are you doing?" she asked as he killed the engine.

He pushed open his door, and the dome light lit up his devious smile. "We're going to sneak out onto the pier."

"Because you want to avoid seeing your parents."

"Come on, Kace." He climbed out of the car and then stuck his head inside. "Where's your sense of adventure?"

She smiled and launched herself out of the car and met him at the front, where he threaded his warm fingers with hers, her skin humming as an electrical current shot through her veins. Their shoes crunched along the rock driveway as they jogged past the four-car garage, past the huge deck that ran the length of the back of the house, and down the path toward the lake.

Kacey sucked in a breath as she took in the beautiful lake, sparkling in the light of the moon and the stars.

"What's wrong?" he asked.

"I forgot how gorgeous the lake is."

"Well, then it's a good thing I brought you here, so you

can remember how much you love it." He led her down the hill to the pier that stretched out over the glistening water.

She breathed in the familiar scent of the lake and looked out across the water toward the lights glowing from the Splendid Lake Cabins and Marina resort, which was run by their classmate and friend Brianna Porter and her family.

When they reached the end of the pier, they both sat down, and she took in the sound of the water lapping against the pier and a dog barking in the distance. The sky was clear as the stars seemed to twinkle for only Kacey and Drew.

"Are you cold?" Drew's voice was a low rumble next to her ear, sending a tremor through her.

She shook her head as happiness bubbled through her. She wouldn't care if the lake was frozen over as long as she had Drew beside her.

She settled into a comfortable silence and enjoyed the view of the water shimmering in the moonlight.

"I've been meaning to ask . . . are you seeing anyone back in Charlotte?"

Her eyes snapped to his face, but he was looking out at the water, his expression unreadable. "No. Are you seeing anyone?"

"No." He gave a little laugh and shook his head. Then his tone became more serious. "Have you ever seen yourself getting married and having a family?"

"Someday, but probably not anytime soon." Kacey ran her hands up and down her legs as she wondered what Drew was getting at.

He nodded and sucked in a breath. "Could you see your-self staying in Splendid Lake?"

With that question, Drew turned to face her. She studied him, wishing she could read his thoughts. "Why all these questions?"

He shrugged and a small smile formed on his lips. "I'm just trying to get reacquainted with you."

She hesitated. "You know I've always dreamed of living in a city."

"So that's a no."

She angled her body toward him. "What about you?"

He let out a breath. "I love it here."

"Any Christmas wishes?" Kacey could think of one of her own.

He chuckled. "I have everything I need."

She scanned the glorious dark sky and felt his eyes focused on her, pulling her gaze to meet his. The intensity in his expression made her lose her breath.

Drew reached up and cupped his hand to her cheek. She leaned into his touch as he tilted his head toward hers. Her breath hitched, and her pulse raced as she waited for his lips to meet hers.

"Who's out there?"

Drew jerked back and looked to where the voice called from the end of the pier. "Dad! It's me!" He jumped to his feet and held his hand out to Kacey.

She latched on, and he helped her up. She pressed a hand to her chest, trying to catch her breath.

Drew's father still stood at the end of the pier. "Why didn't you come to the house?"

"We didn't want to bother you and Mom," Drew said, resting his hand on Kacey's shoulder.

She lifted her hand in a wave. "Hi, Mr. Murphy."

"Kacey Williams," he said. "It's been a long time."

She nodded. "Yes, it has."

"Come inside and visit."

"We should really be going," Drew said.

"Nonsense. I insist," his father said.

"Okay," Drew said, sounding resigned.

While his father started up the hill toward the house, Drew took Kacey's hand in his and motioned for her to slow her pace, putting some space between them and his father. "I'm sorry," he muttered. "I was hoping we could sneak out of here without seeing my parents."

"It's totally fine." Kacey smiled and gave his hand a squeeze.

Drew and Kacey followed his father up the deck stairs and into their enormous family room. She glanced around, spotting new furniture and a larger flat-screen television than she remembered from high school.

Mr. Murphy had also changed. His dark hair was mostly peppered with gray, and his dark eyes were rimmed with wrinkles. He also looked as if he'd gained at least twenty pounds, and Drew was now at least a few inches taller than he was.

"Marilyn," Mr. Murphy called, "you'll never guess who I found out on the pier."

"Who is it, Randy?" Mrs. Murphy appeared in the doorway, and she smiled as she hurried into the family room. "Drew! Kacey! Oh my goodness. What a nice surprise."

Although Drew had received his angular jaw and perfectly proportioned nose from his father, Kacey had always noticed that his gorgeous green eyes and sweet personality came from his mother.

Drew nodded and smiled. "Hi, Mom."

"It's nice to see you, Mrs. Murphy." Kacey shook her warm hand.

"Call me Marilyn." She motioned for them to follow her. "What on earth were you doing out on the pier in this cold weather?"

"We were taking a trip down memory lane," Drew said.

And your son almost kissed me, but your husband interrupted! Kacey pinned a smile on her face as the recollection of that moment made her legs feel like cooked noodles.

Marilyn waved them over. "Come into the kitchen, and I'll make some cocoa."

Randy followed his wife out of the family room.

Drew turned to Kacey. "If you want to go home, we can leave. I'll make up an excuse."

"Hey, it's okay." Kacey took his hands in hers. "We can visit with them for a little bit. It will be fun."

"Drew? Kacey?" Marilyn called.

Drew faced the doorway to the kitchen. "We're coming, Mom."

Kacey and Drew entered his parents' enormous kitchen,

and she felt as if she'd stepped back in time. The kitchen had the same pristine white cabinets, stainless steel appliances, gray tile, and the matching island in the center surrounded by white barstools with gray seats.

The white table and chairs still sat by the sliding glass doors that led out to the deck overlooking the beautiful lake.

"Have a seat," Marilyn instructed.

Kacey sat beside Drew, and his father took a seat across from them.

"Are you back for good, Kacey?" Marilyn asked as she filled the kettle with water and set it on the stove to boil.

Kacey shook her head. "No, I'm just here until I find another roommate in Charlotte. I might just get my own condo. I'm working remotely and helping my sister run her bakery while I'm in town."

"That's a shame. I was hoping you'd say that you were here to stay." Marilyn frowned over at her before retrieving four mugs from the cabinet. "What do you do?"

"I'm a graphic designer. I design websites and promotional materials."

Marilyn smiled. "How nice. I recall how you were very artistic. I still remember your artwork on display at the high school. You even won a few awards and that nice scholarship because you're so talented."

"Thank you," Kacey said.

Marilyn disappeared into their huge pantry and emerged with a box of hot chocolate mix. She pulled out four packets and poured them into the mugs.

"We haven't seen you in a while, Drew." Randy nodded at his son. "What's been keeping you so busy?"

"I'm directing the children's choir for the Christmas Tree Lighting Festival."

"How nice," Marilyn said.

Randy's brow furrowed. "Why would you want to take that on?"

Out of the corner of her eye, Kacey noticed Drew's spine go rigid. "Dana Hansen had an emergency and asked me to fill in."

"Oh no, what happened?" Marilyn asked.

Drew explained how Mrs. Hansen had to rush to Florida to care for her mother.

"Oh dear." Marilyn shook her head. "I'm sorry to hear that, but I'm glad you were able to help her out." When the kettle started to whistle, she picked it up off the stove and poured the hot water into the mugs. She stirred them and then added whipped topping before placing them on a tray and carrying them to the table.

"Thank you." Kacey sipped her cocoa and enjoyed the warm, chocolatey drink. "It's delicious."

Randy gave Drew a pointed look. "So why did you take on the choir?"

"I just told you, Dad." Drew's words were measured. "Dana Hansen needed the help."

"You already said that, but why would you want the hassle? Does it pay well?"

Drew set his jaw and his nostrils flared. "Dad, I happen to enjoy the kids. That's why I became a teacher. As I've told you before, sometimes it's not about the money."

Kacey touched his arm, hoping to ease his tension, but he continued to glare at his father.

"When is work *not* about the money? You know I want to retire, and I'd rather leave the firm to you than to a stranger. You should really consider a career change, so you can afford a comfortable future."

Drew picked up his mug and took a sip, then set it back on the gray place mat. "I applied for a music department head job in Newton, and it pays real money."

"How exciting, Drew!" His mother reached over and patted his hand. "We'll miss you, but what a great opportunity."

Randy nodded. "Have you interviewed for it yet?"

"No, I'm still waiting to hear back."

"What are your plans for the holidays?" Kacey asked, hoping her voice sounded bright as she jumped in to change the subject.

While Marilyn began talking about Thanksgiving, Kacey noticed Drew's posture relax slightly.

When they finished their hot cocoa, Kacey thanked Drew's parents and then walked with him out to his car. They were both quiet as they climbed into the Honda and he backed out of the driveway.

The silence stretched between them while he gripped the wheel and stared out at the road ahead of them.

"Are you okay?" she finally asked.

He heaved a deep sigh that seemed to come up from his toes. "I'm sorry you had to witness that."

"You don't need to apologize."

"I get so tired of having the same conversations with my father. If he knew me, he'd understand I don't want to go into financial planning."

Kacey touched his arm. "I understand you and I'm really proud of you for following your dreams and becoming a teacher."

"Thank you."

When they reached his house, she pulled her keys out of her purse as they walked over to her car together. She looked up at him. "Thank you for a wonderful supper and a visit to the pier. I had a great time tonight." She glanced down, feeling nervous now that they were alone together again, and close enough to touch.

He smiled down at her. "I did too."

"Let's do it again soon."

"Absolutely."

She hesitated for a moment and waited for him to lean down and kiss her, but he took a step back. Confusion buzzed through her. Perhaps she had imagined the moment on the pier. Still, she'd been certain he was going to kiss her before his father had interrupted.

"Text me when you get home," he said. "I want to know you made it okay."

"I will," she said, unlocking her car and climbing in.

Kacey waved to him before backing down the driveway. As she steered down the street, she shook her head to try to clear her thoughts. Perhaps she'd misread Drew, and he still only wanted to be friends.

She couldn't tamp down the disappointment that cast a shadow over the evening.

Chapter 8

E veryone," Drew called over the murmur of conversations in the community center choir room the following Thursday afternoon, "you're all doing great, and practice is almost over. Let's try it from the top again." He played the introduction, and the children began to sing, "Silent night, holy night . . ."

Drew smiled. The choir sounded fantastic today. The children were paying attention, and they all seemed as if they wanted to be at practice instead of somewhere else.

When the song ended, clapping sounded from the back of the room, where a group of adults stood waiting to collect their children. His pulse ticked up when he saw Kacey standing near the doorway. She met his gaze and blessed him with a gorgeous smile.

They had shared a brief conversation Tuesday and traded a few texts, but they hadn't made plans to see each other again. He hoped to remedy that as soon as he had a moment to speak with her.

"Great job today, everyone," Drew announced. "I'll see you Tuesday."

Conversations broke out around the room as the children gathered up their coats and bags and the adults herded them toward the door.

Drew nodded greetings and slipped his music into a folder and then into his backpack. He looked up just as Kacey approached him. "Hey, stranger."

"Hi." She gave him a little wave.

"Do you have plans tomorrow night?"

"What did you have in mind?"

"Dinner and a movie?"

"Sounds perfect," she said as one of the children's mothers walked over behind her.

"Excuse me," the mother began. "I have a few questions about the performance at the festival."

"Just give me one moment," he told the mother. Then he looked back at Kacey. "I'll text you the details."

"Okay." She smiled and Riley walked over, threading her fingers with Kacey's.

Riley waved at Drew. "Bye, Mr. Murphy!"

"Bye," Drew said before Kacey, Riley, and Colleen headed out of the room. He couldn't wait to see Kacey tomorrow.

———

"I have a question, Aunt Kacey," Riley announced after Kacey had dropped off Colleen.

Kacey backed out of Colleen's driveway and then steered toward the end of the street. "Sounds serious." She peeked over at her niece and gave her a feigned frown. "Is it top secret?"

Riley shook her head. "No, not really."

"Then lay it on me."

"Is Mr. Murphy your boyfriend? Are you going to marry him and stay here in Splendid Lake?"

"Slow down there, Riley." Kacey braked at the stop sign at the end of the block and turned toward her niece. "What makes you ask all these questions?"

Riley seemed to eye her with suspicion. "You get googly eyes around him!" She giggled.

Kacey laughed. "Well, we've been friends since we were in middle school, and we like to spend time together."

"I think he likes you."

"What gives you that idea?"

Her niece shrugged. "He always looks happy to see you."

Kacey turned down the street that led to her sister's house as Riley's observation settled over her. During the past week she'd tried hard to convince herself that Drew only wanted to be friends, but the curiosity took hold of her again.

When Kacey arrived at Dani's, she helped her mother and sister deliver their supper—breaded pork chops, mashed potatoes, and green beans—to the table and then took a seat beside Riley.

Soon they were all filling their plates, and the sound of scraping utensils filled the room.

"So, how was everyone's day?" Mom asked.

"Aunt Kacey has a date with Mr. Murphy," Riley announced, and heat immediately filled Kacey's cheeks as everyone turned to look at her, even little Kelly. "I told Aunt Kacey that Mr. Murphy likes her, but she says they're only friends."

Kacey gave a little laugh and then looked down at her niece. "Thanks, buddy."

"That's very interesting," Dani cooed. "That makes three weekends in a row that he's asked you out."

Mom beamed. "Good for you, Kacey. It's about time you dated someone. I can't remember the last time you mentioned being interested in a young man."

"Let's talk about something else," Kacey said as she slid a pork chop onto her plate beside her mashed potatoes and green beans. "Since Mom is hosting Thanksgiving next week, what are you going to bring, Dani? Besides dessert, of course."

Dani lifted her glass of water. "I thought I'd make pumpkin pie and cookies for the kids. Also, Travis's parents would like to join us. Peggy said she'll bring cranberry sauce and green bean casserole."

"You know they're always welcome," Mom said.

"Great." Kacey looked over at Mom. "We can handle the rest, right?"

Mom nodded. "Sure."

Then Kacey smiled over at Kelly, who sat in her booster seat and forked a small bite of green beans into her mouth. "Kelly and Riley need to make up their list for Santa, right?"

"Yes!" Riley exclaimed. "I'm already working on mine, and I'll help Kelly with hers."

While Riley announced her wish list, Kacey glanced over at her sister, who frowned, and guilt filled Kacey's gut. She would get her sister alone and tell her that she'd help her with the girls' gifts this year. She wanted to be sure her nieces had a magical Christmas morning.

Kacey had to write a shopping list. She would find gifts for all her family members and also something special for Drew.

"Dinner was delicious, and the movie was pretty good too," Kacey announced as she and Drew strolled toward his car the following evening.

Drew peered up at the clear, dark sky, the bright moon glowing above them, and the stars twinkling. Then he turned toward Kacey, her face seeming to glow in the streetlights. "You actually liked the movie?"

"No." She laughed and shook her head. "I thought it was really boring and talky."

He chuckled. "I did too. I'm sorry I recommended it."

"It's not your fault. I enjoyed the company." She bumped his arm with her side.

"Me too." He actually had considered holding her hand in the movie theater, but he didn't want to come on too strong and scare her away.

"What are your plans for Thanksgiving next week?"

"I assumed I was going to my mother's house. Why?"

"How about you come to my house for dinner and then go to your parents' house for dessert."

He stopped moving and faced her. "You want to spend Thanksgiving with me?"

"Why wouldn't I?" Her expression was incredulous. "Besides, didn't you once tell me that your mom doesn't like to cook so she doesn't even make a turkey on Thanksgiving?"

"That's true."

"So enjoy a traditional Thanksgiving with me and my family."

"I'd love to."

"Great." Her smiled widened. "I'll find out what time we're eating and let you know."

They made their way to his car and talked about old friends as he drove her to her mother's house. When they arrived, he walked her to the door.

"Thank you for tonight," she said.

"You're welcome."

To his surprise, she wrapped her arms round his middle and hugged him. He closed his eyes and breathed in the flowery scent of her shampoo. Or maybe it was her perfume.

"Good night," she said before slipping in the door.

Drew felt as if he were floating on a cloud as he drove home and pondered how he could convince her to stay.

He was still contemplating his predicament of losing Kacey when he sat down in front of the laptop in his office. He powered up the job website and began searching for teaching positions.

He sat up straight and sucked in a breath when he found

a posting for a music teacher in Charlotte. Then he clicked on the position and began to apply.

———

"Happy Thanksgiving!" Kacey sang as she opened the front door and found Drew standing on her mother's front porch the following week.

He looked handsome dressed in chinos, a plaid button-down shirt, and a black leather jacket.

"Happy Thanksgiving to you." He handed her a serving dish. "I brought mashed sweet potatoes with marshmallows. You might have to warm them up in the oven."

"Thank you," she said as she motioned for him to come inside.

The delicious smells of turkey and all the trimmings washed over them as Kacey and Drew walked into the family room.

"Have you ever met Travis's parents?" she asked Drew.

"I don't think so."

Kacey set the serving dish on the kitchen counter and then took Drew's arm and towed him over to where Travis's parents stood by Travis and her nieces. "Peggy and Tom, this is my friend Drew Murphy."

Tom shook Drew's hand. "Great to meet you."

"We've heard so much about you." Peggy shook his hand next. "Riley was telling us about the Christmas Tree Lighting Festival."

"It's only two weeks away," Drew said.

"If you'll excuse me, I'm going to help serve the meal." Kacey slipped into the kitchen and helped her sister and mother carry the food out to the dining room.

Soon they were all gathered around the table with their bountiful Thanksgiving dinner in the center—a golden turkey, green bean casserole, mashed sweet potatoes with marshmallows, cranberry sauce, biscuits, and gravy.

"Before we eat," Mom began, "how about we each say what we're most thankful for? I'll start. I'm grateful for my family."

Dani glanced around the table, smiling at her daughters and her husband. "I'm most grateful for this family too."

Travis and his parents all echoed Dani's and Mom's declarations.

"I love my doll," Kelly said, and everyone chuckled.

Riley sat up straight. "I'm thankful for my family—even my baby sister."

Kacey turned to Drew, and her pulse picked up speed. "I'm thankful for special friends." She looked around the table. "And I guess my family too," she teased, and everyone chuckled.

Drew studied Kacey for a moment and then he said, "I'm thankful you're back in my life."

Kacey's heart hammered as she stared at him.

"Nana," Riley whined. "Can we eat now?"

"Yeah, eat!" Kelly echoed.

Everyone laughed again.

"Yes, sweeties," Mom said. "Let's enjoy this wonderful meal."

"I don't think I can eat another bite," Kacey told Drew as they climbed up the front steps of his parents' house. She shivered in the late November air.

Drew rubbed his hand on her shoulder to warm her. "But now we're having dessert. That's the best part of the meal."

He opened the door, and they entered a large foyer with an open staircase that led up to five bedrooms. Conversations carried over from the spacious dining room nearby.

After Drew hung their coats in the closet by the door, he took her hand and steered her into the formal dining room, where his parents, grandparents, and a few aunts, uncles, and cousins she recognized sat.

"Here they are!" Marilyn announced. "You're just in time for dessert."

Drew and Kacey greeted his family members and then took a seat beside each other while his mother and two aunts delivered a pumpkin pie, a chocolate cream pie, and a platter of assorted cookies to the table, along with coffee.

Kacey talked about work with a few of Drew's cousins while she enjoyed a piece of pumpkin pie and a cup of coffee.

"So, I hear you're directing the children's choir for the Christmas Tree Lighting Festival," Drew's grandfather said.

Drew picked up his coffee mug. "That's right. The festival is two weeks from tomorrow."

"I think that's wonderful," his grandmother said. "I can't wait to hear the children sing. It truly feels like Christmas has come to Splendid Lake when the tree is lit and the choir sings."

Marilyn nodded. "I agree, Mom. And Drew has more

exciting news. He applied for a music department head job in Newton. That means he'd be in charge of the entire Catawba County Schools music program!"

"Department head. How fantastic," his grandmother said.

His father pointed his fork at him. "Have you heard anything about the job?"

"Yes." Drew nodded. "I have a telephone interview next week."

Kacey turned toward him. "You didn't tell me that."

"There's not much to tell." Drew shrugged.

Kacey tried to hide her frown as she took another bite of pie. Sadness settled over her as she imagined Drew moving to Newton while she headed back to Charlotte.

Now that she had Drew back in her life, she didn't want to let him go, but she also didn't know how to find a way that they could stay together.

Drew parked his Honda in her driveway later that evening and then turned toward her. "You've been quiet ever since we left my parents' house. What's on your mind?"

She heaved a deep breath and tried to put her confusing feelings into words.

"Is it that bad?" A look of worry flickered over his handsome face. "Did I do or say something to upset you? Did my family?"

She shook her head. "No. I'm just wondering why you didn't tell me you have an interview in Newton."

"It wasn't deliberate. I didn't think it was worth mentioning. I have a phone interview, and that doesn't mean I'll get the job."

But what if you do? What will happen to us? She shook off the questions. After all, she was leaving too!

"I'm sorry I didn't tell you," he said.

"It's okay." She smiled before pushing open the car door and walking up to the porch with him.

"Do you have plans tomorrow?" he asked.

"I was going to work at the bakery. Why?"

"I'm terrible at picking out the right Christmas tree. I was wondering if you might go with me to buy one and then help me decorate it."

"Do you want to come inside? I'll ask my mom if she'll take care of the bakery for me." She opened the door and found Mom sitting in her favorite recliner watching *A Christmas Story*.

Mom sat up as Kacey and Drew walked in. "How was dessert?"

"Very good," Kacey said. "I was wondering if you were planning to help Dani at the bakery tomorrow."

"I can. Why?"

Kacey placed her hand on Drew's arm. "Drew asked if I'd help him pick out a Christmas tree and decorate it."

"That sounds like fun. I'll cover for you at the bakery."

"I appreciate it, Mom."

"Thank you, Mrs. Williams," Drew said before Kacey walked outside.

"Call me Monica!" Mom called after him.

Kacey turned to Drew when they reached the porch. "I'll see you tomorrow then."

"I can't wait." He jogged down the porch steps toward his car.

As he started his car, Kacey hugged her arms to her chest. She couldn't wait either.

Chapter 9

Kacey pointed to a full pine tree a few inches taller than her. "This is the perfect tree."

They had been perusing the Christmas tree lot located just outside of downtown Splendid Lake for nearly thirty minutes. Kacey looked adorable clad in jeans, hiking boots, her teal jacket, and a matching teal hat.

"You're positive?" he teased her.

She jammed her hands on her hips and frowned. "You said you invited me because I'm an expert, and now you have the nerve to doubt me?"

He loved when she teased him. "You're right, Kace. I'm out of line. If you say this is the tree, then it is."

She laughed.

After he paid for the tree, Kacey helped him secure it on the roof of his car before they climbed in and started toward his house.

"Could we make a stop?" Kacey asked.

"Sure. Where am I taking you?"

"It's a surprise." She pointed toward Main Street. "Head into town and find a parking spot anywhere."

He parked in front of the Coffee Bean. "Are you buying me a snack?"

"Nope!" Her smile was coy as she gathered her purse from the floorboard and pushed open the door. "Let's go."

"Yes, ma'am."

Drew met her on the sidewalk, and she grabbed his hand before steering him through the crowd of Black Friday shoppers. "Where are you taking me?"

"You'll see," she sang.

She stopped in front of the Christmas Shop and smiled up at him. "I want to get you a special ornament so you'll remember this Christmas. Okay?"

"That's a great idea." Although he was certain he'd never forget this Christmas.

Drew followed her inside the store, where several customers milled around more than a dozen Christmas trees, all covered with lights and decorations. Each one seemed to have a theme. One had white lights and all-white ornaments, including snowflakes, snowmen, and stars. Another tree was adorned with red lights and red decorations, and a third had multicolored lights and matching glass balls.

A spirited rendition of "Deck the Halls" rang through the store's speakers, and a suspiciously strong scent of pine filled his nostrils, causing him to wonder if either plug-in air fresheners or powerfully scented candles were hidden among the decorations.

Kacey fluttered around the store, checking out displays of ornaments. Drew looked out the large glass window, where folks decorated the light poles with garland and light-up candy canes in preparation for the festival.

When he turned, he spotted an ornament for Kacey, and he smiled as he picked it up and headed toward the cashier, where Kacey already stood in line.

After they had both paid, they met at the door leading out to the street.

"Here you go." She handed him the bag.

He held out a bag to her. "And here's yours."

He pulled out a beautiful classic wooden guitar with the year printed on it. He smiled and felt warm all the way through. "It's perfect. Thank you."

"You're welcome." She lifted her chin. "You said it was your favorite instrument."

"I love it." He pointed to her bag. "Open yours."

She smiled as she pulled a banana split ornament from the bag. "Oh, Drew! Is this to commemorate all those times we shared a banana split at Scoops?"

"Of course."

"I love it." She slipped the ornament into the bag and nodded toward the door. "Let's stop at the bakery for some Christmas cookies and then decorate that perfect tree."

Drew and Kacey spent the afternoon decorating the tree, eating cookies from her sister's bakery, drinking eggnog, and listening to Christmas music. They reminisced and laughed, and he couldn't remember the last time he'd had such an enjoyable day.

When the tree was done, Drew turned off the overhead lights, and they stood in front of it, admiring their work.

Kacey smiled up at him. "I was right. It's perfect."

"Yes, you were." He felt the overwhelming urge to kiss her. As he started to reach for her, she crossed the room and flipped on the lights.

She pointed to the television. "How about we watch a movie?"

"Sure."

"Do you have popcorn?"

"Who doesn't have popcorn?"

She laughed on her way to the kitchen. "You find a movie, and I'll make the popcorn. Is it in the pantry?"

"Yes." Drew found the remote, flipped on the television, and sat down on the sofa.

Soon the aroma of popcorn coupled with the sound of popping filled the house, and he smiled. If only he could find a way for this day to never end.

———

Later that evening, Kacey flopped down on the sofa across from her mother's favorite chair. "It was the perfect day, Mom. We never stopped talking and laughing." She told her about decorating the tree and then watching a movie together. "I've never felt this close to a man."

"You love him, don't you?" Mom asked.

Kacey sighed. "Yeah, I do, but we want different things. He's pursuing a job in Newton, and I'm planning to go back to Charlotte eventually."

"What if there was a way that you could find a compromise?"

"How?"

"What if you worked remotely from Newton?"

"Mom, I don't even know how he feels about me. I think he cares for me, too, but he's never said he likes me as more than a friend."

"What if you just asked him?"

Kacey grimaced. "And what would I do if he rejected me?"

"And what if he didn't?"

Kacey huffed and stood up. "How about we start on those Christmas cards?"

"You were always great at changing the subject." Mom headed toward her bedroom. "I'll get out the cards, and you make us some tea."

Kacey headed into the kitchen, her thoughts swirling with her mother's questions.

The bakery was hustling and bustling the night of the Christmas Tree Lighting Festival. Kacey rushed around delivering hot cocoa and Christmas cookies to the customers standing in the line that stretched from the counter to the door. Mom ran the register, and Dani kept a supply of cookies and hot cocoa available. Customers sat at the tables in the dining area while enjoying their festive treats.

Out the front window, Kacey saw townspeople milling about, bundled up in coats, hats, scarves, and gloves while talking, eating Christmas cookies, drinking cocoa, and visiting the stores.

When there was a break in the line, Kacey retrieved her phone from the back pocket of her jeans and found a missed call and message Drew had left ten minutes ago. She was surprised that she hadn't seen him, since he promised to stop by the bakery before the program started.

She stepped into the kitchen, moved to the far corner, and then played the message.

"Hey, Kace. It's me." His words came in a rush. "I need your help. I'm stuck in traffic, and the festival is going to start soon. Can you possibly fill in for me? Give me a call, and I'll let you know what I need you to do. I'll take over as soon as I get there. Thanks."

Kacey called him back, and he answered on the second ring. "I just got your message. What's going on?"

"I was stuck in traffic. I'm almost there, but the festival starts in ten minutes. Can you help me? I'll tell you where everything is. It's easy."

"Uh, I don't know, Drew." Her stomach dipped. "You remember how I froze up every time we had to give presentations at school."

"Kacey," he began slowly, as if speaking to a child, "you can do this. I have faith in you."

She listened while he explained where to find the CD with the kids' music on it and whom to give it to. "I'll try, but you need to promise me that you'll get here as soon as you can, okay?"

"Thank you, Kace. You're the best."

"You're going to owe me, Murphy," she teased.

"I know. I'll see you soon."

Kacey disconnected the call and then slipped her phone back into her pocket before gathering up her coat, hat, and gloves.

"Where are you going?" Dani asked when Kacey returned to the front of the store.

Kacey zipped her coat. "Drew was stuck in traffic, and he needs me to direct the choir for him until he gets here."

"What do you know about directing a choir?" Dani laughed.

"Nothing, and honestly, the whole idea of standing up there in front of all those people scares me to death, but Drew needs help." Kacey rushed out of the bakery and into the community center, where she found the CD and Drew's folder of music.

She exited the community center and wove through the noisy crowd until she came to the thirty-foot-tall artificial tree that towered at the end of the block near the town hall. The members of the children's choir, all wearing elf hats, stood in front of the tree. A podium faced the children, and microphones stood on stands in front of them.

Riley rushed over to Kacey and grabbed her arm. "The festival is about to start! Where's Mr. Murphy?"

"He's on his way, and he asked me to fill in until he gets here. I'm going to take care of the music. You tell all the kids to get ready." She searched the sea of nearby people until she found a young man standing by the electronic equipment, and made a beeline to him. "Are you Brian?"

He gave her a curious expression. "Yes."

"Drew Murphy is stuck in traffic, and he asked me to direct the choir until he gets here." Her hands shook as she gave him the CD. "Here's the music."

"Got it." Brian took the CD and turned to the equipment.

Kacey spotted Mayor Fairmount and dashed over to him. "Excuse me, Mayor."

"Yes?" Mayor Fairmount spun to face her.

"I'm Kacey Williams. Drew Murphy is stuck in traffic, and he asked me to direct the choir." She took a deep, trembling breath, hoping to calm her frayed nerves. "I-I'm ready whenever you want to make the introduction."

"Oh good. Let's get this show on the road." The mayor walked over to the microphone near the tree.

Kacey joined the children and put her shaking finger to her lips, indicating that they should be quiet. When she turned toward the crowd, her stomach plummeted, and her throat began to close up.

Calm down, Kacey! You got this!

Then Drew's voice echoed through her mind: *Kacey, you can do this. I have faith in you.*

Drew believed in her, and she was determined to make him proud.

She found her mother, Dani, and Travis standing beside Travis's parents in the crowd with Kelly perched on Travis's shoulder, waving.

"Welcome, everyone, to the annual Splendid Lake Christmas Tree Lighting Festival," the mayor began. "It's my favorite festival of the year. Now join me in welcoming our community children's choir as they sing us into the Christmas season. Kacey Williams is standing in for our choir director, Drew Murphy, who is on his way. Let's give our choir a round of applause."

While the crowd clapped and cheered, Kacey took a deep breath in through her nose and worked to stop her hands from quaking as she opened the music folder. She looked over at the children and pointed to her eyes, indicating that they needed to look at her.

When the opening to "Jingle Bells" sounded through the speakers, Kacey smiled. She could do this! She just needed to pretend that the entire town wasn't watching her. And just like that, she found confidence deep inside herself.

She directed the children to sing, and their voices rang out over the speakers on either side of the tree. She smiled as they sang in unison, their little voices blending almost perfectly!

"Jingle Bells" ended, and they went straight into "Joy to the World." Kacey smiled as they continued to serenade the crowd. When the song ended, the mayor flipped the switch, and the tree lit up in all its colorful glory. The crowd oohed and aahed as the children began to sing "Silent Night."

When a tall figure filled her peripheral vision, she breathed a sigh of relief. Drew appeared beside her with a sheepish expression on his face.

"Thank you," he whispered.

She nodded at him and then moved off to the side. She hugged her arms to her waist and smiled as the children finished the performance with "Rudolf the Red-Nosed Reindeer" and then "We Wish You a Merry Christmas."

When the choir finished, the crowd clapped and whistled for them. Drew gestured at the kids, and they all took a bow as the crowd clapped and yelled louder.

Drew motioned for Kacey to come back up front, and she joined him. He turned toward her. "You did a wonderful job, Kace."

"I don't know about that, but thank you. When you're done here, bring the choir in for cocoa and cookies at the bakery. It's on the house," she said.

"Thanks. I will."

Kacey hustled back to the bakery, where her mother and Dani were already serving more customers cookies and cocoa.

"You did fantastic, Kacey," Mom said as she handed a customer a receipt.

Dani nodded. "It was great."

"Thanks. I actually overcame my stage fright. I'm going to get some cocoa and cookies ready for the choir. I'll pay for it, Dani," she told her sister.

Dani waved her off. "Don't worry about it."

Kacey had pushed a few tables together and set out cups of hot cocoa and a few plates of cookies by the time Drew led the choir members and their parents into the bakery. "Come and help yourselves, kids. You all did a fantastic job."

The children thanked her as they each sat at the table and dug in.

Drew took Kacey's hand and led her over to the corner, away from the children and parents. "I can't thank you enough."

"You're welcome. I should actually be thanking you."

"Why?" he asked.

"You forced me to overcome my stage fright." She tilted her head and scrunched her eyebrows. "Where were you?"

He hesitated. "I was at a job interview. For the department head in Newton."

"Oh." Her breath hitched, and she tried to stop herself from frowning. "How did it go?"

He shrugged. "It's difficult to tell."

"Oh."

"Aunt Kacey!" Riley called. "Look! It's snowing."

Kacey spun to face the window and gasped as beautiful snowflakes swirled through the air. She moved to the window and smiled at Drew. "Isn't it beautiful?"

His eyes never left hers. "Yes, it is."

"Aunt Kacey . . ." Riley sang as she tugged on Kacey's sleeve.

Kacey looked down at her niece. "What is it?"

Riley giggled and pointed toward the ceiling. "Look up."

Kacey peered toward the ceiling where mistletoe hung above them. She met Drew's gaze, and her knees wobbled.

Drew's lip twitched. "I guess we know what we have to do."

He rested his hands on the sides of her face, then leaned down and brushed his lips across hers, making her lose track of both her surroundings and time. She closed her eyes, savoring the feel of her mouth against his, and a shiver of longing vibrated through her body.

The children began to giggle and hoot, and Kacey came back to earth. She took a step away from him, trying to catch her breath.

She met Drew's gaze, but his expression was unreadable. And the question that had haunted her since senior year bubbled up in her mind.

"Why didn't you ask me to prom?" she asked.

He blanched as if her words had struck him. "I thought— Wait . . . Would you have gone with me?"

"Well, yes, but—"

"Oh no!" one of the mothers called. "You spilled it all over, Braxton!"

Kacey pivoted toward where one of the children had dumped his cup of cocoa on the floor. "I'll get some paper towels."

She hurried to the kitchen and wondered if she'd ever find out if Drew cared for her.

Chapter 10

"So you kissed her?" Garrett grinned at Drew across the table Monday afternoon while they ate lunch in the teacher's lounge.

Drew nodded and heat roared through his veins at the memory of how it felt to brush his lips against hers. "Yes. Thank goodness her niece noticed the mistletoe."

"Surely that means you're finally dating. Good for you."

Drew shook his head as he swallowed a bite of his ham and cheese sandwich. "No, we still haven't talked about it. She started to ask me why I didn't ask her to prom, and we just haven't had a chance to connect and finish the conversation. She was busy with her family the rest of the weekend."

"Wait." Garrett set his bottle of water on the table. "What's the story with prom?"

Drew frowned. "I was planning to ask her, but my best

friend at the time beat me to it. Then they started dating, and Kacey and I grew apart. If I'd mustered up the courage sooner, I could have asked her out myself."

"You know what you have to do. Tell her how you feel now."

Drew's phone buzzed. He flipped it over and found a missed call and a voice mail. He listened to the voice mail and his mouth dropped open.

"What is it?"

"It's about the teaching job in Charlotte. They want me to come in for an interview next Tuesday."

"You applied for a job in Charlotte too?"

"Yeah, it was a whim." Drew took another bite of his sandwich.

Garrett nodded. "Well, I'll miss you, buddy, but Charlotte could be your future."

Drew let his friend's words soak through him, and hope lit in his chest.

———

Kacey perused her work email Friday morning. She found one from her supervisor and began responding just as her phone started to ring. Her friend Jackie Campbell's name was on the screen.

"Hey, Jackie. What's up?" Kacey leaned back in her desk chair.

"I heard you were looking for a roommate. Is that right?"

"Yes, it is. Ginny Sorrentino got married, so I'm staying with my mom until I can find something affordable in Charlotte."

"I might have the solution to your problem. My roommate is moving out January first. Would you like to come back to Charlotte? You'll have a nice big bedroom and your own bathroom."

Kacey sat up straight. "What's the rent?"

Jackie gave her all the details, and the rent and utilities were within Kacey's budget.

"I know you don't go in very often, but it's right near your office too," Jackie added.

"This sounds too good to be true."

"It's not! You'd be doing me a huge favor, because I can't afford this on my own, but I love the location."

"Well, it's perfect. I'm in."

"Fantastic. I'll call you after Christmas, and we'll work out the details."

"Thank you for thinking of me," Kacey said before disconnecting the call. She stared down at her computer screen, and a mixture of gratitude and sadness filled her. She'd been worried she wouldn't find a new roommate in the city she'd grown to love, but she was going to miss her family. And her heart began to break at the idea of leaving Drew behind. What if Charlotte wasn't her future anymore?

As if on cue, her phone buzzed with a text from him:

Dinner tomorrow night? My treat.

She grinned as she typed back:

Yes. Only because you're paying.

Pick you up at 6.

Don't be late.

She sighed and rested her elbows on her desk as she pondered moving back to Charlotte. How would she ever recover from losing Drew a second time?

———

"I have some news," Kacey said as she sat across from Drew at the Little Italy Italian restaurant the next night.

Drew closed his menu. "I do, too, but you go first."

"Okay," she began. "So, it looks like I'm going back to Charlotte after Christmas."

His smile faded. "So soon? What happened?"

She explained how her friend Jackie called and asked if she wanted to move in January first when her roommate moved out.

"That's great, Kace." His smile seemed forced, and didn't quite meet his eyes.

"Yeah, I lucked out. What's your news?"

"I got the music department head job in Newton."

"Oh wow." She tried to sound excited as disappointment overcame her. Would she even see Drew when she came back to visit her family? She tamped down the thought and leaned across the table to place her hand on his. "I'm so proud of you."

"Thanks. It's a big raise."

"That's fantastic. When does it start?"

"After the holidays."

"So you need to sell your house and find a place to live there."

Drew nodded. "Right."

Kacey fiddled with her napkin. "We'll keep in touch, right?"

"Of course."

"Your friendship means so much to me. I'm sorry we missed out on so many years."

"I am too." He reached across the table and took her hands in his. "I promise I'll do better this time."

"Me too," she said softy.

———

Drew walked into Garrett's classroom Monday afternoon.

Garrett looked up from his desk. "Hey, man, what's up?"

"I got the job in Newton." Drew sank down on one of the chairs in the front row.

Garrett's face lit up. "That's great."

"Thanks." Drew rested his right ankle on his left knee. "My father, who only cares about money, said I should take it."

Garrett stood up and walked around the desk before sitting on the edge of it. "But it sounds like you don't want to take it."

"Not really." Drew pursed his lips and crossed is arms over his chest. "Tomorrow I'm going to Charlotte to interview for the music teacher position there."

"And that's the job you want," Garrett said.

"Yes. I want to go there with Kacey and start a life with her."

"Have you told her this?"

"No, not yet. I want to get the job first."

Garrett nodded. "And what if you don't get the job?"

"Then I'll have to think of something else."

"Good," Garrett said. "Oh, you had asked me about IT jobs with the school system. You have a friend who is looking for one, right?"

Drew nodded. "That's right."

"I have a lead for you." Garrett handed him a piece of paper. "Have your friend call Rich Monroe. He has an opening."

Drew took the paper. "Thank you. I'll give Travis a call."

"I can't believe you convinced me to close the bakery today and go shopping with you," Dani said Tuesday morning as she walked inside the small mall located a few miles from the town of Splendid Lake with Kacey and their mother. "You know I need to work."

Kacey faced her sister, pulled a thick envelope out of her purse, and handed it to her. "Merry Christmas, sis."

"What is this?" Dani asked, her blue eyes wide.

Kacey shared a smile with Mom and then looked at her sister again. "Just open it, Dani."

Her sister opened the envelope and gasped at the bills stuffed inside. "I-I can't take this." With her eyes misting over, Dani pushed the envelope back toward Kacey.

"No, I insist. I was saving for a down payment on a condo, but my friend Jackie called me and said she's looking for a roommate. So, I wanted to give you and Travis this money so you can buy the girls gifts and then use the rest for bills until something works out for Travis. Please take it. This is my Christmas gift for you."

Dani's lip trembled as she pulled Kacey in for a tight hug. "You're the best sister on the planet, Kacey."

"You know it," Kacey teased, and they laughed.

Dani put the envelope into her purse. "Did you know Drew called Travis and gave him a lead on a job?"

"When?" Kacey asked.

"Yesterday. There's an opening with the school system. Drew told him to reach out to someone for an interview."

Kacey clapped. "That's great!"

"I know. Travis called and it sounds like a great opportunity."

"What a blessing," Mom said.

Warmth filled Kacey's chest. Drew was such a wonderful man.

"Let's go shopping," Dani said.

Kacey pointed toward a music store. "Let me go in here to find something for Drew and then we'll head to the toy store for the girls."

"What are you going to do about Drew when you go back to Charlotte?" Mom asked.

Kacey frowned. "I haven't figured that out. He was offered a job in Newton."

"Maybe you can try long distance?" Mom suggested.

Dani held her finger up. "Or you can work remotely from Newton."

"When are you going to admit that you two are meant for each other and that you need to find a way to work it out?" Mom asked.

Kacey shook her head as they walked into the music store. "We both promised to keep in touch, but he hasn't said anything about being more than friends." The truth was she couldn't stop thinking about that kiss the night of the festival. She'd never felt such an explosion of desire in her life. The memory sent a flush of bashful pleasure through her cheeks and made her light-headed. And she couldn't shake the feeling that maybe her future could be in Splendid Lake with Drew instead of in Charlotte.

"I think you need to tell him how you feel and then figure out a way to make it work," Dani told her.

Kacey smiled. "Maybe I will."

———

"Merry Christmas!" Kacey exclaimed as Dani, Travis, and the girls walked into her mother's house Christmas morning. She leaned down and hugged her nieces. "You need to go over to the tree. There are presents there for you."

Riley took Kelly's hand. "I'll help you find your gifts." She guided her over to the tree.

Dani hugged Kacey. "We have big news."

"What is it?" Mom asked as she joined them.

Dani looked at Travis as he grinned.

"I got the job with the school system," Travis said.

"Oh!" Mom gasped. "I'm so happy to hear that!"

"Is it the job that Drew recommended?" Kacey asked.

Dani nodded. "Yes. Drew made it happen."

"That's amazing," Mom said.

"Nana?" Riley called from the Christmas tree. "Will you come over here and help us find our presents?"

Mom smiled over at them. "Of course."

"I'll come with you," Travis said as he carried a large tote bag filled with gifts over to the sofa.

"What are Drew's plans for today?" Dani asked Kacey.

"He texted me last night and asked if he could come over."

Dani smiled. "That's good."

"Aunt Kacey!" Riley called. "Come here and open your gifts."

Dani touched Kacey's arm. "You're being summoned."

"We'd better go."

Kacey sat down on the sofa between her mother and sister and watched as her nieces opened their gifts from her and her mom.

Dani pulled out a box of cookies, and Kacey brought in glasses of eggnog while they continued opening gifts, laughing, and enjoying each other.

When a knock sounded at the door, Kacey popped up from the sofa, retrieved Drew's gift from under the tree, and then darted to the door.

She pulled it open and found Drew standing on the porch. Above them the sky was white and it felt like snow was coming. "Merry Christmas."

"Merry Christmas to you."

She opened the door wide. "Would you like to come in?"

"Actually, I was wondering if we could talk out here alone for a few minutes."

"Oh. Okay." She shivered. "Let me grab my coat." She set his gift on the little table next to her mother's rocking chair, retrieved her coat from the closet, and pulled it on. "What did you want to talk about?" she asked when she returned to the porch.

He hesitated and then drew out a ragged breath. "Remember Tuesday when you went shopping with your mom and sister?"

"Yes."

"I told you I was busy all day, and the truth is, I had a job interview."

She studied him. "I thought you already heard back about the job in Newton."

"This interview was for a teaching position. I got the job, and I really want to take it. But I need to tell you something first." Drew paused and swallowed. "You asked me why I never asked you to prom. I was a coward. I had planned to ask you, but I waited too long. The truth is that I love you, and I've loved you since I was sixteen years old. I was never brave enough to tell you, but now I'm telling you that I love you and I want to build a future with you in Charlotte."

Kacey heaved a breath as happy tears leaked from her eyes. "I love you, too, Drew." Then she held her hand up. "Hold on a second. You said you want to make a life in Charlotte with me? Where's the teaching job?"

Drew smiled. "In Charlotte."

"You applied for a job in Charlotte?"

"Yes, I did." He cupped his hand to her cheek. "I wanted to find a way to be with you. I can't let you walk out of my life again."

She sniffed. "Drew, I'm so honored that you did that for me. But the truth is that I've been doing a lot of thinking and I've realized something." She paused, and his smile wobbled. "My life is here now, and I belong in Splendid Lake. How would you feel if we stayed?"

"Actually, I'm relieved to hear you say that."

"But your job in Charlotte—is it a promotion? Are you giving up a great opportunity because of me?"

"No, actually." He shook his head. "My supervisor heard that I was interviewing for jobs, and he offered me a promotion if I stayed here in Splendid Lake. He wants me to be director of our little music department here, and it comes with a nice raise. If you're really happy staying here with me, I would love to accept his offer."

"That's amazing!"

"You're amazing, Kace." He pulled her to him. He dipped his head and kissed her. She looped her arms around his neck and soaked in his nearness. When he deepened the kiss, Kacey melted against him. She was certain she was dreaming, but the heat rushing through her veins was as real as the feel of his lips.

When he broke the kiss, Kacey placed her hand on Drew's chest. She felt something wet hit her face, and she smiled when she realized it was snowing. "I love you, Drew Murphy, and I can't wait to start the new year with you by my side."

"How about we start it right now?" He kissed her again while snow drifted down, swirling around them.

ACKNOWLEDGMENTS

A Perfectly Splendid Christmas

As always, I'm thankful for my loving family, including my mother, Lola Goebelbecker; my husband, Joe; and my sons, Zac and Matt.

Thank you to my mother and my dear friend DeeDee Vazquetelles who graciously read the draft of this book to check for typos. I appreciate my dear friend Maggie Halpin for her research help. You're a blessing to your students!

Thank you to my wonderful church family at Morning Star Lutheran in Matthews, North Carolina, for your encouragement, prayers, love, and friendship. You all mean so much to my family and me.

Thank you to Zac Weikal and the fabulous members of my Bookworm Bunch! I'm so grateful for your friendship and your excitement about my books. You all are awesome!

ACKNOWLEDGMENTS

To my agent, Natasha Kern—I can't thank you enough for your guidance, advice, and friendship. You are a tremendous blessing in my life.

Thank you to my amazing editor, Laura Wheeler, for your friendship and guidance. I look forward to our future projects together.

Special thanks to editor Karli Jackson for polishing the story and connecting the dots. I appreciate your help!

Thank you most of all to God—for giving me the inspiration and the words to glorify you. I'm grateful and humbled you've chosen this path for me.

DISCUSSION QUESTIONS

A Christmas Do-Over

1. Darby Brown, former mean girl, has a lot of past to live down when she comes home for the holidays. Have you known any mean girls? Would you find it hard to forgive someone who had been mean to you?
2. There is often that one "difficult" family member everyone has to deal with. How do you deal with the difficult people in your life?
3. Darby's mother has all kinds of holiday plans for her family, including baking cookies. What is a favorite tradition in your family?
4. We all love those holiday treats. What is your favorite?
5. Darby's former friends sneer at the new improving

her. Have you ever tried to make changes in your life and met with a lack of support?

6. Darby does have one friend who encourages her to keep changing for the better. Do you have someone like that on your life? Would you say you are that kind of friend?

7. If you were Gregory Collier, would you have given Darby a second chance?

8. Is there a scene in the book that resonated with you?

9. Darby and her sister had a troubled relationship. Do you have siblings? If so, what relationship challenges have you faced?

10. What do you think was the underlying message of this story?

Dashing Through the Snow

1. Willow thinks that with the private cabin, she'll get a moment of relief after her hard breakup, only to find she has to make the hard choice of giving it away to someone who needed it more. When is a time in your life when you've done something similar? Was it worth it?

2. After Willow sacrifices her private room, she meets Oliver's father and ultimately Oliver. She was given

a blessing in disguise she may not have received otherwise. When is a time in your life you were surprised by something similarly unexpected that changed your life?

3. Willow had a classic case of settling for things in life instead of risking and jumping into the unknown. When have you experienced the same thing, and what was the outcome?

4. This novella included research into real cross-country train experiences. Would you ever participate in such a trip? Why or why not?

5. The theme of the train trip was experiencing a nostalgic and romantic Christmas getaway. What kind of tour would you like to explore if you went on a train getaway?

6. What was your favorite pit stop depicted in the novella. Why?

7. Who was your favorite character in the book (author answer: mine was the quirky, lovable elf, Ian!) and why?

8. What was your favorite scene in the book and why?

9. Oliver waited until they were nearly at the end of their trip before making a move. Do you agree with his reasons for doing this or think he should have brought up the topic with Willow earlier?

10. Which character did you relate to the most? Why?

11. Willow loved her caretaker job despite its low salary. Would you prefer a job you loved with little pay or a job that was mediocre but the salary was strong? Why?

12. The train tour's goal was to create soon-to-be favorite Christmas memories for its passengers. What are some of the most nostalgic Christmas memories in your own life?

A Perfectly Splendid Christmas

1. At the beginning of the story, Kacey plans to only stay in Splendid Lake temporarily while she finds a way to move back to Charlotte; however, by the end of the story, she decides to stay. What do you think inspired her decision to give up her dream of living in a city and instead build a life in her hometown?

2. Drew and Kacey were the best of friends in school, and they quickly rekindle that friendship when they reconnect. Do you have a special friendship like that? If so, what do you cherish the most about that relationship?

3. Drew is frustrated with his father for constantly pressuring him to make more money and work for his financial planning firm. Did you think his father had a right to encourage Drew to take over the family business? Why or why not?

4. Dani, Kacey's older sister, follows her dream and opens her very own bakery. Do you have a special

hobby or dream that you have fulfilled or always wanted to see come to fruition? If so, what is it?

5. Kacey and her family enjoy the Christmas Tree Lighting Festival in Splendid Lake. What are your favorite holiday traditions? Does your hometown host any holiday traditions or festivals?

6. Have you ever visited a place like Splendid Lake? If you could go anywhere for vacation this weekend, where would you choose to go?

ABOUT THE AUTHORS
Sheila Roberts

Photo by Robert Rabe

USA TODAY and *Publishers Weekly* bestselling author Sheila Roberts has seen her books translated into several different languages, included in *Readers Digest* compilations, and made into movies for the Hallmark and Lifetime channels. She's happily married and lives in the Pacific Northwest.

———

Website: sheilasplace.com
Facebook: @funwithsheila
Twitter: @_Sheila_Roberts
Instagram: @sheilarobertswriter

ABOUT THE AUTHORS

Melissa Ferguson

Photo by Taylor Meo Photography

Bestselling author Melissa Ferguson lives in Tennessee, where she enjoys chasing her children and writing romantic comedies full of humor and heart. Her favorite hobby is taking friends and acquaintances and turning them into characters in her books without their knowledge.

———

Connect with her (and prepare for the possibility of becoming her next character) at melissaferguson.com

Instagram: @our_friendly_farmhouse

TikTok: @ourfriendlyfarmhouse

Amy Clipston

Photo by Dan Davis Photography

Amy Clipston is the award-winning and bestselling author of the Kauffman Amish Bakery, Hearts of Lancaster Grand Hotel, Amish Heirloom, Amish Homestead, and Amish Marketplace series. Her novels have hit multiple bestseller lists including CBD, CBA, and ECPA. Amy holds a degree in communication from Virginia Wesleyan University and works full-time for the City of Charlotte, NC. Amy lives in North Carolina with her husband, two sons, and six spoiled rotten cats.

Visit her online at AmyClipston.com
Facebook: @AmyClipstonBooks
Twitter: @AmyClipston
Instagram: @amy_clipston
BookBub: @AmyClipston